STATE OF THE ORBIT

D RAGONS HAVE ALWAYS HELD an intense fascination for me—
as I believe they do with many people. I am most attracted
to dragons who possess a majestic, inhuman intelligence. The
dragons of Ursula K. Le Guin's *Earthsea* books were very in-
fluential to me, as was Kazul from Patricia C. Wrede's *Dealing
with Dragons*. My favorite fictional dragon, however, is probably Scales from Diana Wynne Jones's fantastic *Dark Lord of
Derkholm*, with an honorable mention to her interpretation of
the White Dragon from *The Merlin Conspiracy*. I see my appre-
ciation of dragons as an extension of my childhood romance
with dinosaurs—I hold both in high esteem, but for different
reasons. Dinosaurs impress me because they *actually happened*,
and fill me with reverence for the natural world. Dragons are as
much an embodiment of a powerful mind as they are of physical prowess. I find depictions of dragons as dumb (if ferocious)
beasts disappointing, and I recoil at the thought of applying the
term *dragon* to a giant reptilian beast with *no forelegs*. Dragons
may have feathers, scales, even fur; they may be serpentine or
quadrupeds; they may have two wings or eight or none, but for
some reason I cannot conceive of a dragon with hind legs and
wings and *no* forelimbs. Perhaps this is because we already have
a word to describe such a beast: *wyvern*, and I feel it's unfair to
the wyverns not to recognize them.

In this issue of Apsis Fiction, celebrating the aphelion of Earth (the period of time when the Earth's orbit takes it farthest from the Sun; this year it occurs on July 3rd), I clarify this distinction in the very first story: "Griffin's Blood" (*Bouragner Felpz Volume II, #4*) primarily concerns itself with the fate of a griffin, but there are rather a lot of dragons (and wyverns) clustered around the edges of it. It marks the first time dragons have appeared prominently in my fiction, and with it I hoped to represent, not only the majesty and terror of these beasts, but also their variety. So if you like dragons, be they small and hissing or large and noble or overpoweringly huge and god-like, I hope you'll find something to like in "Griffin's Blood." In contrast, "The Three Fates of Talias Minn" (*Bouragner Felpz Volume II, #5*) is a more whimsical tale. One thing I like to do with serial stories is show that the characters' lives are not a constant life-or-death struggle, and that you can have an entertaining adventure without anyone being seriously injured.

"Griffin's Blood" and "The Three Fates of Talias Minn" are from Volume II of my *Bouragner Felpz* series; the first three installments of which can be found in *Apsis Fiction* issues 1 and 2 (*Mesohelion 2013* and *Perihelion 2014*), while the first eleven stories comprising Volume I have been published in *A Study of Magic* (*The Adventures of Bouragner Felpz, Volume I*). All from Heliopause.

"The Trickster and the Devil" came out of a conversation with my brother about the nature of Job and how his story could be interpreted as having a *very* different moral. It leads into another story with devilish characters: "Sex, Blood and Rock 'n' Roll" (*Driving Arcana #4*). The preceding episodes of *Driving Arcana* can be found in *Mesohelion 2013* and *Perihelion 2014*, and published together as *Driving Arcana: Rotation One*.

"How Riding Got Her Red Hood" is another instance of me being deeply dissatisfied with an old story, and trying to hammer out a version I could believe in. As the title implies it is a re-envisioning of the classic "Little Red Riding Hood," and I wrote it after the style of Rudyard Kipling's *Just So Stories*—which made more of an impression on my childhood mind than any of Grimm's fairytales.

The Semi-Annual Anthology of Goldeen Ogawa

Volume 2, Issue 1 • Aphelion 2014

CONTENTS

author • illustrator • editor • book designer
GOLDEEN OGAWA

a HELIOPAUSE PRODUCTION

Apsis Fiction: The Semi-Annual Anthology of Goldeen Ogawa
Volume No. 2, Issue 1, Whole No. 3 (Aphelion 2014).
Published semi-annually by Heliopause Productions.

FICTION/Science Fiction/Short Stories

FICTION/Fantasy/General

First Edition 2014

ISBN: 978-06922575-3-1

Finally, getting back to the theme of dragons in this issue, "The Dragons of Geda" (*Professor Odd #5*) concerns dragons in a more abstract sense. I suppose a more accurate title might have been "The *Dinosaurs* of Geda," but as someone points out in that story, the dinosaurs are not dinosaurs as we would know them. I had long wanted to tell a story about dinosaurs living alongside humans a la James Gurney's brilliant *Dinotopia* books, but when the time came I discovered the story was about something else altogether. The previous *Professor Odd* episodes have all been published individually from Heliopause.

The cover of *Aphelion 2014* is a colored-pencil illustration depicting the double moonrise of a Gedan evening. It also includes a dinosaur that very much existed on Earth: a *parasaurolophus*, which was my favorite dinosaur as a child.

—GOLDEEN OGAWA
California
June 2014

"Griffin's Blood" comes fourth in the second volume of Bouragner Felpz *stories. These are set in a fantastical world reminiscent of late nineteenth-century England, and chronicle the exploits of the magician Bouragner Felpz, as told by his friend and companion, Corianne Birch. "Griffin's Blood" follows "The Ghost of Castle Hill" which appeared in* Apsis Fiction 1.2: Perihelion 2014. *It was written in May, 2013.*

GRIFFIN'S BLOOD

SOME OF MY READERS have been disappointed at how little I have spoken of my daughter in these semi-autobiographical tales. They have expressed a certain amount of curiosity about the young woman who, as I mentioned before, "has gone far on the backs of dragons."

I do not find this surprising at all. The fact is, however, that although my daughter leads an exceptionally interesting life, it is very much her life, and I believe that when the time is right she will tell her own story in her own words. So I have taken care not to become sidetracked with her affairs, as these stories deal in the doings of my friend, the magician Bouragner Felpz, and not those of my daughter, the dracologist.

Once, however, their two paths did cross. The result was so extraordinary that reports of it have already been published in several newspapers and scientific journals. My version I present here, not only as an example of my friend's remarkable powers— but also to shed some light on the doings of that incurably adventurous woman, Milain Harper Birch.

It happened in the long days of that glorious summer of 2315. The past two years had been exceptionally busy ones for me, for as some of my older readers may remember, 2313 was the year in which I began to publish the accounts of my adventures as a young girl with Mr Bouragner Felpz. Though the first installment was met with no great fanfare, I was surprised and heartened to receive many letters requesting more stories about my friend, and the fulfillment of these requests served to fill my days to the brim. Furthermore, that year I was quite overwhelmed with collecting those stories into the volume which would later become *The Adventures of Bouragner Felpz: A Study of Magic*.

So I had not been on any adventures of a magical nature in some months, and those of the past year had all been small, quiet affairs—amusing enough to regale friends with over dinner, but hardly worth the trouble of writing down—when I received an urgent letter from my daughter.

Letters from Milain were not so unusual; we corresponded regularly and frequently, and many of these stories of Felpz began as letters to her. Similarly, I have been carefully filing all her letters to me against the day she inevitably decides to write her own memoirs. No, it was not the letter that surprised me, but the manner in which it was delivered.

I was sitting up in bed one morning, so absorbed in my writing that I ignored the call to breakfast. From the sitting room I heard a sharp tapping on the window, but dismissed it as one of the ravens that frequently delivered messages to Felpz. This assessment was confirmed a moment later when I heard Felpz greet the creature and let it in. I heard the flapping of wings and a muffled crash as it landed among the breakfast things. Then there were steps in the hall, a rap on my bedroom door, and Felpz put his head in.

"Ah, Corianne," he said. "Do you mind setting aside your quill for one moment? Only there is a wyvern in the other room who, if you do nothing, will eat your breakfast."

"Me?" I cried, jolted abruptly out of my world of ink and words. "Wyverns are your province, Felpz. Tell him to go away yourself."

"You would not love me if I did so," Felpz said. "He brings a message from your daughter."

Disbelief washed over me. I set aside my notebook and hurried into my dressing gown and across the hall. The door opened onto the bright, cluttered room, and I entered to find the breakfast table even more crowded than usual with the small wyvern perched in the middle of it.

For those of you who have not seen a wyvern, a small distinction must be made: they are not, as my daughter has told me many times, dragons. Though they appear reptilian, and have similar leathery wings and long, toothy snouts, they lack the third set of appendages that form a dragon's forelegs, and they cannot breathe fire—though adults can hiss jets of steam. They do not grow as large as dragons—the largest documented specimen being only twenty feet long—and cannot use magic to assist their flight.

This particular wyvern was either a juvenile or one of the smaller species. He—and I trusted Felpz's word on this—was the size of an albatross, with the addition of a stubby tail. He had a smattering of red feathers around his head and across his shoulders, and his scaly skin was a deep mahogany hue. His wings were currently folded tightly along his sides, with the fingers that protruded at the wyvern equivalent of a wrist held questioningly over my plate of biscuits.

He looked up guiltily as we entered, and I remembered more of my daughter's lectures on wyverns: though they did not have the vast, inhuman wisdom of dragons, they were of an intelligence and temperament similar to a human child. With this in mind I cleared my throat politely and wished him good morning.

"Good morning," said the wyvern. He had a high, chirping voice, but his words were clear and precise. "Message for you from Birch girl. Urgent. Am to wait for your reply. Came long way this morning. Hungry." He looked longingly at the tray of sweets.

"You may have one biscuit," I said, coming to sit at the table. "I do not think my daughter would thank me if I sent you back with an upset stomach. What do you normally eat?"

The wyvern turned around on the table, flaring his wings for balance. Their webbing was a brilliant orange, and as they opened and closed it looked like a flash of fire.

"Biscuits?" he said hopefully, extending one of his legs to which had been secured a roll of paper.

I looked helplessly at Felpz as I removed the document.

Felpz cleared his throat deferentially. "I am sure we can provide you some roast chicken, which will no doubt agree with you better."

"You may have two biscuits while you wait." I relented at the wyvern's drooping crest, and unrolled my daughter's letter.

While the wyvern helped himself I read with interest the following message:

Draco Abbey, Crogard.
21st June 2315, 3:30 AM
Dear Mother,

I hope Radcliffe has found you safe and swift. I would have written in the ordinary way, but something has come up and I need your advice as soon as possible.

Two weeks ago the dragons began acting very strangely. They will not talk to me, which is troubling. More troubling still, earlier this evening one of them killed a sheep and carried it away. This is the second poaching in as many months—the first was a fortnight ago—and it has undone all the progress I have made with the local farmers, who are understandably upset. It is further troubling because these are lesser fire dragons, and they only hunt when their young are hatching—which they have no eggs to hatch this season.

I have been up half the night flying around on Tero, who at least still helps me, trying to discover if there is a nest. Around midnight we were nearly knocked out of the sky by a greater elder dragon gliding up from the south. This is serious: we have not had elder dragons here in over five hundred years. None of us have any experience with elder dragons, and I am at a loss for what to do.

My colleagues on the farm are full of ideas, but they strike me as foolish and dangerous. Dr Vayar, the director, is considering writing to a preeminent draconic scholar from Aldonica. However, I know that neither of them has had direct contact with elder dragons—merely studied them extensively through the writings of medieval experts. But these stories and anecdotes from history are contradictory at best, and allegorical most of the time. What we need is someone who has known these dragons, and knows how to speak to them.

However, there is no one of my generation or the five previous who have even seen an elder dragon, much less spoken to one.

Which is why I'm writing to you, mother. I believe you do know someone who has direct experience with these dragons: your friend Mr Felpz. If you could convince him to come up and advise us I would be immensely grateful.

I have attached a description of the dragon in question, in case Mr Felpz might recognize it.

Wishing for a swift reply,
Your loving Milain

As I read this remarkable document I could feel my eyebrows slowly climbing up my forehead, and by the time I finished they must have been close to my hairline.

"I trust all is well with your progeny?" Felpz asked from across the table.

I looked up to find him watching me intently, his dark eyes sparkling. On the table the wyvern—Radcliffe—had polished off the biscuits and was eyeing my breakfast hopefully.

"Well with her, I believe so," I said. "Her world, perhaps not. Here." I thrust the letter and the attached slip into Felpz's eager hands, and began upon my breakfast before Radcliffe could steal it.

While I ate, I watched Felpz's expression of mild surprise and curiosity slowly harden into sharp concentration. When he got to the attached description he was so enthralled as to read it aloud, interspersed with his own thoughts.

"Greater elder dragon—this means nothing to me—reptilian, short bodied—that would make it a northern drake—wingspan of . . . three hundred feet or more? Well. That certainly narrows it down. Could be Armandoros . . . or Therangaar . . . but they have been far out of this world. I would have felt it if they had returned, I am sure. Mordicade? No, that is a fanciful notion. Let me see . . . she gives no mention of its colour, or the style of its spinal ridge. Understandable, given the circumstances. No, I'm afraid I cannot identify it from this. And it may be a dragon unknown to me—I have known dragons, my dear, I have not known them all . . .

"Well, I suppose we must arrange a trip to Crogard at the nearest possible moment to see if we can't resolve the matter."

He spoke lightly, but I could tell from the tenseness about his form and the gleam in his eye that this was an unusual and serious situation. I knew also from my daughter's tutelage that dragons came in three kinds—mostly. The lesser or common variety, which still inhabit the high rocky areas of this country; the greater dragons, which have mostly moved into the inhospitable heights of the Dragonridge Mountains; and the elder dragons, which as far as I could tell consisted of a few named individuals of the sort found in stories and legends—none of whom had been seen in Kyreland for many hundreds of years. What she could have meant by a greater elder dragon, I could only guess.

"Still hungry," Radcliffe chirped. "Chicken?"

"Have a care with how you eat," Felpz chided. "Lest you lose your ability to fly. Now take this note, my good drake," he said, scribbling something on a slip of paper and handing it to the wyvern, "and take it back to your mistress."

Radcliffe took the note in one spiny claw, eyeing Felpz cagily.

"She's not my mistress," he said. "She is the Birch girl." And with a clatter and a snap of leathery wings he was at the windowsill, and a moment later he was gone.

"What do you make of it, Felpz?" I asked, getting up to close the window.

Felpz shrugged. "I make nothing of it as yet," he said. "A dragon will do as a dragon does and to question it is folly. Still, there can only be four or five dragons of the size your daughter describes, and I should like to meet this one—whether or not the situation requires my attention. You will come, of course?"

"I should not dream of missing this opportunity," I exclaimed. "Besides, it has been years since I visited Crogard."

Felpz clapped his hands. "Excellent," said he. "Now I have one more letter to write, and then we may be off."

He was as good as his word. It was a sign of just how enthusiastic my friend was that all our luggage appeared at the door already packed—quite literally by magic. I took this as a sign in general that the journey would receive similar assistance, and indeed the interminable train ride passed much more quickly than I remembered.

The last time I visited my daughter had been in the fall of '12, when she had only recently become installed at the Draconian Institute at Crogard. Then the mountains had been bleak and forbidding, the air cold, and the weather a miserable combination of spitting rain and stinging snow. The dragons had made themselves scarce in their caves, and apart from showing me around the venerable buildings of the Institute, there was not much we could do.

Now it was summer, and the mountains rising from the southwestern lowlands were high and green and refreshingly cool looking. Here and there among their pine-covered sides I could see the occasional cliff or peak of brilliant gold stone—a reminder that Crogard was, under its cloak of Kyrish soil and vegetation, a part of the great Dragonridge Mountains: that mighty range that stretched the length of our entire continent. Hewn into sharp spires by the fire of ancient dragons, they are an everlasting reminder that, though those dragons are now a rare sight in our world, they were once the indisputable rulers of it, and their legacy will last beyond the scope of humanity. Indeed, it abides in the very bones of this earth.

We alighted in Rivenstone, the small town that had gathered around the College of Rarities—that most isolated and idiosyncratic branch of Redling's University of Magic—from which it was only a short journey by coach to Draco Abbey, as the locals had affectionately dubbed the Draconian Institute. As we waited for our bags to be unloaded, I caught Felpz looking intently around the station, as if expecting to see a familiar face. This puzzled me, as despite our long friendship he had never set eyes upon my daughter—whom I was expecting to meet us.

But Milain was nowhere to be seen, and it was a different figure from my past who eventually presented himself by the door to Main Street: A small, silver-haired boy in a disheveled brown suit and pale bare feet, who saluted us as we drew near.

"Abharus!" I cried, swooping down and embracing him. "This is a most welcome surprise!" I knew that, though he still appeared to be a child of no more than twelve, he was in fact over ten years my senior. Nevertheless I could not resist the habits I had developed when my daughter was young, and he bore my attentions with admirable fortitude.

"Hardly worth making a fuss," he chided me, patting my arm. "Didn't Mr Felpz tell you he called me?"

"What? Why, no!" I looked about distractedly. Abharus's choice of words was curious, but I did not think they were inaccurate. Abharus traveled in and out of our world, and for all I knew Felpz had summoned him from some distant adventure. "Where have you been?" I asked. "How did you get here before us?"

Abharus coughed modestly, and nodded towards the coach waiting outside. This coach was nothing unusual—it looked like any sober black cab—but the horse than pulled it was . . . difficult to look at. It had a shimmery, ethereal quality to it that made the eye want to slide away. I got the impression of hooves and a wild, feathery mane and tail, and a pillowing turbulence above its withers that might have been a disturbance of air, or might have been restless wings. Its colour was even harder to describe, like a patch of sunset on a cloudy day sitting in the street.

"Ah, Abharus," said Felpz, sliding up beside us with a porter in tow. "And you've brought Yuragorn, excellent. This way, Jecab."

"Yuragorn?" I asked while our luggage was being stowed.

Abharus looked up at me through his silvery bangs, and smiled angelically. "Yuragorn is good to have around when you're dealing with dragons," he said.

We climbed into the coach, and I saw that although Abharus sat in the driver's seat he held no reins, gave no command. Yet as soon as we had settled in, the coach moved smoothly off, and we began to pass swiftly through the town, heading steeply up Main Street towards the abbey.

Felpz leaned forward and proceeded to spend the remainder of the journey deep in quiet conversation with Abharus. I sat back and let them converse without even trying to eavesdrop; I had learned long ago that my friend would explain all when all would be clear, and I would not get a morsel of information before then.

Draco Abbey had once been the cornerstone of a large convent that lay just beyond the town at the top of a low hill. Since the nuns had moved out and the dracologists had moved in nothing had changed about the exterior—save a few modifications that made it easier for small dragons and wyverns to land on the roof. The gardens that extended down the far side of the hill had been converted into hatcheries, nests, and a long strip of scorched grass where the larger dragons could land comfortably, but approaching from the town, the only visual clue was the bordering wall; this had been built of natural flint which had slowly chipped away, leaving sharp glassy spikes at the top, and the intact bricks, glossy blue-blacks and deep browns, gave the impression of scales. Milain had told me that when the scientists moved in they thought the wall looked so fitting they left it as they had found it.

Today there were a number of people gathered around the gate, angry farmers and craftsmen by the look of them. They were shouting heatedly at two burly young men who stood on either side of the gate looking bored and long-suffering. As we drew nearer I saw why they seemed so relaxed despite the throng around them: they were guarded by the presence of a dragon that sat in the middle of the gate.

It was curled tightly in on itself, its wide, webbed wings furled against its back, and the giant head resting serenely on feet with talons the length of my forearm. It was, I thought, a very beautiful dragon, deep chocolate brown with flecks of orange and crimson, like frozen flames, speckling its scales. Its spinal ridge flared red with gold tips, and the great eye that opened at our approach was improbably pure and blue.

At this movement from the dragon the crowd drew back abruptly, and we slipped through. The two youths at the gate did not seem to notice our strange excuse for a horse, but I was certain the dragon did: its crest went up like a fire being stoked, and it backed away from the gate almost respectfully.

Milain had told me it was best to be polite but direct with dragons; that they could sense fear in humans, but respected those with the self-control not to show it. So though my heart was pounding at the sight and my limbs shook a little, I boldly poked my head out of the carriage and said:

"Good-day, we are here to see Milain Birch. Could you please tell us where to find her?"

The dragon blinked at me, its eyes like two huge pools of sapphire flickering in firelight. Then it spoke.

To one who has never heard a dragon speak, it is important to understand that they do not speak as we do; their mouths and lips and tongues are the wrong shape for human language. Some dragons, with a lot of practice, have learned Kyrish and other languages, but these are rare. Mostly, dragons speak with intent. The sounds that come out are predominantly growls and hisses, which form themselves into words somewhere between the dragon's lips and a person's ears. Like many things about dragons, it is a magic not well understood, and not all dragons do it. (Whether because they cannot, or more likely, choose not to, was one of the things my daughter was studying.)

This dragon was fairly good at it, and its words came across clear and precise.

"Birch girl is not here," it said. "I wait for Mother Birch and Purple One. I lead; you follow." With that it flowed to its feet and began walking down a side road that led along the edge of the abbey. We had to wait for several moments, as the dragon was a long and slender one and had a lot of tail.

We followed the dragon around to the back, where there were stables for such livestock that the Institute required. The dragon stopped outside and sat down on its haunches, curling its tail around its legs like a cat—except because the dragon's tail was so long it made several complete circuits.

"Leave your cart here," it said.

We disembarked, and a young stable boy came running to take our luggage. As Abharus helped him load it onto a handcart I tried again to get a look at our horse, but found it quite impossible.

As the boy wheeled the cart away the dragon raised its spiny head, nostrils flared, and then glided to its feet.

"Follow," it said, and began leading us out of the stables and through the gardens behind the abbey.

We followed the dragon—and the strange, horselike creature, having detached itself from the coach, followed us—through an orchard of hardy-looking apple trees, past a high hedge smelling strongly of herbs, and finally out onto a wide field, spotted with clumps of grass, but so covered with scars and gouges and charred black earth that it could hardly have been called a lawn. From where we stood it sloped down in a gentle curve to a cleft where a small river divided us from the towering heights of the Crogard mountains.

There was activity on this field. People running about and two dragons—even larger than our guide—crouching, as small figures climbed down off their backs. One of these was a slender person whose rusty-blond hair was valiantly trying to escape from her helmet in the gusting wind blowing up from the river. She dropped lightly to the ground, impatiently unsnapping the helmet and tugging it free. Then my daughter walked up the hill to greet us.

Milain Birch is taller than her mother by almost a head—nearly as tall as her father. Her hair was pale flaxen when she was a girl, but now it has darkened to a light reddish-blond. Her skin is similarly reddish from all her time out of doors, and her eyes are very small and bright and blue. She favors leather and heavy cotton clothes in tones of tan and brown, and categorically refuses to wear skirts. That afternoon she was dressed in a leather tunic fastened around the waist by a thick belt from which hung many pockets and pouches. She wore sensible trousers tucked into knee-high leather boots, and was just in the process of pulling off her thick leather flight gloves when she reached us.

"Thank you, Spheron," she said to the dragon next to us. Then she reached out and embraced me. "Mother!" she cried. "I am so happy you came at once. Radcliffe said you would. And these must be your fr-friends—" It was to her credit that she stumbled only a little in her speech as she beheld Abharus and Felpz standing beside me. For she had been hearing stories of the Purple Magician and the immortal boy with the silver hair all her life, and having them appear so suddenly in her own world must have been a shock.

But a woman who works with dragons soon learns to conquer her base emotions. Managing somehow to make it look natural, she bent almost double and offered her hand to Abharus.

"Milain Birch," she said.

"How do you do?" Abharus said gravely, shaking the proffered hand.

Milain rose and looked at Felpz. I cannot guess what went through their minds, but I know mine was all in turmoil seeing these two equally important—and until now mutually exclusive—halves of my life put together for the first time.

"Mother has told me all the stories," Milain said by way of greeting Felpz. "Even the ones she didn't put in her books. She told them to me first."

Felpz smiled. He raised a hand and tapped a long finger against his lower lip—a habit I noticed he performed when something interested him greatly.

"Miss Birch," he said, cocking his head forward like a bird of prey that has spotted a target. "I'm sorry, I must ask—what have you got in your pockets?"

Milain started in surprise, then smiled to herself. "I should have expected as much, coming from you. Well, we've made some progress since I wrote to Mother, and this is the result." She reached into a pouch on her belt and removed a small glass bottle, half full of a dark brown liquid.

Felpz leaned forward until his nose was almost touching the glass. He sniffed.

"Explain," said Abharus.

"In order of events," Felpz added, taking the bottle from her. "Preferably. Leave no detail out."

My daughter smiled a little bemusedly. "As you wish," said she. "Walk with me, won't you? Tero wants to meet you."

"I caught a few hours of sleep after I wrote you that letter," she continued as we made our way slowly down the hill to where one dragon—a deep blue one—still waited. "Then we went out on a dawn patrol. There has been no sign of the elder dragon since it arrived, but the eyries are in an uproar; all the drakes, even the wyverns, felt it arrive."

"This elder dragon," Felpz said, enunciating the qualifying word with elaborate care. "Can you be more precise as to its appearance?"

"It was large," said Milain flatly. "The night was dark. I only got an impression of its size and shape. You'll have to ask Tero; she got a better look at it than I did."

Felpz seemed to accept this. "Go on." he said.

"Thank you. Well, I couldn't see how a dragon that large could have disappeared without a trace—even in mountains such as these. So I've had every rider out searching, and around noon today Marigold found . . . well, he called it a murder scene, but to be honest I'm not certain if it was murder. Something was killed there, though. That bottle is filled with some of the blood we found."

"Yes, and interesting blood it is," Felpz remarked.

"It is not dragon's blood," Milain announced, as if this somewhat diminished its interest as far as she was concerned. "But there was a lot at the scene; I am satisfied it is not human. There was no body," she explained. "Though it looked as if something had been dragged away. There were dragon footprints there too, which concerns me."

"Dragons do kill, sometimes," Felpz remarked gently, as one introducing an unpleasant truth to a child.

"Yes, but all our dragons are adults," Milain said, the problem at hand distracting her. "They feed almost entirely on ambient energy discharge. Wind and sunlight, the waterfalls of the river. Trains, they love the energy of trains. I wish more people understood that—how they eat the energy of a thing, not the thing itself. Some of them have gone as far west as Hexindale, following the southern railway line. It's caused some worry. And then of course Crogard is rich in ore—they have no need to hoard treasure."

Felpz considered this, and shrugged. "Have there been any new developments since?"

"None at all," said Milain. "I'd only just returned from visiting the site when I heard you had already arrived. Here we are. Tero, this is the magician."

Tero was a magnificent dragon, if I consider myself any judge. Even bigger than Spheron, tall and sleek and blue-black, she had a crest of spines that shimmered in the sunlight, and this was raised to its full height as she watched us approach.

Felpz stepped forward, and the dragon bent her head so they were almost nose to nose. Man and dragon stood motionless for some minutes, until Abharus lost patience and cleared his throat.

Felpz looked around at us, as though we had woken him from a doze.

"Well, it is certainly no dragon I know of," he said, straightening his lapels. "Though that isn't saying much. This blood, though, does trouble me." He held up the little bottle and frowned at it.

"You know whose it is?" my daughter asked.

"No, but I think I know what it is. Corianne, can you tell me what you had for breakfast two weeks ago?"

I gaped at him. "How can I possibly be expected to remember that? And what relevance does it have to our case?"

Felpz smiled a little twinkling smile at me, and handed me the bottle.

"Try answering now. What did you have for breakfast two weeks ago?"

"Two slices of toast with strawberry preserves, a cup of tea, a biscuit and a small bowl of porridge," I said promptly. Then I gasped and clapped a hand over my lips. The words had formed in my throat and got out of my mouth before I realized they were there. "Felpz, what is this?" I cried.

Abharus snatched the bottle from me, and holding it tightly said with dead certainty:

"It's griffin's blood, Corianne."

"A griffin? In Kyreland? But how did you—"

My daughter nudged me gently with an elbow. "Griffins are emblems of truth. They say it's impossible to lie when in the presence of one."

"A somewhat inaccurate description," Felpz said, plucking the bottle from Abharus's unresisting hands. "The truth—and be sure I speak it here—is that griffins possess the element of truth. This manifests itself by compelling honesty in people who are nearby. Holding a piece of a griffin—such as its blood or bone—magnifies the effects tenfold. It will summon the truth out of you, even if you have forgotten it or are unsure."

My daughter, who had been listening to this shrewdly, nodded once. "Well then, Mr Felpz, what has become of the griffin whose blood this is?" she asked.

Felpz frowned. "I'm afraid that I do not know, and so this blood helps us little in that regard. However, if Tero will be so good as to show me the way, I would like to take a look at the place where you found this sample."

"Oh, but Tero isn't—" Milain began, intending no doubt to begin a long explanation of how dragons are not horses and do not carry people on their backs unless they know and respect them, but Tero was already fanning her wings and extending one long, spiny foreleg towards Felpz.

Instead of mounting the beast, Felpz stepped gently onto Tero's claw and took a firm hold of the spike protruding from her elbow. He made us a stiff bow.

We watched in astonishment as the dragon's huge wings spread wide, the long fingers embedded in the webbing like dark branches, with the membrane between glowing from the sun shining through. For a moment we were enveloped in a deep blue shadow, and then with an almighty clap Tero leapt into the air.

We were buffeted by a sharp stinging wind, and I felt a tingle along my skin from the blast of pure magic the dragon used to fling herself into the sky. I ducked and turned my head away from the turbulence, and when I looked again Felpz was only a tiny figure clinging to the leg of the soaring beast as she veered off across the low peaks.

Milain was staring after them with the look of one who has just witnessed a railway accident.

"Tero allows no one to ride her—no one but me." Then she shook herself. "No, I should not be so surprised, should I? Where has Spheron got to?"

"If you plan on chasing after him," I said sternly, "make allowances for at least one more passenger; I am coming with you."

"Yes—you are?" My daughter looked around distractedly.

"I'll find my own way," Abharus said, and quietly disappeared. I am convinced only I saw him go; Milain was too preoccupied pouring instructions on Spheron to notice.

Spheron, it appeared, was not so obliging as Tero. He agreed to carry us, but not on his back: Milain had to run back to the stables and fetch out what she called "the basket."

This was a contraption I was already familiar with. On my previous visit Milain had coaxed me into taking a short dragon flight in the basket, an experience I spent the following days trying hard to forget. The basket was a stiff sack made of heavy canvas laced to a metal ring. A person could stand in it, and the ring would come up to her shoulders if she were my height. Attached to this ring was a muddle of ropes which the dragon carrying the basket held in its claws. In this way a person could travel by dragon in relative safety, if not comfort, without the dragon suffering the indignity of carrying that person on its back.

As it turned out, even though Milain was a good deal slimmer than her mother, the basket could not be made to fit both of us. The solution Milain concocted did not please me: she sat on the metal ring with only her feet inside the sacking, holding onto the ropes.

"Goodness, Mother, calm down," she said in response to my concerns. "I've done this countless times!"

I need hardly point out this had the opposite of the intended effect.

It was with my heart in my mouth that Spheron took off with us suspended so hazardously below him. The storm of wind and magic whipped up by the dragon's wings was many times worse when stuck under it, and I was temped to crouch right down in the bottom of the basket. As it was I held on tight to the metal ring with one hand, and my daughter's leg with the other.

Milain tells me the mountains are a beautiful sight from the air, being able to look down between ridges and peaks to the narrow, glittering rivers and the tops of trees so distant they look like models on a child's play set. I have to take her word for it: I was far too terrified to notice any details beyond the great expanse of sky overhead that threatened to swallow us up, and the stinging wind in my face. For though the dragon used magic to augment its flight, this applied in no way to us, and I was overly conscious of the fact that only a layer of cloth and some hemp ropes prevented us from plummeting to our doom.

After a tumultuous flight, Spheron set us down in a remote valley where an ancient landslide had left a wide sandy beach pillowed up beside the stream. Beside this sat Tero, her large blue bulk standing out sharply against the yellow sand and stone of the canyon. She was watching Felpz, equally conspicuous in his purple suit, who in turn was regarding the center of the sand bar with extreme gravity.

Once I had extracted myself from the basket I could see why: it looked like a large animal had been slaughtered there. Old blood stood in pools and lay in streaks; the sand was turned and gashed so deeply even the more recent footprints of my daughter and her colleagues could not disguise it. Flies gathered profusely at the edge of the pools, and the whole place smelled vile.

It was late in the summer afternoon now, and the tall peaks rising on either side cast the whole scene in a soft blue twilight, yet still the blood glimmered in that way peculiar to the substance, and it was present in such volume that I felt my stomach clench. I am not by nature a weak-nerved person, but since my youth I have had an aversion to copious gore, and the sight put me off balance.

Milain, on the other hand, had banished any such weakness as she had apparently banished her fear of heights. She strode right up to Felpz, put her hands on her hips, and said: "Well? What do you make of it?"

For his part, Felpz did not seem at all surprised to see us. He looked up from his contemplation of the ground and blinked.

"Clearly, someone was killed here, or at least mortally injured," he said. "You observe the gashes in the ground, the disrupted soil?"

"Yes," said Milain, as if answering a painfully obvious question.

Felpz ignored her tone and carried on. "It crashed here. Attempted to take off again . . . failed. Then, it appears, someone came to its aid . . . " Felpz had circled the mess as he spoke, and now came to a halt beside a peculiarly smooth patch of sand. It looked as though something very large had blown on it, scattering the grains to cover any track. Felpz looked up at Milain, a hard crease between his eyebrows.

"Are all the resident dragons of Crogard known to you?" he asked. "Aside from this interloping elder dragon you speak of?"

"We have fifty-two adults on our books," Milain replied promptly. "But these are only the ones who have come forward and allowed themselves to be known. We estimate close to five hundred live in Crogard, but . . . " she glanced deferentially towards Spheron and Tero, who were standing loftily apart and not deigning to look at us, "dragons don't take kindly to their territory being invaded, and that is the last thing we want to do."

"Rather late to develop a sense of propriety," Felpz remarked with a sigh. "Still, late is better than never I suppose. Yet it doesn't help us now. There was a dragon here, I am sure. You see the traces of a body being dragged away? Yes, well, they go nowhere. They disappear into this . . . " he waved at the patch of wind-blasted sand, "obfuscation."

"You think a dragon carried the body away?"

"I am sure a dragon did," Felpz said. "The question is, which one? And why . . . is this a dragon's kill? Or is it something else . . . ?" He trailed off, letting his gaze wander over to the two dragons.

Felpz squared his shoulders and walked over to Tero and Spheron. Though they towered above him, Felpz somehow gave the impression of being their equal in size. The purple ghost of billowing sleeves and a trailing cape flashed on the edge of my vision, and I got the strangest sense of potential power, like water behind a dam, welling up behind him in this strange, distant way. Felpz, the man Felpz, was but the lid on a much deeper well—and we could only perceive its presence now because he wished us to.

Or at least, he wished the dragons to.

"You'll find it is in your best interests to answer my questions plainly," he said to both of them in such tones of authority that Milain's jaw dropped.

The dragons did not appear agitated; they regarded him impassively. Felpz took their silence for acquiescence.

"Do you have an interest in this matter?" Felpz asked, waving a hand at the nearby scene. "Specifically, do you have an interest in whether or not we learn the truth of it? If you are ignorant of the truth and have no objection to our untangling this mystery, please continue to assist us. If you are not. If you do not wish us to follow this trail to the bitter end, then I must request you remove yourselves and no longer provide us with false service."

Milain was staring in horror by the end of this speech, and I half expected the dragons to roast Felpz on the spot.

Instead they turned to one another, mantled their wings in a draconian shrug, and then as one leapt into the air, the force of their wingbeats like small thunderclaps as they soared away into the sky.

Felpz straightened the collar of his coat and smoothed his hair down.

"Just as well," he said, turning back to us. "Now we may make some actual progress."

I had never seen my daughter struck speechless, but there she stood staring at Felpz, her mouth still agape. I could see a torrent of outrage slowly building behind the shocked façade, however, and I hastened to intercede.

"Do I take this to mean those dragons are somehow involved in all this?" I asked.

Felpz dusted off his hands and returned to the messy scene. "Involved, yes, there is no doubt. But on which end I am not so sure. I see your daughter has inherited your talent for glaring holes in the side of my head. Please do not look so betrayed, Miss Birch. Once I get to the bottom of this I have no doubt your dragons' actions will seem perfectly reasonable."

"You sent them away!" Milain exclaimed, fighting back a slew of insults I could tell were boiling in her chest.

"I merely asked them to remove themselves if they were here on false pretexts," Felpz said rationally.

Milain looked ready to launch into one of her lectures on the proper treatment of dragons—powerful magician or no—when there was a shimmer in the air and the soft sound of feathered wings. A gust of wind smelling faintly of wet grass and flowers lifted the hairs on my neck, and Abharus stepped out of nowhere onto the sandy beach.

Or not quite nowhere. It appeared to be out of nowhere, but I got the distinct impression that he had just dismounted from a horse—or horse-shaped being.

He looked pale in the summer twilight, with a tightness about his mouth that boded ill for the news he brought.

"I found her," he said, gesturing at the blood. "The griffin, I mean. I found her body, or what's left of it."

Felpz's face darkened at that. "Near or . . . ?"

"Not far," Abharus said. "But hidden, and rather hard to get to. Hold on, Yuragorn can open a door on our end if you can do the rest here."

"Do so," ordered Felpz, and Abharus took firm hold of some-thing invisible and vanished.

"Felpz," I said, laying a hand on my daughter's elbow. "Would you be so kind as to explain? What is this about doors?"

Felpz looked confused for a moment, as if surprised I should ask.

"Why, it's only a simple translocation spell. Similar to what I often do, but working with Yuragorn we can cross a greater distance in no time at all."

"And who," said Milain with steel in her voice, "is Yuragorn? I can't see him . . . her . . . it properly."

"Keep looking then," Felpz said, turning his back on us—but not before I caught the sly grin on his face. "When you see her you will understand."

The door that Felpz created was unlike anything I'd ever seen before. It was as though he pushed his hands clean out of the world and pulled aside a flap of curtain. From this breach a ring of light rose, sending out arms and tendrils like a spider's web, encircling him. At the center of this web, where the light was brightest, a small picture appeared: I caught a glimpse of a deep blue sky and high, red mountain peaks. A wind blew out of this image and brought with it that same smell of wet grass and flowers—a smell I was beginning to associate with the creature Yuragorn.

"After you," Felpz said, beckoning to us.

For once it was I who led the way, perfectly confident in Felpz's magic, and my daughter who clung to my hand—as she had not done in many years—as we walked down the glittering strands of web and into the picture.

We came out the other side into a gust of sharp wind. It was so strong I had to turn my face away in order to breathe, and I hunched my shoulders against it.

Abharus stood not far away, posed in a mimicry of Felpz, and beside him was the vague impression of wings and feathers and glimmering horn that was still all I could see of Yuragorn.

We appeared to be on a wide ledge near the top of a mountain: the evening sun was full upon us, but the air was noticeably colder and I felt light-headed. I was glad of my daughter's strong grip on my arm, and we steadied each other as Felpz came through, the closing of the portal causing the wind to back and buffet us irritably. I sank to my knees, all too aware of how much sky there was, and how little ground. This, however, only served to bring me closer to the reason for Abharus's summoning.

The bones and eviscerated skin of a griffin were laid out on the rocky slab.

Only the fear that I would tumble off into that great expanse of sky should I move kept me from writhing backwards.

The thing had clearly been dead for days and had been picked clean of meat and fat in that time. Only the skeleton, jumbled and scattered by the activity of scavengers, and pieces of hide, with here and there a few feathers, remained. The skull, which was as big as a horse's and had a beak a foot long, lay on its side near the cliff, and even from the distance of several feet I could see the movement of countless insects as they crawled over it, cleaning the curves and crannies of the bone.

Felpz came through so energetically that he nearly stepped right into the middle of this mess. He let out a surprised shout and danced sideways—towards the side of the mountain—and there crouched, observing the scene with grave eyes.

"I thought you said dragons only hunted when they had hatchlings to feed!" I exclaimed to my daughter, who was staring at the remains with equal surprise.

"So I said, but that hasn't stopped them poaching sheep," she said. "This is strange indeed. It could only have been a dragon that moved a creature of this size all the way up here, but why?"

"This death was not caused by a dragon," Felpz said from his perch by what had once been the griffin's tail. "And this"—he gestured at the scene—"was not the work of a predator." He leaned forward and began to crawl among the bones, turning them over and running his fingers across the sandy stone beneath.

"I don't believe I follow you," said Milain frankly.

Abharus, who had been standing very quietly with his hands behind his back, looked up at us with large, sad eyes.

"Dragons do not die," he said quietly. "They fly away into the sky and become stars. Griffins are creatures akin to dragons, being part bird—which are descended from the ancient dragons that once lived all over the world—and part cat—which have been friends of dragons since they first evolved. But a griffin cannot fly out of this world and rest in the ethereal sky—a griffin does die—so the dragons have done the next best thing." He waved a small hand at the bones scattered across the rock. "They gave her a sky burial."

"Some human cultures practice it as well," Felpz remarked from the middle of the bone field. "They lay out their dead on a cliff top, and the vultures come and eat it, carrying the flesh away with them . . . quite the kindest sort of burial, I always thought . . . " He was crouched on his tip-toes, running his fingers around and around, until with a cry of triumph one hand darted forward and snatched at something. Standing up, he leapt nimbly out of the bones and held out his hand to me.

There in his palm was the squashed remains of a lead bullet.

Milain stared at it, wide eyed.

"I don't understand," she said. "What does this mean? And . . . how do you know this individual was female?"

Before Felpz could answer, Abharus made an inarticulate gasping sound, and I caught a sharp whiff of Yuragorn's scent as the creature swept her wings out in alarm. A second later I smelled something else: something scorched and burned, hot and dry; the smell of a desert baking under the sun.

A new wind blew across the mountain. Where before all had been cool—almost chill—and smelling of clear mountain air with a hint of pine . . . now I felt a rough, hot wind on my cheek. It blew not up, from the canyons and valleys below, but down, out of that wide, blue sky.

A sky that had become much darker for the great shape that was sailing, like a spiky black thunderhead, down upon us. Its wings stretched from peak to peak across the nearest valley, and in its shadow Tero and Spheron, who were flying below, looked as small as sparrows.

"Felpz?" I said uncertainly. I was surprised I could speak at all; for I felt as though my heart was in my throat and beating fit to burst.

"Get behind Yuragorn," Felpz commanded, and he turned and leveled a piercing stare upon Milain. "For your future edification," he said pleasantly, "that is not an elder dragon. That is what is called, by the people who are in a position to call them anything, a Royal Dragon. A ruling drake. They usually remain in the Dragon Lands."

"Then what is it doing here?" demanded Milain.

"That is one of the questions I will ask, when it arrives," Felpz replied. "Whether it answers, that is another matter."

The dragon was definitely making for our mountain by this time. It was circling above us, each circuit bringing it lower and lower. Every time it passed, it brought another gust of hot, dry wind.

In colour it was a glossy, iridescent black, pricked with glimmers of purple and blue. Its webbed wings, which must have been three hundred feet long each, were slightly translucent, pale sky showing through them. I could make out a dark latticework, like tree branches, that stood out against the grey-blue of the membrane. It was soaring in the manner of raptors, with its wings fully outstretched, and along with the sharp sting of magic, I could feel waves of heat radiating down from it.

This dragon, I thought, did not need to breathe fire—it could set the mountains alight with a beat of its mighty wings.

There was a gentle tug on my hand. I looked down to find Abharus there, his face very pale but set in a determined expression.

"Come stand with me," he said. "Let Felpz do the talking."

He led us to a corner where the jutting ledge met the sheer rock of the mountainside, beyond the remnants of the griffin. It felt just as exposed—now the great dragon was level with us, circling the mountaintop and drawing ever closer— but then I heard the gentle rustle of feathers, and a draft of cool air smelling of wet wildflowers washed over us. By this time I could almost see Yuragorn's wings as they enfolded Abharus, Milain and myself, and I got the strongest impression of a large, horse-shaped body. A long, jagged horn like a piece of starlight leveled at Felpz, who stood brashly at the edge of the cliff, his purple coat-tails flapping in the hot wind of the dragon's flight.

It passed before us once, twice more, the last time its wingtip grazing the mountainside. Then it dropped out of sight.

I do not think the mountain actually shook when the great dragon landed, digging its claws into the rock as if it were made of clay, but that was my strong impression. Certainly there was a horrible, thundering noise like several avalanches, and I felt the rock vibrate beneath my feet.

Felpz stood calmly through this all, his feet in a wide stance and his hands clasped modestly behind his back.

Slowly, its horns like the masts of a sunken ship rising from the deep, the dragon's head came into view. Up close I could see more clearly the contrast between its shiny black, and iridescent blue-purple, scales that shone in its dark skin like vivid stars. It had many rows of black horns, all smooth and curving, save one or two that looked somewhat mangled, and a string of plate-like protrusions that began between its eyes and disappeared behind the ridge of its head, creating heavy, forbidding brows.

Its eyes were deep blue pools set in black caves, and its thin-lipped mouth looked wide enough that, should it open, it could have swallowed all of us in one gulp. I could not see any teeth, but there were enough spines and spikes decorating its snout to make it appear as though it were snarling.

The dragon breathed out through its wide, flaring nostrils, and the air around us caught fire.

The sight of Felpz disappearing into those flames is not one I will ever forget, nor something I ever wish to see again. I felt my cry of horror die in my throat as the wall of fire hit us.

Then at last I saw Yuragorn. For the flames did not wash over us as they had Felpz, but hit an object that stood between us and the dragon, and there died. In the dying fire I saw the shape of a large horse, its limbs strong and graceful with thick feathers about its feet. Its tail was like that of a peacock, with long, flowing feathers, and in place of a mane, a crest of feathers. The wings spread wide above us to block the fire, and for a moment I saw its head, the profile of a noble equine with a jagged horn protruding from its forehead, its ears pinned back along its neck.

Then the shape against the fire turned. I saw its feathers, stretching like the fingers of spread hands, and the creature reared up onto its hind legs and beat its wings.

A rush of cool air came out of nowhere, the scent of wet flowers almost overpowering, and the dragon's fire rolled back, thinned, and died away entirely.

Felpz still stood at the edge of the cliff, his coat not even singed. The dragon's face regarded us, its eyes narrowed to glinting slits. Yuragorn was invisible once more.

"That was entirely uncalled for," Felpz said placidly, dusting off his shoulder.

The dragon snorted, sending jets of steam out of its nostrils. I saw Felpz move his hand over the jets of hot air as they passed him, and by the time they reached us the air was cool.

"We are not your enemies," Felpz said calmly. "We only wish to learn the truth."

The dragon stared at us. In its mountainous face I thought I could discern an expression of skepticism. Its breath washed over us, hot and clean and burning, like the first direct ray of sun on a desert morning.

"Will you not speak to me?" Felpz asked eventually.

The dragon's eyes flickered in their caves, and I felt the beam of its attention fall on me. Memories of the demon I had faced years ago rose in my mind, but the dragon was something very different. Where the demon's voice had felt like burning acid, the attention of the dragon felt like being dunked in a river of hot water. It made my mind sluggish and slow.

Then the dragon moved its attention to Milain, and while I was still reeling from the sensation Abharus jumped forward.

"I'll do it," he said loudly. "I will speak for you!"

There was a disturbance in the air around Yuragorn, and the dragon's gaze focused on Abharus like a searchlight.

What happened next I found difficult to understand at the time, but I now see it this way: the dragon beckoned to Abharus, even though its forelegs were currently clinging to the mountain. Abharus walked forward, stiffly, until he stood before the dragon's great spiny snout, and there turned to face us.

Only it was no longer Abharus. It was as though we only saw the shell of him, and something else entirely looked out at us through his eyes.

"I have read of this," whispered Milain, her hand clamped on my arm. "Some of the elder dragons cannot speak to humans at all, so they find one whose mind is attuned to theirs and use them as a translator!"

I shook my head, trying to clear it of the dragon's presence, and watched in mute horror and fascination as the dragon began to speak in Abharus's delicate, child voice.

"This . . . is not your concern, human mage." Abharus's mouth moved, and it was Abharus's voice, but it was the dragon's words and the dragon's will. It spoke slowly, as though getting used to this new, small mouth and tongue, but its words were quite clear. "Go back, humans. Go back to your cities and your little wooden houses. Go back. Play your music. Leave this place where my children live, and do not meddle in the affairs of dragons. If I catch you again, I will not be so gentle."

Abharus wobbled on the cliff edge, steadied himself, and then it was Abharus who stared back at us, his eyes wide and his mouth gaping open. It was undoubtedly Abharus who said:

"Felpz, she's got me. Her name is Kasarvo and she is very strong. Don't worry," he added, even as he walked backwards until he came up against the dragon's snout, hooking his arms over the two nearest spikes and holding on as if for dear life. I understood why a moment later when the dragon raised her head, lifting Abharus with her.

Abharus shouted something, something that was lost in the hot wind of the dragon's breath—which burned now more than ever, and I guessed Yuragorn had left us—and I saw Felpz run to the very edge of the cliff, clearly intent on catching Abharus's words.

With a mighty rumble the dragon leapt back from the mountain, her wingbeats hurtling air at us with such force that Milain and I were thrown back against the rock. In the strange way of things I did not feel the burst of magic the dragon used to propel herself upwards, but tasted it like hot sand in my mouth. The sensation was so intense that I actually bent over and spat, thinking I had somehow got a mouthful of dust, but nothing came out, not even spittle; my mouth was perfectly dry.

As the wingbeats of the dragon faded to distant thunder Felpz came back from the cliff, smoothing down his hair which had been blown all over by the dragon's breath and fire. He was frowning to himself, but did not seem particularly upset. Perhaps it was this relative serenity that caused me to fully realize what had just happened.

"That... that overgrown lizard!" I cried. "She took Abharus!"

"He will be in a better position than we," Felpz remarked, going over to the bones of the griffin—which had been blown up against the side of the mountain during the encounter. He took off his coat and laid it flat on the ground, then began carefully piling the bones into it. "This situation is indeed puzzling."

"P-puzzling?" cried my daughter, clearly thinking several steps ahead of us. "This is downright inconvenient. How will I explain this to the director? If we can find a way to get back— without Tero or Spheron to help it will be rather difficult." She looked accusingly at Felpz.

Felpz actually chuckled, and went right on collecting bones. I patted my daughter on the arm.

"Felpz has ways of making distance inconsequential," I explained. "Remember, he is a magician."

"Yes, yes, space folding," said Milain, looking bleakly around at the mountaintops surrounding us. "I can't see how that helps us here."

"You work with beasts who by nature are intensely magical," Felpz said, tying the sleeves of his coat together to secure the bones. Holding this odd bundle in both hands he stood up and smiled at us. "Have a little more faith in my magic. Corianne, be a dear and hold this." He passed his burden to me. It was large and bulky, but astonishingly light. "Now, it will be easiest if we join hands," he said, looping an arm through mine and extending the other to Milain. "Can you picture the landing field behind the abbey?" he asked as she took his hand reluctantly.

"Yes, easily," she replied.

"Good," said Felpz. "Imagine it in every detail—close your eyes if it makes it easier. Now hold that image in your head . . . "

There followed a jarring transition so abrupt it made my teeth hurt. It was as though the piece of the world we stood in were torn away, and behind that the field of Draco Abbey pushed forward. For one horrible moment I was uncertain whether I stood on the mountain cliff or on the singed grass of the field. Then the latter scene solidified, and I breathed in thicker, sweeter air and caught a whiff of horses from the stables. I found my feet planted in short, yellow grass, and a little ways off loomed the dark body of the abbey. The mountains were distant spires rising above us once more, silhouetted against the setting sun.

"Oh . . . my goodness," said Milain in a small voice. "You never said he could do that."

"He never has in my experience," I replied, once I could speak again.

Felpz, who might have taken issue with this conversation, appeared not to hear; he was striding away towards the abbey, beckoning to an astonished stable lad as he went. Finding I still held his bundle of griffin bones, I made haste to hurry after him.

Bouragner Felpz moved like a man on a mission, and we did not catch up to him until he was seated at the head of a long table in the reference library while young interns ran and fetched him book after book. A tall, grey-haired man with sloping shoulders and a burn scar on one cheek, whom I recognized as Dr Asifian Vayar, the director of the Draconian Institute, stood at his elbow looking bemused. His gaze hardened when he saw Milain, and he frowned disapprovingly at the bundle in my arms.

"We do not make a study of the griffins in this area," he said to Felpz, clearly answering a question that had been asked before our arrival. "They migrate through twice a year, but are not permanent residents. It would be highly unusual for one to be seen here during summer."

Felpz moved aside the book in front of him and picked up from the table the small lead bullet which he had found in the griffin's remains.

"Rare enough to surprise a farmer, already set on edge by having his stock in close proximity to dragons?" Felpz asked.

"That is an extraordinary claim," said the director uncomfortably. "What proof have you besides a lone bullet . . . " he trailed off as Felpz beckoned to me to hand over the bundle, and taking it he shook out his coat so that the scorched bones tumbled forth over the book-laden table.

A young intern cried out and snatched a particularly aged volume out of the way, but the rest were buried under the deluge of griffin remains.

"What is this?" cried the director, understandably affronted.

"These," said Felpz, spreading his hands over the bones, "are the remains of a griffin who came to these parts under duress and met with a very unfortunate end. It was shot, escaped, only to perish in the mountains. There the dragons found it, buried it after their fashion, and are in their way looking after its affairs."

"Its affairs? What affairs could these be?"

"My associate is looking into that as we speak," Felpz said placidly. "I expect an answer before morning. In the meantime, Miss Birch," his eyes rose and fixed themselves upon my daughter, "the first sheep that was killed . . . are you certain beyond a shadow of doubt that a dragon killed it?"

"I . . . " Milain seemed taken aback by this idea. She swallowed her initial affirmation, and a contemplative expression crossed her face. At last she sighed. "I assumed," she admitted. "The animal was well grown—nothing but a dragon could have carried it off."

"The name of the farmer to whom it belonged?" Felpz asked.

"Er, it was McMorris I believe?" she looked questioningly at her director, who nodded.

"Edther McMorris has the largest lease in the grass valleys," he explained. "We've had complaints from him before, but nothing as serious as this."

"And he reported the poaching of the first sheep? The one lost two weeks ago?"

"Aye, that is so," said the director. "It was he also who complained of losing one two days ago."

"Can you get a message to him? By human courier, preferably," Felpz said, scribbling a note.

In due course a courier was drafted and sent running with Felpz's letter. Milain, clearly impatient and uncomfortable under the disapproving eyes of the director, twisted her hands and muttered ominously.

"Wyvern would have been faster."

"Ah, yes, I nearly forgot," Felpz said, his face brightening. "Where is that charming fellow Radcliffe? I have a favor to ask."

Radcliffe arrived minutes later, accompanied by a small flock of other wyverns. They crowded onto the sill of the largest window and peered in excitedly as Felpz went to greet them.

"I need something found," he said frankly. "It may or may not be there, in which case I need to know one way or the other. You are looking for the remains of a sheep, well-grown, colour . . . " he glanced at Milain.

"McMorris keeps Borerays, most of them are white—he's very proud of them," she supplied.

" . . . likely dropped not too far from McMorris's farm. Give the mountains there a good sweep and report back. There will be—" he raised a finger at the ensuing clamor of high wyvern voices "—there will be biscuits for all who participate, whether a corpse is found or not."

The clamor's nature changed from protest to enthusiasm, and in a storm of leathery wings the wyverns scattered into the evening.

Felpz returned from the window and surveyed the table of books. He picked up his coat and shook it out, then put it on again and sat down. He looked up at our expectant faces with an expression of perfect innocence.

"Friends," he said, giving us a beatific smile. "Please, sit down. I imagine it will be a little while before Mr McMorris arrives, no need to pass the time on your feet."

So it was we were all seated around the table, which was still covered in old books and griffin bones, when a red-faced and breathless intern put in his head and announced, "Mr McMorris of Lower Rivenstone—" before Edther McMorris pushed him aside and entered the room.

He was a large man in both height and girth, with a forthright bearing and an expression that declared he was not best pleased.

Despite our visitor's daunting appearance Felpz leapt up and greeted him like an old friend; jumping out of his seat, he fairly danced across the room and clapped the man on the shoulder.

"Mr McMorris you are just the man I wished to see," he said jovially, shaking the astonished farmer by the hand.

"I have to admit you have me at a loss," McMorris said, with understandable reserve. He eyed Felpz's bright purple suit with distaste. "I'm here to answer a summons from Dr Vayar, who claims to have apprehended the one responsible for poaching my stock."

I did not bother to look, but laid a calming hand over the director's, who sat next to me. "Leave all to Felpz," I whispered to him. "He may be inscrutable, but he always has some clear end."

"A thousand apologies," Felpz said, throwing his hands up. "I did not mean to mislead you—for it was I who wrote that note, not the director. Forgive me, I am Bouragner Felpz, a magician of some small ability—but I do have your poacher."

"Indeed," said McMorris, narrowing his eyes at Felpz. "That news gladdens me." His manner was anything but glad; he made an involuntary jerk to put some space between himself and the magician. "Where do you have him restrained?"

"Restrained?" cried Felpz with a laugh. "No restraints are necessary. For you see, she—er, it is rather more likely that it was female, you see—is right here." He flung a hand out to the table covered in bones, the griffin's skull staring wanly from the center, and in that moment all his benevolent good nature quite deserted him. His tone grew chill and his face grave, and he looked very hard at McMorris as the man took in the grim sight.

I watched with interest as the farmer's ruddy expression went from suspicious to confused, and was just building into offended when Felpz spoke again.

"Mr McMorris," he said in that peculiar resonant voice that was quiet yet piercing at the same time. "Did you shoot a griffin that you caught hunting on your land two weeks ago?"

McMorris's head jerked up. He looked furious, but he said quite readily:

"Why, yes I did, the damn beast was harassing my sheep. She'd got one of my best ewes in her claws by the time I got there. I had my rifle with me, and I took a shot. The damn thing flew off but I'd do it again given the chance." The man's mouth snapped shut, and a look of panicked horror rose in his eyes as he realized what he had just said.

"That is . . . I meant to say . . . " he stammered. The words seemed to catch in his throat and drown in it. "How did you—?" he gasped.

Felpz smiled humorlessly. "I direct your attention to the contents of your left waistcoat pocket," he said. "Which contents, I admit, are entirely my doing."

McMorris groped in his pocket, his face now very pale, and produced the familiar vial of black blood.

"What—" his mouth worked wordlessly on lies the blood would not allow him to say "—is this?" he managed at last.

"A griffin's blood," Felpz said softly. "The blood of the griffin you killed. She may have flown on, but she left behind enough of herself to allow me to trap you."

McMorris gaped and stammered, clearly attempting to deny this accusation, but the vial of griffin's blood sat heavy in his hand and did not allow the lies to pass his lips. At last Milain went over and plucked the item off him.

"While I do not condone Mr McMorris's actions," said the director sadly, "by law he has done nothing wrong; he is perfectly within his rights to defend his stock, and griffins are not a protected species here; it is perfectly legal to shoot one."

"It is not the arm of the law Mr McMorris has to fear," Felpz said coldly. "It is the animosity of dragons, which I shouldn't need to point out are a law unto themselves."

"But the Institute said—" McMorris began.

"Have you forged a pact with their brood mother?" Felpz demanded, fury rising behind his eyes. "Have you sworn your soul to them under the old stars? Have you walked into the fire and called it friend? If not, then you mean nothing to the dragons. You are a pest, an intruder who has killed one of their allies, and no human promises can save you. There is nothing left to be said. I will not wish you a good evening, but I recommend you have a care on your way home."

McMorris was actually cowed by this onslaught, and seemed to shrink back in on himself. He turned to go and shuffled miserably out the door.

"You mean to just let him go?" Milain said indignantly.

"What else can I do?" Felpz said. "As your director says he has broken none of our laws. The dragons will deal with him in their own time."

The director blanched visibly at this thought, and after a moment Felpz took pity on him.

"Well," he said with a great sigh. "Perhaps Mr McMorris can be induced to move his farming elsewhere? To Gaela, perhaps? I understand there are no dragons on Gaela."

"None of this tells us what the dragons are doing," I pointed out. "Or what has happened to Abharus . . . "

"One, I hope, should explain the other," Felpz said cryptically. "But don't fret over Abharus; he's been in hotter places and has more experience in these matters than you might think."

Nevertheless I did fret over Abharus. All through supper and into evening I spun disconcerting narratives in my head, working myself into a shocking state of nerves.

We were seated in one of the small turrets that had historically been used for star gazing, but was now the wyvern's rookery, when events finally began to unfold.

Milain sat at a desk in the corner going over a pile of paperwork, while Felpz sat astride the windowsill, one leg dangling outside and kicking lazily at the stonework. With nothing better to do, I took a stool by the door and attempted to write in my journal, but found by this point I was too nervous to write anything. I had only got so far as "At least he has his Yuragorn creature with him . . . " when, as if in response to my thoughts, I smelled the scent of sweet grass and rainy nights, and a cool breeze blew into the little room out of nowhere.

Felpz kicked his leg inside and looked about alertly while Milain and I got to our feet. There was a whorl in the air by the wall, and I recognized the beginnings of another portal.

"Felpz?" I said tentatively. "What does it mean?"

"It means it is time to discover what this has all been about," Felpz announced, and strode through the portal almost before it finished forming.

Milain and I looked at each other across the space where he had been, then throwing aside our pens and paper, we dove after him together.

We came through into a confusion of darkness and hard stone. I groped about, grazed my hand on a sharp rock, and then found Milain's arm.

"Where is this?" she cried indignantly. "Mother, what has your magician gotten us into now?"

"Quiet," came Felpz's voice out of the darkness, and I swallowed back my reply.

I reached out, tentatively, hoping to find him, and instead felt a warm and furry flank which heaved under my hand. Whiskers brushed my face, and raising my hand to push them aside I felt the unmistakable shape of a horse's nose; soft and a little wet. It breathed out cool air that smelled of a wet night and flowers.

I remembered the shape in the flames.

"Yuragorn?" I said. "Where is Abharus?"

"Here," came Abharus's voice from somewhere near the ground. He sounded tired, but strangely triumphant. A tight knot that had been in my chest the whole evening finally loosened.

"Felpz, could you manage the light?" he asked. "I'm exhausted."

In response, a gentle yellow light bloomed, and by it I saw Felpz bending over the shape of Abharus, who was leaning up against the wall of the cave we appeared to be in. In his lap was sprawled a creature covered in downy white fur with short, stubby wings. Its beak was long and hooked, like an eagle's, and it rested comfortably across Abharus's right arm. It was fast asleep.

Felpz stood up and looked over at Milain with shining eyes.

"You were right after all, after a fashion," he said. "It was a hatchling."

"But not a dragon," said Abharus, gently extracting a hand and stroking the creature's feathers.

Responding perhaps to our voices, perhaps to the light, the creature made a crooning noise and lifted its head. It blinked, then stared up at us with eyes the colour of amber.

"A griffin kit?" Milain whispered in astonishment. "What on earth is it doing here?"

To her second question there was no immediate answer, but it was unmistakably a baby griffin which lay across Abharus. I could see now its front and rear legs, which were that of a cat, and its long feline tail which had not yet sprouted the stiff feathers that would enable it to steer in flight.

"Some crisis must have driven its mother to hatch her egg here," Felpz said, gazing at the animal with sad, fond eyes. "What that may have been, likely we shall never know."

The kit was not afraid of us; it got up—kneading Abharus painfully in the stomach—and walked on wobbly, uncertain legs towards Felpz.

Milain, with her natural affinity for strange animals, came forward and intercepted the griffin with wide, steady hands. She spoke to it softly, her voice low and cooing—not unlike a large bird. She dipped a hand into one of the pockets of her belt and produced a small strip of dried meat.

"I always keep some handy for the wyverns," she explained, offering it to the griffin. When the animal turned its nose aside Milain simply put the meat into her mouth, chewed it, then spat it back out onto her palm. Now the griffin found the food attractive, and snapped it up with a flash of beak.

"Have you ever cared for a griffin before?" Felpz asked.

"None as young as this," Milain admitted. "I usually see the regulars when they come through in the fall and spring. Sometimes we give them a meal."

"Griffins possess a human intelligence," Abharus explained, shifting into a more comfortable position. "This one is only a few weeks old. She keeps crying for her mother."

"Oh," I said, my heart sinking. "Oh dear."

"Is this what Tero and Spheron were hiding?" Milain asked, but without rancor; she was too distracted trying to measure the griffin kit while feeding it more chewed meat.

In response, a great noise filled the little chamber. It was not a roar: it was too calm and deliberate to be called a roar. It was merely a vast exhalation of air into a large and echoing chamber. For the first time I thought to wonder what lay beyond the sphere of Felpz's little yellow light.

"Oh dear, she's back," Abharus said, getting stiffly to his feet. "Kasarvo. Felpz, I meant to tell you. Kasarvo once served Eldis and Aldor—she knows griffins—that's why the other dragons called her in; they didn't know what to do with the kit after the mother was killed. Kasarvo has been protecting—"

He was cut off by a roar as the far wall of the cave burst into flames.

I looked again, and saw this was not quite so: the far wall was no wall at all, but a great window onto a vast cavern beyond. Something had just breathed a wreath of flames past the aperture.

Far from being distressed, the griffin kit squealed in joy and took off at an unsteady trot towards where the fire—now spent—had flared.

Milain, clearly expecting it to injure itself, followed hunched over, her hands hovering protectively around the animal's head.

"Oh, Milain!" I cried, as I had in years past when she had done unexpected and perilous things. But now—as then—she ignored me, and followed the little griffin until it stopped, propping its feet up on the ledge of rock that marked the end of our little cave.

Felpz moved his hand and the light grew stronger, revealing the great face of the huge dragon as it peered in.

Milain looked up, saw the mouth large enough to swallow her in a single bite, saw the deep, glimmering eyes, and put her hands on her hips. Then, to my shock and horror, she began to berate the dragon.

"Don't you dare think of breathing fire at me, drake," she said loudly. "Not with your little one right here. What have you been thinking? Leaving her all cooped up in the dark? Abharus seems to think you know a thing or two about griffins, but I'm not so sure. And what did you mean trying to roast us all earlier today? Did you really believe because one foolish and frightened human shot the mother we would only be interested in killing her child? Well! You may be a very ancient and learned dragon, but you clearly don't know much about humans."

She paused, her chest heaving, and still the dragon did nothing. The baby griffin mewled and pressed its feathery head against Milain's nearest hand.

"Abharus, what is she saying?" Milain asked, the tenseness audible in her voice at last.

"Nothing," replied Abharus from the back of the cave. "She is thinking."

With a faint shuffle Felpz went to stand across the griffin from Milain. He put a protective hand on her shoulder, then said:

"Forgive me, but there seems to have been a great misunderstanding here. We have no intention of harming this child. Indeed, I will do everything in my power to keep her safe."

The dragon's face regarded us with thoughtful, distant eyes. Then a white crack appeared along her snout, rows of pearly sharp teeth shining in the dim light as her scaly lips peeled back. Yet still no fire rushed out, and I realized with a jolt that she was smiling at us. Her mouth opened, but all that came out was a huge, satisfied sigh. Then the great head vanished downwards into the dark.

"I don't understand, what just happened?" Milain said in confusion.

"Kasarvo says, 'it is good,'" Abharus supplied. "She says she will take us back to your . . . um . . . lair. She says to wait."

"Wait?" cried Milain. "For how long?"

For answer there was a rumble from beyond the window, and the little griffin yipped excitedly. It scrambled up onto the ledge, and then jumped.

Milain shouted. I ran over, catching myself on the stone ledge, and gazed out.

The baby griffin was only a few feet away, apparently scrambling over a steep and spiky cliff. Felpz raised a hand, and his ball of light drifted free of the cave and shone more brightly.

I saw then that the dragon had not gone away, but merely turned about so that her great, wide neck was even with the cave entrance. The griffin sat atop it, its claws spread wide to grip the uneven surface.

While we stared in amazement, Abharus calmly pushed past us, making the short jump across nothing to land among the jumbled spikes and scales of the dragon's neck. He took up a perch behind the griffin and turned to us.

"She says to get on," he said. "Before she changes her mind."

I do not like to think of what followed. Even with Felpz in front holding my hand and Milain pushing me from behind I barely made it over the gap and onto the dragon's neck. Then I lay there gasping, clutching it with both hands. I felt ridiculous as Milain leapt over nimble as a mountain goat and came to sit behind Abharus, while Felpz sat comfortably beside me, but I was glad of my grip a moment later, when the great shape we were riding began plummeting through the dark.

Any cry of surprise that managed to escape my throat was quickly whisked away in the rush of air. I felt Felpz's steadying hand on my shoulder, and I reached out and grabbed his arm.

We fell through the black and empty cavern. The dragon's scales were warm to the touch, smooth as water-polished rocks, and smelled of a hot day under the sun.

With a great rush we came out of the cave and into the relative brightness of a night sky pricked with countless stars. By craning my neck I could look back far enough to see along the dragon's spine and down her tail, to where a huge, gaping maw of a cave in the base of a mountain yawned.

The wings of the dragon spread, and like dark sails they filled and we were whisked off over the mountains.

Strangely, now that we were out in the open sky my fear subsided. Having ridden magical flying animals before, I recognized the feeling of weightlessness I had experienced when riding a night mare, and I knew this dragon was using not only its wings to push the air about, but also a great deal of magic to make its substantial body much lighter, and by extent its passengers as well. However I still clung fast, as we were traveling at such speeds I feared the wind would blow me off otherwise.

The dragon's head was just visible before us as a large, black silhouette with craggy spires of horn jutting out from it. It eclipsed the starry sky and must have cast an even greater shadow over the land below.

After a time we were joined by two other dragons whom I recognized as Tero and Spheron. They twirled in the air about us like sparrows around a hawk. Milain laughed and shouted something at them, to which they replied by letting out piercing wails. To my consternation this caused the griffin kit to respond in kind, and the noise became truly terrible. It was almost a relief when the giant dragon let out a long, low, rumbling roar, drowning out the keening of its smaller brethren.

When the noise of that had faded away all was silent but for the swishing of the night wind, and we were descending low over familiar spiky mountains.

I heard later that the landing of Kasarvo at Draco Abbey sounded like a thunderstorm and woke the entire town. She came in so low her wings blocked out everything, and many people thought it was a cloud of black smoke. They said that when she touched down the ground shook, and several of the more delicate windows in the abbey were shaken out of their frames. The wyverns in the rookery were sent into fits of extreme agitation, and many of the animals not secured in their stalls bolted.

Dr Vayar tried to storm out onto the landing green to see what the commotion was about, but was prevented by Kasarvo's left forefoot blocking the door; the dragon was so huge she could barely fit in the field without crushing some fence or building, and so filled it entirely. Indeed, this was the reason for the small earthquake: rather than landing at a run as dragons preferred, Kasarvo had been obliged to drop vertically out of the air. We all felt it when she landed.

Abharus, moving in that strange, stiff way that suggested that the dragon was in control, not himself, dismounted and went to speak to the director, but not before he beckoned to the little griffin to come with him.

It took both Felpz and Milain working together to get me down off Kasarvo's neck, and for the final plunge off her foreleg Felpz was obliged to levitate me down.

I arrived in a storm of leathery wings. All the wyverns had focused on Felpz, yammering in their high, childlike voices.

"No sign of it?" I heard Felpz say. "Well, the dragons must have come back and picked it up. No matter. I shall speak to the cook about your biscuits, Radcliffe, now if you'll excuse me . . . " Felpz began forging a path after Abharus and the baby griffin, while Milain and I followed in his wake.

When we arrived, the director was speaking, somewhat distractedly, to some vague point halfway between Abharus and Kasarvo's face. He seemed to have realized Abharus was merely acting as the dragon's mouthpiece, and wasn't sure which entity he should direct himself towards.

"It's not that we don't like griffins. We are quite fond of griffins. I'm merely saying that we have no experts on griffin behavior."

"I should hope not," said Kasarvo through Abharus. "A griffin must learn to invent herself. What she must know about flying and hunting she can learn from us. No, I do not want you to teach her how to be a griffin. I want you to teach her how to be human."

"I'm sorry?" stammered the director. "Isn't that rather . . . um . . . presumptuous? Surely in time she may be reintroduced to her own family . . . "

"A griffin is not a dumb wild animal, it is an intelligent wild animal. Specifically, it has a human kind of intelligence. She cannot learn your tongue, your art, your music from us. This we entrust to you. We shall take care of the rest."

"Excuse me," Milain said, coming up and tapping at Kasarvo's claw, which was all she could reach (the dragon's head being a dark shape hovering two stories off the ground). "Do you mean to say, you want us to educate this griffin? But she's hardly a month old!"

"Griffins learn fast," came the answer out of Abharus. "She should begin early. It will be easier for her. Your language is harder than you think for one not born to it."

It was difficult to tell in the dark, but I thought the dragon's face took on a rueful expression at this.

"Well, in that case . . . " Milain looked around at the director.

"An elder dragon has just entrusted us with the care of a baby griffin," he replied with a stern glare. "Of course we accept."

"She's a Royal Dragon, really," Felpz sighed. "But that does settle things nicely, I think."

It was not quite so simple, of course. Farmers complained. There were concerns over the sudden and continued presence of a dragon the size of a small castle outside the town: for Kasarvo made it quite clear that she did not intend to simply abandon the griffin. She took to roosting behind the abbey, watching all the comings and goings with fascination. The positive aspect of this was that no one so much as commented on the arrival of the baby griffin—who came to be known as Rumpus, for obvious reasons—though McMorris did indeed sell his farm and move away after the first month—more likely because of Kasarvo than Rumpus.

Felpz and I stayed for a week. He spent a lot of time sitting with Kasarvo, speaking in a tongue none could hear but them. As a result, after six days Kasarvo could speak Kyrish in simple sentences—albeit in voice so rumbling and breathy it was almost impossible to understand—and Abharus disappeared with a sigh of relief.

To my delight Milain took charge of Rumpus's education, so I received a continual string of letters in the following months. She grew very well, her white down quickly shedding out to reveal a reddish brown coat with stark, black and white wings and tail feathers. Spheron taught her to fly by jumping with her off the highest tower in the abbey. By the time the fall migration passed through, she was more than ready to rejoin her tribe. It was a bittersweet day when I received the letter informing me that Rumpus had left Rivenstone, but a joyous one indeed when I learned the following spring that she had returned and decided to stay for the summer. Griffins were all well and good, she declared, but they did not have a library, and Rumpus wanted above all to learn to read.

As for Kasarvo? The great dragon remained at Rivenstone for Rumpus's first summer, and after the initial shock—after she showed no interest in raiding farms or setting the town on fire—the people accepted her as part of the landscape. She even allowed the dracologists to observe and study her, and I understand that the unique opportunity to see a living elder dragon—as the dracologists insisted on calling her—in the flesh more than made up for the disturbance that Rumpus caused.

Kasarvo left one night in early autumn, presumably returning to whatever distant world she originally came from, and has not been seen since.

Rumpus still lives at Draco Abbey, and though she is not strong enough to carry Milain about on her back as the dragons do, she follows my daughter on most of her expeditions. Milain tells me her intelligence rivals that of Dr Vayar, and that she wants to become a dracologist, like Milain.

"A griffin studying dragons!" Felpz exclaimed when I told him. He laughed. "That will be something. Oh, Corianne, can you not wait to see the books she will write?"

AUTHOR'S NOTE

Eldis and Aldor, to whom Abharus refers in reference to Kasarvo's experience with griffins, are the legendary lieutenants of Bandur, one of the old Rian earth dragons. Eldis is described as a snowy white griffin while Aldor is pitch black. According to legend they are the mothers of all modern griffins. With this in mind it is not surprising that Kasarvo, having once served them, would be sympathetic to one of their descendants—no matter how much time had passed.

The Dragon Lands, which Felpz alludes to, are a hypothetical world that exists beyond the boundaries of our own. Very little is known about them, save that they operate by a very different set of rules.

Yuragorn is an alacorn: an extremely rare creature thought to be the origin of both unicorns and paragaids (winged horses). Alacorns exist on their own frequency, and so are difficult for most people to see. By all accounts they are intensely magical, and rarely form alliances with humans. How Abharus came to be such good friends with one is a story in itself, which shall be told another time.

Returning to the world of Bouragner Felpz, "The Three Fates of Talias Minn" is the fifth story in the second volume of Bouragner Felpz sto‑ *ries. Chronologically it is set almost a year after the events of "Griffin's Blood," but as the two stand alone it is not strictly necessary to read them in that order. It was written in July of 2013, and will be followed by* "The Stone Man" in Apsis Fiction 2.2: Perihelion 2015.

THE THREE FATES OF TALIAS MINN

IT WAS IN THE EARLY HOURS of a wet morning in the autumn of 2316 that the curious character of Talias Minn entered our lives. He did so quite memorably, knocking the ancient Mrs Bryce over in his desperation and bursting into the sitting room before we had even begun breakfast.

He would have been an ordinary and rather plain young man under normal circumstances, but now his face was so flushed from exertion it was red as a cherry, and he wore a bright gold and blue knit scarf wrapped around his neck and thrown over one shoulder. This stood out against his otherwise conservative attire and neat, sensible brown hair. His eyes were very wide and darted about the room in frantic confusion before settling on Bouragner Felpz, who was in the act of pouring tea.

"Oh, Mr Felpz! Mr *Felpz!*" he cried, darting forward. Then he froze, his chest still heaving, and shut his eyes. With them still closed he said in tones marginally more calm: "Please make no mistake: I am not a lunatic, but I have been put through such unusual stress I feel on the verge of losing my mind. Say you will help me, for I fear no one else can!" He passed a hand over his face and wobbled on his feet.

I took the opportunity to leave the table and draw up a chair for him.

"Sit *down* young man," I said, guiding him into it. "It's not like me to make promises on behalf of someone else, but rest assured Mr Felpz will do all he can for you."

Thus reassured, the poor youth buried his face deep in both hands and began to shake with silent sobs.

Felpz leant over and offered him the cup of tea he had been pouring for himself.

"See that he drinks this, Corianne," he told me. "And there is the bottle of whiskey on the mantel which may prove useful. Look after him while I see to poor Mrs Bryce, will you?"

Mrs Bryce, though aged, was a solid old woman and more amused by the incident than anything else. Once she had been set up in an armchair in her kitchen with a pot of her own and some biscuits, she sent Felpz right back up to "see that young one straight, like you always do."

By the time Felpz returned I had coaxed our new guest into drinking his whiskey-fortified tea, and he was more or less composed. He had taken off his scarf and now wound it nervously around his hands, while he looked up at us in hopeful distress.

"I am so sorry," he choked out at last. "It is only . . . the last few days . . . well, how could you know? My life flows in a very different channel from yours, and there is no reason that an important city magician should know about the trials and tribulations of a country bumpkin such as myself."

"Yet I am willing to learn," Felpz said, pulling up a chair and sitting down opposite. "Whatever could have caused you to alter the course of your life in order to interrupt my breakfast *must* be important. Now, the first thing you can do is tell me your name, and then explain very slowly and calmly exactly what has driven you into such a state."

The young man looked on the verge of tears again, but he mastered himself with a supreme effort and drained his cup before beginning.

"My name is Talias Minn," he said, a little shakily at first. "I live in Milton Drew, which is a little village outside Corvisgate. I am the son of the vicar, and have spent much of my life preparing to succeed him—or to move to a nearby town and perform the same duties. As a result I have little knowledge of practical magic—though I have a great deal of learning regarding the mystic acts of the saints—and I blame my ignorance entirely for allowing myself to become entangled in the unfortunate situation I now find myself.

"First, some background, which will help. Growing up in a small village, you must understand I had a very small social circle. There were my parents, my cousin Molly, who came to live at the other end of town when I was very small, and my uncle Samiel. I grew up playing with the other children my age, but as we have matured they have one by one left our village and gone to pursue careers in the cities. There was a good score of us when I was young, but now there is only myself and two others: Darik, who I was never very close to, and Falchone, who came to our village from Fortau two years ago. Her Kyrish was not very good at the time and, as the most learned person close to her in age, I nominated myself to tutor her. We found we got on very well. So well, in fact, that by the end of the first year we had determined to get married. We have been engaged for three months now and plan to be married at New Year's. And this is where all the trouble began.

"Two weeks ago was the annual autumn festival, and my cousin Molly insisted on dragging me to the fair. Once there it was not enough for me to stand back and watch her 'ooh' and 'ahh' over the attractions; she took me to one of those cheap diviners with a crystal ball and demanded I have my future read.

"I tell you Mr Felpz, I have never believed in any sort of divination except that performed by the angels and the saints. Just as well, because the future predicted by the festival's witch was not at all attractive. She divined that my steps would be dogged by birds, every day a new bird, until the day when one hundred birds were following me at which time I would lose all my hair and come to a sudden end.

"Cousin Molly laughed at this and told me to try another witch to see if I didn't have better luck. And although I didn't believe a word of the prediction, I did feel it was an ill omen for a fellow about to get married, so I agreed. She took me to a witch who lived outside of town, and I sat down in her parlor and she gave me this prediction:

"I would live happily until the day before my wedding. However in the months leading up to that day I would meet a stranger in the village who would give me ten crests to hold for him until he returned. If I refused him I would die on the eve of my wedding. If I accepted and then spent the money my-self, my fiancée would die on the eve of our wedding. And if I accepted and was faithful to him, my fiancée and I would have a long and happy marriage but without any children.

"None of these outcomes seemed at all desirable to me, and I was flustered by the certainty of the witch. When she saw how upset I was she patted my hand and told me to visit her mother who lived on the other side of Corvisgate.

"In my right mind I do not think I would have accepted, but I was already agitated from the first two predictions and now more than ever wanted some reassurance. Falchone thought I was being silly, but as I could not get the two predictions out of my head she agreed I should go, on the condition that once I got a favorable prediction I would cease talking about it.

"Well, I went to the witch's mother's house, which was on a modest farm outside Corvisgate. There she grew vegetables and kept chickens, and I was at first put at ease by the wholesome appearance of her home. No sooner had she got me into her kitchen, however, than I was gripped by an unusual fear. I could not describe it and so tried to ignore it, but as she began to tell my future it only grew and grew.

"This third and final witch—more aged than the other two—told me to stay away from dogs, because each dog from now on would be more and more aggressive towards me, until finally I would meet one that would leap upon me and tear out my throat. I asked her if there was any way to prevent this, and she told me that the only thing to be done was to avoid dogs.

"I went away very shaken indeed, but on the journey home I managed to convince myself it was only so much twaddle. I put the whole distasteful matter out of my head and began working on preparations for the wedding.

"But now . . . " The poor man leaned forward, covering his face with his hands. "Now I simply don't know what to *do* . . . "

Felpz put his head on one side and looked at our guest cu-riously. "Why such distress?" he asked softly. "Is one of the predictions coming true?"

Talias Minn raised his face, and his eyes were wide as saucers, his cheeks blotched white and red.

"No, Mr Felpz," he said in an agonized whisper. "They *all* are."

Such was my experience with my friend the magician that I could almost see the searchlight of his attention snap to Mr Minn; it was something in the sharpening of his gaze and a tenseness about his mouth, though to the casual observer he must have seemed unchanged.

Talias Minn certainly thought so.

"You *must* believe me," he said, extending his hands pleadingly. "My neighbor's little dog, which is usually the sweetest thing, has taken a set against me, and now I cannot pass their door without the dog running out and trying to bite me. The butcher's dog growls at me if I come too near. It has gotten so that I avoid dogs as much as I can, lest one of them attack me. Furthermore, ever since the day of the festival I have been followed by birds. More and more each day. And then, yesterday . . . yesterday I met a man in the village; a man I had never seen in my life before. He approached me out of the blue and handed me a ten crest note, saying he would have to go away for a time and he couldn't take it with him.

"I was so frightened I nearly ran off, but I remembered what the witch said would happen to me if I refused. After the dogs and the birds I did not find it so absurd."

"You took the note?" Felpz asked sharply.

"I have it here," replied Talias Minn, reaching into his breast pocket and drawing out a crisp, white bank note.

Felpz took the paper between his long deft fingers and held it up to the light. I saw his eyebrows rise, and he passed it to me with a low whistle.

"You have me at a loss, I am afraid," I told him, examining the note. "It looks perfectly ordinary to me." I handed it back to Minn.

"It *is* perfectly ordinary," Felpz said. "As ordinary as you could please. Just as I suspect this stranger is ordinary in his way."

"You think this is all a great coincidence?" Talias Minn exclaimed, a flush of anger in his pale face.

"I never like to rule it out," Felpz remarked pleasantly.

"Ha!" cried Minn, leaping up and darting to the nearest window. Thrusting open the blinds he pointed out into the street, where a healthy beech tree was in full, autumn splendor. Standing out sharply against the fiery foliage was a mass of black birds. Some were recognizably ravens, others smaller and sleeker—crows—and others were smaller still: blackbirds and starlings.

They sat eerily still, but I saw their little heads move to keep Talias Minn in their sight. The effect then was like dozens of eyes in a great bushy face, all staring at you. It was quite unnerving.

Felpz frowned. He got up and went to the window. Pushing it open he put his head out and called to the birds, as if they were a passel of children who had been misbehaving.

"Now what is this all about?" he asked. "Come, explain yourselves."

But the birds only shivered in the tree, and then they scattered, taking off in a mad whirring and whumping of wings, causing a shower of orange leaves to fall on the pavement below.

Felpz brought his head back inside, his frown even deeper than before.

"What does your fiancée, Miss Falchone, think of all this?" he asked, closing the window.

Poor Talias Minn, who seemed entranced by the departure of the birds, shook himself out of his daze.

"Oh, she thought it was nonsense at first, but recently she has become as concerned as I. It was she who recommended you to me. Apparently she read of your exploits in Elgany some years ago and was quite impressed."

Felpz raised an eyebrow at that and shot me a sardonic smile. "Ah, the matter of Kliser Kurn," he said. "I don't believe I told you about that one, Corianne. Too dark, too distasteful. Though I managed to sort things out well enough."

"If you could apprehend one of the most dangerous criminal magicians in modern history, surely you can tell me what is going on?" Talias Minn burst out. "My means are modest enough, but rest assured I will pay you whatever you deem worthy—"

Felpz raised a hand at this, and Minn's speech stopped abruptly.

"Let us not talk of payment," he said. "It can cloud one's judgment. Put that matter out of your head until this issue is resolved. And yes, I believe I can tell you what is going on, though at present I cannot tell which of the many possible explanations that have presented themselves is the correct one.

"You say that dogs have taken a set against you; you say that birds follow you—as we have seen—and now this mysterious stranger with his ten crest note. Have you considered the possibility that there are more mundane explanations for these events?"

"Mundane—how?" gasped Minn, perplexed.

Felpz came and sat in a chair opposite him, twisting his hands together expressively. "It is unusual for such prophecies to take root so strongly. Is it possible that someone has learned of these prophesies and is making them *appear* to come true? It is not as hard as I wish it were to place a spell upon someone that makes birds flock to them, or makes dogs dislike them. That stranger could have been an actor hired to be part of an elaborate prank."

Talias Minn looked flabbergasted. "But . . . but who would *do* such a thing?"

Felpz shrugged. "Someone jealous, or vindictive, or just plain malicious. Is there anyone in your circle who would or could harbor such feelings towards you? Anyone, perhaps, unhappy with your impending marriage?"

Talias Minn's whole face wrinkled in thought as he pondered this.

"No one that I can imagine," he said unhappily. "My family is overjoyed, and Falchone's relatives, though they are abroad, have been nothing but supportive." He ran a distressed hand through his hair and sank into his chair. He was such a pathetic sight that I felt my heart swell in sympathy.

"Well, that is hardly helpful," Felpz said, the picture of clinical disappointment. He went around behind Minn's chair and bent down, as if inspecting the back of our guest's head. "Don't move, I beg," he said when the man started in understandable surprise. "I can at least rule out the possibility that you are under an enchantment . . . " and so speaking he began to run his hands through the air a few inches away from Talias Minn, making short flicking motions, as if he was brushing dust off an invisible coat.

"Don't fret child," I said, trying to soothe our troubled visitor. "I've seen Felpz pull people out of far more perilous predicaments than this."

"That is some . . . er . . . some comfort," Talias Minn admitted, holding himself stiffly still as Felpz worked over his right shoulder and down his arm.

Felpz snorted, but it was only in frustration at his task.

"Nothing," he said, standing up abruptly.

"What does that mean?" I asked sweetly, for I could tell he would not explain himself without a little prompting.

Felpz turned around from heading into his own room, apparently thinking of something else already. His lavender dressing gown swirled about him.

"Oh," said he. "Well, you're not under any enchantment that I can see. The problem is, if it is fate, I can't read that either. To tell the truth you *look* like any other thread, as free as Corianne or I. That is to say," he went on, seeing our clouded expressions, "someone under as dire a fate—not to mention *fates*—such as yourself usually appears to have a . . . a sort of *weight* about their spirit. You do not. That was what led me to believe that your perceived fates might have been practical constructs . . . but I cannot find any evidence of the spells necessary for that either. It's problematic. I need more time. But you will hear from me soon, have no doubt."

"Oh," said Talias Minn, sinking into his chair. I could see how much this worried him—it was thoroughly worrying, after all—and I could tell he had been hoping Felpz could give him some immediate assistance.

"Felpz," I said, catching him as he made another dart towards his room. "Is there nothing we can do for him *now*? Surely there is some charm or amulet you could give him that might alleviate the negative effects of the birds and the dogs?"

"Oh," said Felpz, and he actually stamped his foot—just like a child—in his impatience. "It is not as simple as that. I am not some general practitioner handing out placebos. No, it would be better to monitor their progression—we may learn something from it."

"In that case," said I, mentally striking the next week off as a loss on the writing front, "why don't I accompany him, so that I might observe the effects first hand? It would do well for him to have someone to confide in, at least."

Felpz blinked, as if this were the first thing I had said that he understood. His eyes sharpened, as they did when his mind was working furiously, and he looked from Minn to me and smiled slightly.

"Yes," he said at last. "Yes I believe that would work very well. You do not mind staying for a little breakfast, Mr Minn, while Corianne packs? It will not take long; she is really the most capable and efficient woman."

I could tell that Talias Minn was somewhat let down by this compromise, but he hid it well, and by the afternoon we were on our way out of Redling bound for Milton Drew.

Milton Drew, for those of my readers who have not had the pleasure of visiting the western lands of our country, is one of the many satellite villages surrounding Corvisgate, set among the rolling hills and hedge-lined lanes south of Barsbury Plain. In summer it is truly idyllic, but even in fall the place has a comfortable sort of beauty. Indeed, I found the country so delightful it was easy to forget what mission had summoned me.

I was reminded the moment we disembarked from our train when a large shaggy dog, who until then had been sleeping peacefully at the edge of the platform, roused himself and lumbered towards us, growling deeply with his ears laid back.

"Oh dear," cried Minn. "You see? You *see?* Even old Rumsfield now!"

I looked around, surprised to see that no one seemed at all concerned that a young man was being menaced by a large dog. I saw a middle-aged woman walk past and pause to stroke the beast on his reddish back, ignoring the malevolence he was radiating as he stalked towards us.

I do not have any unreasonable dislike of dogs, but I was not in a hurry to put myself in the way of such an ill tempered animal. Yet I still felt protective of Talias Minn, and I remembered how the birds had scattered when Felpz tried to speak to them.

Gathering up what courage I had, I stepped between Minn and the dog, and taking the firm tone I used on Felpz when he was being difficult, I said: "What is the meaning of this? Stop that growling nonsense at once and explain yourself."

To my intense relief—and Talias Minn's surprise—the dog stopped in his tracks, a startled expression on his wrinkled face. Then he shook himself and lumbered away.

Talias Minn let out a great sigh, and for a moment I feared he was going to swoon. I took his hand and flagged down a porter for our luggage, leading him into the station. Yet I glanced back as the doors closed behind us, and saw there, perched on the signal arm, a sleek black crow. It watched us intently until we passed out of sight.

In the cozy waiting room a tall woman with straw-colored hair leapt to her feet. She was young—about Minn's age—and quite handsome in a chiseled sort of way. Her clothes were well made but clearly old, dark and conservative with a high, stiff collar, yet she carried herself with such energy that she made them appear modern.

"Talias, Talias what happened to you?" she cried with a pronounced Fortaun accent, and I guessed that this was his Miss Falchone. She came forward and carefully took him off my hands, muttering soothing words in her native language.

"It's quite all right, Fal," Minn said, shaking himself out of her grip. "Just had a bit of a turn coming off the train." Clearly it was acceptable to show weakness in front of an old maternal figure such as myself, but not in front of one's fiancée.

Falchone looked at her betrothed in a shrewd way that suggested she knew exactly what had happened. "Didn't the magician help at all?" she asked.

Talias Minn brightened at that. "He has agreed to look into my case. And see, he has sent his friend Mrs Birch to look after us until he comes himself. Oh, Fal, you should have seen what she did to Rumsfield! Just one strong word and he slunk away like a chastised puppy!"

"Are you a magician as well then?" Falchone asked, turning to me. It was like being faced with a particularly rough-hewn marble statue: her skin was flawlessly smooth and pale, but the face it was stretched over was an angular one with high, jutting cheekbones like cliffs, and sharp curling lips. Her eyes, though I could see they were blue in color, remained dark, and so it appeared she had two black pools resting under her pale brows. This striking appearance was somewhat offset by her open and cheerful expression, and I took only a moment to collect myself.

"No, I'm afraid not," I said in answer to her question. "Merely an old friend. But I've assisted Mr Felpz on a number of cases, and I'm not inexperienced with this sort of thing. You may find me useful."

Falchone's face, which had darkened a little at my admission, brightened again.

"He has told you then, about the birds and the dogs and the stranger with the bank note? You still have it, don't you *chére?*" she asked sharply.

For answer Minn patted his breast pocket.

"Mr Felpz is pursuing many avenues of enquiry and hopes to have a solution very soon. In the meantime I am here to observe and offer whatever assistance I can."

"Oh, then you must come and see Miss Molly," Falchone exclaimed. "She was the one who got him into this mess. I've tried talking to her about it but she refuses to take me seriously. Perhaps now that the magician's assistant is here she will listen to reason!"

Smiling inwardly at the position that had been unilaterally assigned to me, I followed Falchone's tall, straight back as she led the way out of the station.

It was late in the afternoon and growing dark when we reached the vicarage where Minn and Falchone lived. This was a large, sprawling estate near the center of town guarded by rows of birch trees and flanked by two evergreens that stood on either side of the gate.

"It is good to have a guest," Falchone said as she let us in through the kitchen door. "Talias's father is away visiting his mother, and the place is too big and rattling with only the two of us. Here, come and sit. You find us in such a distressful time I don't see the point of hiding anything from you. Would you like tea and biscuits? Oh, I also have Hersian coffee—we have it all the time in Fortau but I must order it specially here—it is much stronger than tea though."

I sat a little bemusedly in their modest kitchen, gazing around at the blue and white plates on the wall and the faded salmon wallpaper. Here and there more exotic knick-knacks could be seen—evidence, no doubt, of Falchone's foreign roots. All in all it struck me as a good and unpretentious place—very much like what I had seen of the people who lived in it—and I felt it was a shame that their lives should be so disrupted.

Coffee was eventually agreed upon, to revive us from our journey, before we called upon Molly Minn. ("She lives close by, will be an easy walk. Good for your legs.") And as we sat and drank, Talias Minn began to recover somewhat. He was almost jovial when we left the vicarage, bundled tight against the cool autumn night.

Molly Minn lived at the top of a large house and turned out to be an older woman, closer to my own age. She was a little irritated at being roused from her relaxing evening, and even more irritated with Falchone, who let herself in without so much as a knock. When she saw Talias, however, she softened.

"Is this about those silly predictions?" she said, wringing her hands. "I told him not to take things so seriously, but it is all my fault really: I should never have taken him to see those witches."

"It is no good to make self-recriminations now," Falchone said briskly. "You can at least help us solve the problem. Look, here is Mrs Birch, who has come in place of the magician who is helping poor Talias. Tell her what you did."

Molly Minn, who was in her way quite a handsome woman with dark hair salted with grey and very large brown eyes, glared at Falchone. But she came around and said to me, quite civilly, "It began as a harmless enough joke, I assure you. Everyone knows these carnival witches do not *really* tell the future, but instead give positive, if vague predictions. I thought, with Talias so excited about his upcoming wedding"—here a sharp glance in Falchone's direction—"that hearing some reassurance would do him good. But instead the witch began spouting this nonsense about *birds* and suchlike.

"Well, I assumed it was malicious nonsense, but Talias took it mightily to heart—"

"I never did," interrupted Talias. "Until the birds started to follow me!"

Molly Minn waved a hand as if this were nothing important. "So I suggested he see a *second* witch, who would be more agreeable. But she was as disastrous as the first, rattling on about strangers and ten crest notes. I thought, this is getting ridiculous! I took him over to Corvisgate to see Mrs Dolhume—who I *know* is the best witch in the county and doesn't make up silly predictions—and *she* comes back with this thing about the dogs. Which I don't know what to make of. Dogs usually get along fabulously with Talias. But now all they do is growl at him. Is it true then, and those *really were* predictions?"

"It certainly looks that way," I admitted, at which the woman's shoulders sagged.

"Oh . . . I *am* sorry love," she said, patting Talias on the hand. Falchone sniffed.

I glanced from one woman to the other, and decided a change of tone was in order.

"Nevertheless, I am *sure* Felpz will be able to sort this out. He's very good at solving magical problems."

"Oh, I do hope so," said Molly Minn anxiously.

In truth I was hoping Felpz would turn up sooner rather than later. I had not the foggiest notion of how to proceed, and the effects of Minn's fate made themselves noticeable as soon as we left Molly Minn's house. The tree outside her front door was filled with the round, dark shapes of owls, and these watched us intently as we left, before following us silently through the town. I tried shooing them off, but they only scattered to the nearest rooftops and sat there, waiting until we had progressed farther down the street.

We walked fast, wishing for the relative safety of indoors, but not fast enough to outpace the lean dog who fell in behind us after a few yards. Hearing its growl I steeled my nerves and turned around, prepared to scold it away, only to find it was actually three dogs, with a fourth lurking in a nearby alley. Their ears laid back along their heads and all of them growling low, they made a truly sinister sight. I did not blame Talias Minn for giving out a despairing wail, but I did wish he hadn't. At the sound of their quarry all the dogs darted forward.

"Get him away!" I cried to Falchone, waving in the direction of the vicarage.

The woman, bless her, did not have to be told twice, and Minn not at all. They pelted up the lane, while I put myself firmly in the way of the dogs.

"Now see *here*—" I began, but then they were already upon me.

Then they were past me, lunging silently through the night. I cursed, and turned to run after them, and found myself staring up at a jagged roofline covered in birds.

"You!" I shouted, forgetting how silly I must have looked in my frustration. "Why can't you do something *useful!*" I strode towards them, and they fluttered away.

All but one. This one was darker and leaner than the others, and I saw with surprise that it was no owl, but a raven. It looked down at me out of beady black eyes, and I remembered how Felpz often received messages via raven.

"You could at least tell Felpz about this," I shouted up at it. "I need him here *immediately.*"

The raven put its head on one side, as if considering. I thought to add, just in case, "I would appreciate it very much!" and then hurried after the stricken couple. I heard the sharp whir of its wings as it passed by overhead, and I wondered whether it would deliver my message or if I had just been playing the fool.

When I arrived at the vicarage it was to find a crowd of dogs sitting silently around the front door. They were arranged in a semicircle and were staring at the door as if they were cats watching a mousehole.

Thinking better of attempting to reason with them I went around to the kitchen door and let myself in there. I was confronted immediately by a white-faced Falchone wielding a carving knife, which she lowered as soon as she saw me. Behind her, in the hall, they had pushed the sofa against the front door and piled chairs on it. Minn sat halfway up the stairs looking down on the scene, huddled in a blanket but apparently unharmed.

"They aren't mad anymore," I explained. "They're just waiting around the front door. Still, I wouldn't recommend venturing outside until they leave."

Minn whimpered and put his head in his hands. Falchone set down her knife and went to comfort her fiancé, while I secured the back door.

It turned out to be a long night. Minn refused to go to bed, and so we were obliged to sit up with him in the parlor all night. This was a cozy little room well equipped with soft, comfortable armchairs, but even the most comfortable chair in the world can become a torturous device if sat on for too long.

Such was my fate, and I spent the night awkwardly dozing until, in the wee hours of the morning, my body succumbed to exhaustion and I fell asleep despite it all.

I was roused by an almighty crash from the hallway as the pile of chairs toppled. Half asleep and disoriented I could not remember for a moment where I was. Then I heard the familiar sound of Talias Minn's moan, and it all came back.

Minn was standing on the chair that had until recently served as his bed. Falchone had picked up a lamp and was hefting it menacingly—truly a most competent woman—before I managed to lever myself out of my own chair, which seemed to have half-swallowed me during the night.

There was a desperate scraping as the sofa was pushed aside, and I leaned into the hall to find none other than Felpz standing in the open doorway, the morning sun shining in behind him, as he surveyed the pile of furniture with some perplexity.

"Felpz!" I cried indignantly. "You could have *knocked!* You'll frighten Minn to death at this rate!"

Felpz's features sank into a tired, long-suffering expression, and he called out over his shoulder to someone unseen:

"Quite lively as I see. Thank you, and I apologize if she was rude."

There was a muffled *cawing* and the flap of wings. Felpz picked his way inside.

"My raven, it worked?" I asked in surprise.

"Rork is not 'your raven,'" Felpz explained. "She is a very kind and generous friend. I asked her to keep an eye on you during my absence, which she did most faithfully. Apparently you had some trouble last night with the town dogs? You may come out now, Minn, I can assure you *they* are not here anymore."

Talias Minn crept forward into the hall on tip-toe, clearly prepared to flee at the first sign of anything canine. When he saw it was only Felpz he relaxed slightly and let out a long breath. "Are *you* the magician?" Falchone said, striding forward. "Does your presence mean you have a solution to our problem?" I saw Felpz's eyes widen at the sight of her, but otherwise he remained unmoved. He put his hands in his pockets and cocked his head at us in a quizzical manner.

"Not a definitive solution, I'm afraid. I was hoping to make a few more advances before joining you, but Corianne's call from last night sounded so urgent I thought it would be best if you accompanied me for the remainder of my investigation."

"Investigation?" Minn said. "What is it you have been investigating?"

Felpz shrugged. "The witches, of course. They were a little hard to track down, and none too obliging when I did find them. I am satisfied, however, that the two I have managed to interview did not intentionally cast malicious fates upon you, nor do they have the skill to do so even if they wished to."

"But *Felpz*," I interjected. "There is something *very* strange and quite dangerous going on here."

"No doubt," Felpz said, wincing a little at my tone. "As I said, I *had hoped* to make further advances before I saw you. You remember I have only spoken with two. There is still the third witch who lives on the other side of Corvisgate. I had intended to visit her this morning, and if there are no objections I do not see why you should not accompany me."

"Excellent," said Falchone before either of us could reply. "Is a splendid idea, but first we must have breakfast. At least let me pack something for the train."

Felpz gave her an amused look, and at the challenging expression she threw his way he turned to me and shrugged dramatically.

Taking his meaning, I said to Falchone: "Felpz does not travel by train for such short distances. He has a much swifter means of transport. We might as well have a comfortable breakfast here before we set off."

It was late in the morning and the sun was peeking over some low clouds in the south when we again left the vicarage.

Felpz strode in front, as was his wont, with Talias Minn fairly clinging to his coat-tails. Falchone and I took up the rear, and as we walked I attempted to explain the spatial folding magic Felpz performed in order to speed us on our journey.

"Imagine our world laid out on a sheet of cloth," I said, remembering the manner in which this practice had first been described to me, so many years ago. "We are like ants creeping across this cloth. Normally, it is stretched smooth and tight. What Felpz does is to create a fold in this cloth so that two points that would normally be far apart are now close together, and the ants—that is to say, *us*—may step from one point to the other and pass over all the distance in between."

Falchone's eyebrows went up at this, and she looked around at the little village intently.

"I see no folds," she said, a little skeptically.

"I've never actually *seen* it happen," I admitted. "But I've felt the effects. You will notice something, I am sure."

We reached the edge of the village, and though I noticed nothing odd, Falchone and Minn each exclaimed and pointed. According to them, it appeared we were now outside Corvisgate itself—not Milton Drew—and were heading down a narrow country lane leading away from that town.

It was a short walk from that point to the bottom of the lane where the witch kept her farm. Though Minn told me it was a full morning's journey when he went with his cousin, we arrived at the high, wooden gate within minutes. It appeared to be an ordinary farm at first glance, with a little barn and a cozy-looking house nestled in the fold of a hill. The drive was a dirt track, heavily rutted from the recent rains, which wound between low fences made of piled stones. On the other side a trio of goats watched us curiously.

Though the place had an aura of comfortable dilapidation, the wooden gate swung open at our approach as smoothly and silently as the best oiled steel door. Felpz gave it an approving look as he passed inside, and we followed close behind.

The door to the house itself opened in a similar fashion as we drew near, and Felpz walked boldly inside. When we entered, however, we discovered that the door's mystical action was explained by the presence of the witch herself, who had been standing behind the door and was revealed as she closed it behind us.

Mrs Dolhume was a short, wide, grandmotherly woman with a head of thick, silvery hair piled in a lopsided bun. She wore a faded blue dress under an apron with little dogs and cats printed on it, and large gold rings in her sagging ears. These glittered at us as she wagged her head in greeting.

"I can't say this is a surprise," she said in a cheerful, creaking voice. She shook a bony, bulbous finger at Felpz. "And I have to say it's a relief to see it's *you*. When Mirabell told me there was a *magician* asking after the fates of the Minn boy I worried he'd enlisted the help of one of those hard-mouthed college men who can't tell a rune of fire from a pig's arse. But now *you're* here, Mr Felpz, maybe we have a chance of sorting this mess out."

"My dear Mrs Dolhume," Felpz said, so startled by this greeting that he let slip a surprised smile. "It appears you already have intimate knowledge of these events. I have been hard pressed to find any concrete evidence, perhaps you may be able to enlighten us?"

"Come in then, come in," said the witch, leading us briskly through the little parlor and into a kitchen so large and cavernous I could not credit it with fitting into such a modest building, and I wondered if the witch had enchanted her house so that it was bigger on the inside.

This kitchen had a huge, wood-burning oven taking up an entire stone-faced wall, and a high ceiling strung with ropes from which hung bundles of herbs and strings of drying fruit. A long, wooden table ran the length of the room, and Mrs Dolhume rattled down it, scooping off dirty plates and mixing bowls and cutting boards, piling them on top of each other, and setting the lot unceremoniously next to a deep, stone sink. The whole place had a strange, uneven feel to it, which I soon realized was due to fact that the entire floor (paved with tightly fitting stone slabs) sloped down towards the center, where a thick, iron grate covered the aperture of a drain, half hidden by the table.

At the very end of this table sat the most unusual thing yet: a tall, slender person with the head and face of a deer, and a pair of large, impressive antlers. They wore only a simple loincloth, bound about the waist by a belt containing many pouches, and they were completely covered by a coat of fine, honey-colored fur. They were hard at work shelling nuts into a large bowl, and looked up at us with huge, dark eyes for only a moment before dropping back to their work.

"Sit, sit," commanded Mrs Dolhume. "Don't mind my assistant, Jeserry. Now, I think tea is in order, and then talking. Biscuits, anyone?"

It was some minutes before we were settled to Mrs Dolhume's satisfaction, but once we had been provided with piping-hot cups of tea, and a plate of biscuits each, she got down to business with the same brisk efficiency.

"I knew there was something strange the moment Mr Minn walked in my door," she said. "It was as though his destiny—which ought to have been in a state of constant flux—had divided and hung in two ghostly clouds above him, as if he had the *potential* for two fates, neither of which had crystallized yet. I thought to myself, I thought: what is this young man, who ought to have no very strong fate at all, doing with *two* potential ones hanging about?

"I should explain, as I believe I did the first time Mr Minn came here, that what I do is merely *read* the fate that is already there. I don't *lay* destiny upon anyone. The only difference in a person after they have been to see me is that they *know* what their fate is—which can itself drastically affect how events play out, let me tell you. So I sat down, intending to muddle through and hopefully dispel these clinging half-fates, as they did not look at all nice, when the most peculiar thing happened.

"I set about drawing up the strings of fate, as I usually do, and I came across a knot of sorts. It was this knot that contained the information about the dogs that so upset Mr Minn. Really it shouldn't have had such a pronounced effect, but as soon as I told him, it was as though all three fates—the two which had come with him and the one I had just foretold—suddenly solidified and became equally real.

"It was the most peculiar thing, and I'm afraid to say it so surprised me that I could not at first articulate what had happened. It wasn't until the next morning—long after Minn had left—that I managed to puzzle the thing out with Jeserry's help. Even then I could not imagine what could have led to such a ridiculous circumstance, until yesterday when my daughter came to visit me all in a fluster.

"My daughter, as you already know, is Mirabell, a witch herself. She came to me in such a state as I haven't seen her in since she was a child. 'Mother!' she cries to me the moment she's in the door. 'Mother, I have done something utterly foolish and I don't know how to fix it!'

"So I sits her down, like I have you, and she tells me about how, maybe a month ago, this young man comes to her and pays her a great deal of money so that, should a Mr Talias Minn come asking for his fortune told, she would read the most dire fate she could imagine.

"Now Mirabell's a good girl, and she would never do such an underhanded thing—there's enough charlatan witches out there to give us real practitioners some problems with credibility—but the young man was ever so insistent and made it to sound as if the whole thing was a great joke and he would reveal it to his friend later and they would all have a good laugh. Mirabell was still reluctant, but there's not a lot of money floating around in the life of a young witch, and so she took the job. She saw Mr Minn, told him a fortune she thought was safely ludicrous enough never to come true, and then tried to forget the whole nasty experience. But then, oh, but *then*—then yesterday she gets a call from a fearsome magician who is working on behalf of Mr Minn, and *he* says not only has the fate she predicted come true, but so has the one predicted by that poser, Narla Roost, *and* the one foretold by me, her own mother!"

Mrs Dolhume sat back in her chair and sipped her cup of tea serenely.

"She hadn't the heart to admit to you what she had done, poor child," she went on. "But now you're here be sure I've told you the truth, and perhaps we can set about clearing this mess away."

Felpz leaned back and crossed his legs, looking down the table at Talias Minn, who was sitting like a statue, holding Falchone's hand as if it were a lifeline.

"Thank you, Mrs Dolhume," Felpz said after some thought. "This has been immeasurably helpful. Yes. I do believe it explains what is happening to Mr Minn."

"It doesn't explain it to *my* mind," I pointed out. "You'll have to clarify, Felpz."

Felpz snapped his fingers in impatience.

"Have a little sympathy with those of us who do not have your vast experience," Mrs Dolhume chided, endearing herself to me in an instant. "I'm afraid I am still rather at sea over this myself."

Felpz stared at us in amazement.

"Is it not *obvious?*" he asked. "Why, it's as clear a case of the female trinity phenomenon as I have ever seen."

"The female what?" Falchone asked, speaking for both myself and Minn.

Mrs Dolhume, on the other hand, let out a sharp breath and said, "*Oh!* Now why did I not see that?"

"Likely because you were yourself a part of it," Felpz said mildly. "Practically the vertex, in fact. But let me explain properly or Corianne will have my hair. The female trinity effect, which is also called Shovid's Law—after the three-faced goddess of witchcraft—is the otherwise unexplainable sudden increase in the power and efficacy of magic when performed in concert by three women. It can also be used to describe that particular kind of magic that is attendant on groups of women who work in threes. Trios of women are often more successful and more powerful than the sum of their members. Strangely, it does not affect men—though there is a male equivalent, which applies to men who work in teams of two—hence the *female* trinity effect.

"What we have *here,* in this particular case, are three prophesies made by three witches. Each one, with her prophesy taken individually, should not have been able to influence Talias Minn's fate—since two were false prophesies and therefore no more indicative of what would happen than a layman's fantasy, and the third should have been an honest reading; that is to say, *descriptive* rather than *prescriptive.*

"However, because there were *three,* well, what Mrs Dolhume saw hovering over Minn when he entered her house was clearly the potential for these fates to become real—should they receive the boost of power they needed—and this they received when Mrs Dolhume performed her own fortune telling—because of Shovid's Law. Also, because Mrs Dolhume alone was attempting to perform a true reading, that trueness managed to bleed into the false fates, thus overwriting whatever mild, mutable destiny Talias Minn ought to have.

"Is that clear enough for you?"

Talias Minn stared at the table for some minutes, apparently puzzling through this. Then he looked up, and there was an odd kind of light in his eyes. That of fever and panic, but also threaded with wild hope.

"So . . . " he said. "These fates . . . they are not my *true* fates?"

"Very few people have true fates," said Felpz. "In reality, we construct and reconstruct our fate every day. What you have, to be more precise, are artificial, malevolent destinies. They are not uncommon—some curses use them—but I've never seen three of them at work at the same time."

"But . . . but they weren't real?" Minn asked. "Were not *intended* to be real? Not until Mrs Dolhume completed the triangle and then this . . . this *Shovid's Law* came into effect and made them real?"

"That is a simplification," Felpz said blandly. "But more or less accurate. Ironically, one could say you brought them on yourself; if you had stopped at one witch or two, their false predictions would have remained merely suggestions."

"Felpz!" I cried. "That is *not* helpful."

"What *would* be helpful," said Falchone, a steely glint in her eye, "would be to know who this young man who wished to frighten my Talias was. I should like to have words with him!"

"I should like to have a great deal more than that!" Minn said, a touch of color returning to his face, even if it was the flush of anger.

"He is undeniably important," Felpz remarked, turning to Mrs Dolhume. "He is the ultimate catalyst for these events—for I have no doubt this mysterious young man who bribed Mirabell also bribed Narla Roost—and if we are to untangle Minn from his unwanted fates, we will need his cooperation. I do not suppose your daughter described him to you?"

Mrs Dolhume looked up in surprise. "Described him? Why, she knew him. Did I not say? It was Darik Shaw."

* * *

"Darik *Shaw!*" Minn groaned, and not for the first time.

We had left Mrs Dolhume's farm and were walking back the way we had come. The witch accompanied us ("It's partly my fault you're in this mess, love, must do what I can to clean it up"), while her assistant, Jeserry, followed at a respectful distance. He carried a large sack strapped over his shoulders and walked with a long, twisted staff hung about with crystals that swayed and clinked as it moved.

"I have only met *Monsieur* Shaw once," Falchone stated. "He did not strike me to be very much of any sort of man. Not memorable, I mean to say."

"Perhaps Mr Minn knows more about him than he has divulged," Felpz suggested.

"About Darik?" said Minn distractedly. "We were at school together years ago, grew up in the same village, but you know I don't think I've exchanged more than a dozen words with him? He was always about riding his father's horses while I took a more scholarly interest."

"So you can think of no reason why he would wish such ill luck upon you?"

Minn stared off into the distance, his eyes wide and tired. "Not a reason in the world," he said.

Darik Shaw lived in a grand old house on the edge of Milton Drew. When we arrived, however, we were greeted by his housekeeper who told us Mr Shaw was not at home.

"Been out with his horses all day," she said, eyeing Jeserry with some curiosity. "Must say he hasn't quite been himself this past week. Better not to disturb him." And she shut the door on us.

"Queerer and queerer," Felpz murmured.

"Shall we wait?" asked Falchone.

Mrs Dolhume chuckled. "My dear child, you are not in the company of people who wait, not when they have a means to find what they want." She made a clicking sound with her tongue, and Jeserry came over, bending his antlered head until it was level with the witch's shoulder. Mrs Dolhume spoke to him in a low voice, full of clicks and hisses, and then Jeserry nodded. He walked out into the middle of the drive and turned around in a slow, full circle. Then he gave a little shiver, and with a bound, took off across the lawn, using the staff he carried like a third leg, the crystals clinking and flying, the sack bouncing on his shoulders as he went.

We followed his dark, cloven tracks at a more sedate pace, though Minn looked as if he wished to run—perhaps for fear of losing Jeserry.

The creature waited for us, however, whenever he reached the edge of our sight. Like this he led us in a jerky sort of way across a field and down into a dell where there was a large stable with an adjoining house. There we met a group of people, who stared when they saw Jeserry, but nevertheless came plodding up the hill towards us.

They appeared to be stable hands and groundsmen, from the way they were dressed, each one in a state of dejected frustration.

"See here," cried Minn, recognizing one—an older man with a short, grey beard. "Mr Kilnner, what has happened? Is something wrong?"

Mr Kilnner shrugged unhappily. "Wrong indeed, Master Minn," he said. "That there Mr Shaw has given us all the sack. Up and turned right to the devil, and there we were all going 'bout our business all good and proper."

"But he is still there?" Felpz asked intently.

"That he is," said Mr Kilnner, giving Felpz a strange look. "But good luck getting much sense out of him. And mind he may call the constables on you!" This last was shouted after us, as Felpz, not waiting for Jeserry's lead, had bounded off down the hill towards the stable.

He did not get far; at the bottom of the hill, just before the stable, was a veritable sea of dogs. They crowded round, all shapes, sizes and colors, and when they saw Minn, they growled.

Felpz stopped in consternation, and Jeserry understandably hung back. On their heels Minn steadied himself and glared back at the dogs—but from the safety of behind Felpz's elbow.

"Can't you send them away?" he was asking when I arrived, slightly out of breath.

"I'm afraid I already did," Felpz said, a little chagrined. "As soon as I received Corianne's message, in fact. I laid it on whatever was assailing you to return to its source. A long shot, as I was unsure how well the magic would work when performed at such a distance. But see? It has worked perfectly. Oh, Mr *Shaw!*"

The stable had a high barn of the sort with two stories and a door opening on the gable end—presumably to drop hay through. Beyond the crowd of dogs I saw this door open, and a disheveled, dark figure appeared.

It was hard to make out much of Darik Shaw from this distance, but I could see he looked to be in rather worse shape than Talias Minn had been when he'd first called upon Felpz.

Then, suddenly, the figure crumpled in on itself, and a flock of birds came swooping out of the door.

Minn flinched visibly, and Falchone, Mrs Dolhume, and I all raised our arms in defense. But the birds fluttered harmlessly into a nearby tree and from there watched us curiously.

"Did you lay it on *everything* that was assailing Mr Minn?" I asked Felpz, unable to keep the accusing tone out of my voice.

"From that distance I was unable to be specific," Felpz replied sharply. Then, turning back to the barn, he called in a much more soothing tone: "Oh, Mr Shaw. Do come down, Mr Shaw. There has been a grave mistake, but with your cooperation I see no reason why we should not be able to put all to rights."

The figure of Darik Shaw, still just visible in the open door, shuddered and unfolded into view. He wore good clothes, I saw, but these were so tattered and misused I wondered what sort of fit had come upon him, or if the birds, in their frenzy, had injured him. Yet when he came closer to the edge I saw no blood on him, and he appeared to be unharmed.

"What do you want?" he called out in a broken, anguished voice. "Go *away*. I told them all to go *away*."

"I am afraid that won't be possible," Felpz said. "Not until this is resolved. Mr Shaw, you *do* know why this is happening, do you not?"

"Stupid witches," mumbled the figure in the barn. "Stupid, *sodding* witches"—Beside me, I felt Jeserry stiffen, and Mrs Dolhume laid a hand on his arm—"it's all their flaming *fault*."

"Fault may be assigned evenly, in this case," Felpz said mildly. "However, the credit for the instigation still rests squarely on your shoulders, Mr Shaw, and I am going to need your help in order to undo it. Tell me, why *did* you wish to frighten Talias Minn?"

This question gave Darik Shaw pause. He peered out at us, and for the first time seemed to realize we were not his employees. He stared past Felpz to Falchone. His hand rose, pointing a shaking finger.

"It was your arrogance that drove me to this!" he cried, his face red with emotion.

Falchone gaped at him in response, utterly at a loss for words.

"Why did you pick that wretched, sniveling little rat over *me*? You should have been *mine!*"

Talias Minn sputtered indignantly at this, but Falchone looked from one man to the other with complete composure. She looked from Shaw, red-faced and overcome with emotion, to Minn, white-faced and shocked.

"I should think," she said in a softly dangerous voice, "that would be obvious to anyone with a shred of common sense!"

Darik Shaw grimaced at her. Falchone folded her arms.

"Now will you do as the magician asks and help us?" she asked.

But Darik Shaw was already shaking his head. "No . . . no . . . " he groaned.

"Do you not wish the fates lifted?" Falchone pushed on.

"No!" cried Darik Shaw, and began to laugh hysterically. "No, no, you're welcome to them! If they drive you half as mad as I, it would be worth it!"

"Please stop that," said Felpz.

The crazed laughter stopped with a choke, and Darik Shaw stumbled backwards into the barn and out of sight.

Felpz rubbed his eyes, as if the whole situation were giving him a headache. From the trees the birds watched, and the dogs began to sit or lie down.

"What an inconsiderate young person," Mrs Dolhume said.

"He is certainly not making my life easier," Felpz replied tiredly.

Falchone, who seemed to have been doing some hard thinking, turned to face us and clapped her hands dramatically.

"I see what we must do," she said in her decisive way. "He will not help us undo the fates, so we must do it *ourselves*."

"That will be easier said than done," Mrs Dolhume began to point out, but Falchone cut her off.

"You say this happened because three women predicted fates for my Talias? Because of this Shovid's Will they are all coming true? Well, what I see here is that *we* are also three women, and *we* don't want the fates to be true. I don't see why three women can't undo what three other women have done." She put her hands on her hips and cast a challenging look at her audience.

Felpz, who had listened to this announcement with moderate surprise, now began to smile. He was positively grinning when he turned to Mrs Dolhume.

"She makes an excellent point," he said. "That you were also one of the three original witches should help you in undoing it."

"I'm still not sure it can be done," Mrs Dolhume said skeptically. "Undoing fates as strong as these, when the instigator is so set on them, would be very dangerous. However, we might *move* them. Transfer them to another person, that is."

"Excellent," said Falchone. "Then we move them to Darik Shaw. That is as good as reversing them."

"But," said Talias Minn. "I don't wish these fates on Darik Shaw, much as he's proven to be a scoundrel."

"Then it shall be easy for me to dispel them, once they are shifted." Felpz said, patting him comfortingly on the shoulder.

"If I may," said I, speaking up at last, "I would draw your attention to the fact that, aside from Mrs Dolhume, neither of us has any practical magical skill."

And do you know, they all turned and laughed at me? Quite kindly of course, but I was rather affronted by it. Seeing this, Mrs Dolhume touched me gently on the elbow and said, a twinkle in her eye, "Don't you worry about *skill*, I've got enough skill for the three of us. No, it's power we're wanting, and between you and Falchone, if I do say so myself, I think we have enough power to move mountains."

"Particularly if you're working *against* the nature of the fates," Felpz added. "Corianne doesn't like to mention it, but she has a natural talent for rejecting malevolent magic."

"Then it is settled," said Falchone. "How do we begin?"

Feeling somewhat ridiculous, I allowed Mrs Dolhume to guide me into position alongside Falchone. We stood before the crowd of dogs—who seemed oblivious to our presence—and joined hands. I felt Falchone's wiry grip and the witch's hard boney one, and tried to not let my hands be crushed between them.

Mrs Dolhume began to rock forwards and back upon her heels, her head weaving about, as if searching for something.

"Oh!" cried Falchone. "I've *found* it!"

And suddenly I could see what she meant: the fates were tied around Minn like a knot of fine, almost transparent filaments, drawn impossibly tight. The ends stretched out of him, over our heads, and into the barn.

"Don't try to to untie it," Mrs Dolhume commanded us. "Help me shift it. *Slide* it."

Sliding is a good word for what we did, as little sense as that makes. Imagining myself taking firm hold of the knot of fates I pulled, and pulled, and slowly the knot did begin to slide along the translucent strings.

I know it may seem confusing to think we did all this while standing still and holding each others hands, but that is how we did it. It was as though my mind put out hands and arms of its own, and that was what I used to drag the knot away from Minn.

We had got it roughly halfway when all of a sudden it became much easier, and the knot fairly slipped along, disappearing into the barn. I realized it must have switched to Darik Shaw, like a magnet turning, and let go just in time.

There was a snap through the air like an invisible whip-crack, and suddenly all the birds gathered in the tree turned their collective attention from us to the open door.

At about the same time all the dogs—held at bay by Felpz's magic—turned and rushed towards the building, growling and barking.

"Quickly, Minn!" cried Felpz, urgently. "Do you wish your fates upon Darik Shaw?"

Minn wavered for a moment, but only because he had not seen what we had done and so was confused.

"N-no, I said so. Of course not!" he stammered.

And I saw how the string of fates—their ends still attached to him since Darik Shaw held the knot—broke free and spiraled through the air.

Felpz reached out—in the same manner as we had—and I saw him take hold of the loose ends and unravel the knot of fates bound to Darik Shaw, like someone pulling a thread out of a sweater. He pulled and pulled, casting the strings free into the sky, where they hung briefly before dissipating into the open air.

The baying of the hounds stopped abruptly, and the birds took off in a great rush of flapping wings. One by one the dogs left the barn, disappearing into hedges and through the surrounding fields, returning to their ordinary, inoffensive lives.

Lastly, Darik Shaw himself emerged from the barn, blinking and bleary eyed. Talias Minn marched up to him, and for a short moment I feared he would do the other man violence, but he only reached into his breast pocket and, taking out the mysterious ten crest note, thrust it into Shaw's hand.

"There," I heard him say. "You can riddle what to do with it. Good-day, sir. Good-*bye*."

He left Shaw staring bewilderedly at the note, and taking Falchone by the arm began leading us in the direction of Milton Drew.

After seeing Mrs Dolhume home and Falchone and Talias safely installed in the vicarage, Felpz and I decided we would better serve everyone by going home again—it still being fairly early in the afternoon. But the couple insisted on seeing us off, and as we waited for our train, Falchone took me aside, a strange pink tinge to her otherwise marble complexion.

"You must forgive me, Mrs Birch," she said. "I feel so very silly. I only just remembered—I must have been more distracted by Talias's fates than I realized—but I think I've *read* one of your stories before. That's how I knew the name Felpz. But it was so wild and fantastical, though I knew the magician was real I doubted the story was. Let me assure you I harbor no such doubts *now*."

I laughed and told her I was merely pleased one of my narratives had been of help.

"Do you think," asked Falchone with a sly twinkle in her eye. "Do you think, one day, perhaps this will make another story?"

"Well, that entirely depends," I replied. "Would you and Minn terribly mind being the subjects of one of my little ramblings?"

Talias Minn, who was standing nearby, only shrugged and smiled at Falchone, who clapped her hands delightedly.

So although in the past I have been obliged to change the names of the participants in order to protect their identities, in the case of the protagonists here I have made no such alterations. The reader will be pleased to know that, not only did the mysterious stranger never return, but the couple never received any trouble from Darik Shaw either. I am happy to say that Talias Minn and Falchone deQuivier were successfully married the following spring and are currently raising their first child. But if you visit Milton Drew you will not find them there; after the wedding they decided to move away, and where they went is one thing I have promised not to say.

"The Trickster and the Devil" was written on the last day of July 2013. It can be placed in the same rough continuity as "The Husbands of Hel" and "How Eve Left the Garden" (Apsis Fiction 1.2: Perihelion 2014), which reimagine the mythos of religions as if they all existed together. As with "How Eve Left the Garden," "Trickster and the Devil" focuses on characters from Judeo-Christian and Norse mythology.

THE TRICKSTER AND THE DEVIL

WHEN THE NAMELESS GOD cast Lucifer into the pit he was not too careful about where the fellow landed. So it was that Lucifer ended up in a field of ice not far from Hel's domain. (That is *Hel*, the daughter of Loki and goddess of the dead, not the place which would become Lucifer's home.) After a while she came out to greet her new neighbor, and they began to talk. She was immediately sympathetic to Lucifer's plight, Odin having once done something similar to her.

"The worst of it," Lucifer moaned, "is that no matter how horrible he is to *us*, people will always love him, because he's so good and kind to *them*."

"Oh," said Hel. "I know just the person who can help. You should go speak to *my* father, Loki. He is very clever, and he has no love for the Nameless God!"

So Lucifer went to see Loki, sometimes called the Trickster, who it must be remembered had been chained to a rock in a cavern under the earth where a giant serpent dripped venom upon him. I am sorry to say Lucifer had a bit of a laugh at seeing this, but after a time he grew tired of Loki's screaming, so he tore off the serpent's head and told Loki's wife, Sygyn, to go have a holiday while he talked to the Trickster.

Loki, though he was relieved to have a reprieve from his torture, was not inclined to help Lucifer. But Lucifer patiently pulled up a nearby rock to sit on and explained everything. After hearing the whole tale the Trickster's eyes flashed green and red, and he smiled very wide.

"Allow me to take your form, O son of the Nameless One," said he. "And I will show him such disgrace as never was seen even in Asgard!"

Lucifer, who had heard a thing or two of what went on in Asgard, agreed, and lent Loki his form.

So Loki, disguised as Lucifer, flew up to earth and found the Nameless God looking over his favorite people.

"See here," said Loki (pretending to be Lucifer), "it isn't fair that you are loved and I am reviled, for you do all these nice things for people and look after them. That is the only reason that they love you."

"You are wrong," said the Nameless God. "They love me because I am their one true god and always shall be."

"Prove it!" cried Loki (still pretending to be Lucifer), and pointed to the most prosperous and affluent human—a man named Job. "There is a man to whom you have given everything: a beautiful and loving wife, many sons and daughters, healthy livestock and a prospering farm. Of course he loves you and prays to you. But take it all away and *then* see how he treats you!"

"So I shall!" said the Nameless God. "And once I have proved my point I'll throw you down even deeper than before!"

And the Nameless God took away Job's wife, and one by one his children, and his livestock, and his prosperity, and his health.

But through it all Job remained true to the Nameless God, and called him his Lord and prayed to him and loved him. Even as he lay dying, homeless and destitute, shunned by his former friends, and his body riddled with disease, he still loved his god.

Then the Nameless God turned to the person he thought was Lucifer and said in triumph: "There! You see! They love me though they be rich and happy or poor and miserable. You are wrong, Lucifer; I have won, and now I shall banish you!"

But even as the Nameless God took the devil by the collar, ready to hurl him down into the underworld, the Trickster's eyes glinted green and red, and his face curved into a wicked smile.

"Have you, oh lord?" said he with hissing breath. "For the way I see it—*I*, who am supposed to be the scourge of mankind and the bringer of all evil, have stood back and done nothing, while *you*, O wise and lofty lord, have tortured one of your own subjects, the very beings whom you created in your image and whom you claim to love! What god are you, who pretends such goodness but bends so easily to evil?"

Then the Nameless God, in understandable fury, hurled the devil from earth, and he landed with a mighty crash back in his cave. There Loki shrugged off the disguise and sat up, rubbing his head.

"What did I tell you?" he said to the real Lucifer, wincing triumphantly.

In the end everything turned out for the better: Odin was so amused at Loki's antics that he never bothered to send another snake, and Lucifer was much inspired, saying: "I believe you have given me some ideas for what to do next . . . "

And the Nameless God was so embarrassed that he took Job's soul straight up to Heaven, to be rejoined with his wife and children. But the Nameless God also made the recording angel strike Lucifer's last words from the scroll, so when the story was passed down to humans it was somewhat misinterpreted.

"Never mind," said Loki when they heard the news. "What happened has happened. Even the Nameless God cannot change that."

Then Lucifer smiled at the Trickster, and *his* eyes smoldered gold and black.

"Sex, Blood and Rock 'n' Roll" is the fourth episode in the Driving Arcana saga, which began with "The Sword and the Shield" and "Highway Unicorns" (Apsis Fiction 1.1: Mesohelion 2013) and continued with "Shadows in the Valley of Death" (Apsis Fiction 1.2: Perihelion 2014). These are set in a near-future version of our own world in which supernatural forces are real, but poorly understood. It follows the narrative of one woman seeking to change that, and her two reluctant bodyguards. "Sex, Blood and Rock 'n' Roll" was written on friends' couches across Northern California and Oregon in August 2013, and finished at home that September. It will be followed by "God, or Aliens" in Perihelion 2015.

SEX, BLOOD AND ROCK 'N' ROLL

*Well I'm a jack ripper
And I'm a greedy god
I'm an idol for the opiate masses
Maybe I'm not your savior
But I'll still have your
Love and lust and guts and blood.*

*Sex, blood
Rock and roll
Sex, blood
Rock and roll*

*You wanna give me life
Well I will give you death
I will give you all the things that you want to fear
In return I ask for your worshipful heart
And the hearts of the gods you created!*

THE MUSIC FADED OUT, and the camera, clearly handheld, panned across a line of people dressed in everything from fishnets and leather to fishnets and nothing else. Hair styles were spiked as high as white glue and hairspray would allow, and on the ground, groups had formed around those members with the foresight to bring their makeup supplies. Others, not so fortunate, stood resolutely in the Nevada sun while heavy eyeliner smudged and white foundation became streaked with sweat. Despite this there was a general air of excitement and happiness—almost rapture—among the crowd. The announcer's voice, clipped and professional, spoke over the ambient murmur.

"Outside the Hotel Castle in Las Vegas, Nevada, fans of Johnny Bathory have been standing in line since early this morning, hoping to win one of the five coveted backstage tickets. Originally these were sold to the highest bidder, now Bathory chooses the recipients himself, and they must present themselves for inspection before the show. With attendance in the thousands, only a few dozen will actually be seen by the rocker; the rest will be turned away as soon as the five have been chosen. Asked about the fairness of the situation, Bathory is unapologetic . . . "

There was a fade, and a man's face filled the screen. It was difficult to tell what sort of face it was since half of it was painted dark red, the other half white. Three jagged lines, like claw marks, ripped over from the red side to the white side, crossing his nose and mouth. He wore obviously fake contact lenses, which made his eyes look bright yellow with pinprick pupils, and his hair seemed to be a bird's nest of improbably black locks. The voice that came out of the face was similarly disconcerting: soft and weak, hoarse from too many cigarettes and too much shouting.

"It used to be, you know, I'd be getting people paying ridiculous amounts of money for these tickets. In the beginning it was great—I needed the money—but after a while it just felt greedy. So I started donating the money to charity. Oddly, people were willing to pay more because of that. I had this heiress once—they won't let me say who—who wanted to basically have her bachelorette party in my hotel room after the show, with four of her best friends. And she—well, her father—named this ridiculously high number, and I had to tell him no. Because what had happened was these people who had and were willing to pay out their asses were not actually people I wanted to hang out with. I didn't like them. And that's what the backstage tickets are all about; getting to hang out with some of my fans. What's the point of doing that if they're not people I like? So now we have this much better system; all you need to get a backstage ticket is to be there when I come out to choose people. You don't even have to have bought a regular ticket."

"But what about the sheer number of people who turn up?" the interviewer asked. "You can't possibly see everyone. Realistically, only the first fifty or so actually have a shot—because you usually pick the five from them and that's it."

The man stared past the camera, his face expressionless. He didn't blink.

"You know, before the show is a real hectic time," he said. "There's sound checks, light checks. We have a pretty big production and I need to be there for most of it. So I only have maybe fifteen minutes to see people beforehand, and I'm just looking for people I think would be fun to hang out with. Usually, I find those five people in the first batch. But sometimes it takes longer than that. You never know."

There was a cut again, this time to a crowd of people packed into what looked like a holding pen, with the man with yellow contacts standing on a platform above them. A line of large, humorless men stood on the ground, keeping people back. Even so, the crowd's arms were outstretched, reaching for the man on the platform as if he were some kind of idol. The announcer's voice spoke over it:

"As to the allegations that only the young and the beautiful have a chance of being chosen, and that he unfairly favors female fans, Bathory merely says . . . "

Fade back to the yellow-eyed man with half a red face.

"I mean the biggest demographic of my audience is people aged fifteen to twenty-four. They're *all* young and beautiful. And you know, most of the people who go for the backstage tickets *are* women. So yes, I'm going to favor them. But I had a guy up the other night, you know, and he was wonderful."

"What about the allegations that you use these fans, many of whom border on obsessing about you, for easy sex?"

For the first time, the faintest expression flitted across the man's face, under the makeup. It happened so fast it was impossible to tell just what it was. The next moment the man rolled his yellow eyes extravagantly and laughed.

"Yes," he said. "Because after two hours of dancing around on stage in high heels and leather underwear"—the camera cut to the same man doing just that—"singing my lungs out, getting all sweaty"—cut to a shot of the man, in profile, backlit, shouting into a microphone so forcefully that flecks of spit could be seen arching through the air—"what I really want to do is the horizontal tango with a person I've seen for maybe thirty seconds in a crowd three hours before."

"It's totally an orgy, isn't it?" asked the interviewer, but there was a teasing tone in her voice.

At last the man cracked a grin. He had very white teeth, and the canines were noticeably longer. "Yes, Margie," he said, with complete sarcasm. "Yes, that's exactly what we do."

"Many Christian associations have decried Bathory, some going so far as to call him a devil-worshipper, and several right-wing groups have staged protests at his shows. Nevertheless, attendance remains high and—"

Selene paused the video and hit "escape" so that the window shrank and the rest of Jill's screen came into view.

Jill, who was sitting next to Selene on the hotel bed, looked at her skeptically.

"Really?" she said.

"You asked if there were vampires," Selene said. "That there is the most famous vampire today."

"But . . . Johnny *Bathory*," Jill said. "Even *I've* heard of him. It's an act. A show. Like Alice Cooper and that band Snog—"

"Kiss," Clara interjected from behind a mountain of newspapers.

"Whatever." Jill forged on. "I've read his *Wikipedia* entry, Selene. His real name is Doug Reed, he was born in *Minneapolis* or something. And you're telling me . . . he's a *vampire*?"

Selene raised an eyebrow. "Is it *really* so hard to believe?"

"Belief doesn't enter into it," Jill said. "There is evidence that shows him to be an ordinary human being—albeit one underneath a lot of makeup—and none that I've seen which would point to him being a vampire. What exactly *is* a vampire, anyway?"

At this, both Clara and Selene stared at Jill as if she had sprouted a second head.

"Puh-*lease* tell me you've seen *Buffy the Vampire Slayer*," Selene moaned.

Jill blinked at her, hard-faced. "I don't watch television," she said. "And I'm serious: what's a vampire? Because in every book or movie they're always portrayed differently. They are weak to crosses ... or they're not. They burst into flames in the sunlight ... or they don't. They can dissolve into mist, turn into bats ... or they can't. About the only thing that's consistent is that they drink blood. But sometimes it's the blood of a human, or animal ... or it can only be from a living human ... or ... "

Selene put her hands up, as if to shield herself. "All right, all right. I get it."

"What is a vampire, exactly, and *how does it work?*" Jill pressed on.

There was a rustling as Clara put down her paper. Her huge form—all six feet, four inches of her—spilled out of the flimsy motel chair in the form of long, leather-clad legs like tree branches. She had her leather jacket unzipped, cracked open to reveal the tight black undershirt. Above this her pale face hovered, angular and high-browed, her light yellow hair shaved right down to the quick. She rubbed a hand over the back of her head as her brow furrowed in thought.

"A vampire is a form of the undead," she said. "Similar to wights and zombies, but far more sophisticated. A vampire will present as dead, with no heartbeat and no pulse. They are defined by their need to feed on living blood in order to survive. Other than that ... " she shrugged. "It depends."

Jill frowned, nonplussed. "Depends?" she said. "Depends on *what?*"

"It depends on the vampire," Clara said simply. "Their capacity to withstand sunlight, their susceptibility to Christian or other religious iconography, their taste in blood, and their ... other abilities."

"Other abilities?" Jill said, pulling her computer onto her lap and beginning to take notes.

"You mentioned a few yourself," Clara said. "Powers of transformation, illusion, transmutation, mind control, flight ... "

"Whoa, whoa," said Jill, hitting backspace several times. "Did you say *mind* control? And ... and *flight?*"

"I tracked a vampire in Texas once that could fly," Selene mused. "That was . . . annoying."

"Did you catch him?" Clara asked, with professional interest.

"*Her,*" corrected Selene. "And yes, boy did I ever."

"Okay, so vampires can do pretty much everything," Jill said, skepticism positively dripping from her words.

"Not any *given* vampire," Selene said. "You don't get *flying* vampires much at all, and sun-resistant vampires rarer still. I think it's just skill. Different vampires develop different skills. Like some humans can do backflips, or figure skate, or play the trumpet. Vampires learn to manipulate people's minds, move super-fast, transform into animals, or mist, or fly. *Most* vampires can't do a fraction of that; they can only manage a little misdirection or mental pushing here and there. But they're pretty strong overall."

"What about sunlight?" Jill asked.

"Now, you'd think *that* would be universal," Selene said with a grin. "And actually, most vampires, they don't like the sunlight too much. Think really bad, really fast-acting sunburn. They don't *actually* burst into flames—not unless you douse them in kerosene first—but it ain't pretty, and it slows them down but good. But some vampires . . . I dunno . . . they just have a natural immunity, I guess. They are super-rare, though. I've never seen one."

Jill looked at her notes in some perplexity.

"Aren't you going to ask how to kill them?" Clara prompted.

"How they die does not interest me so much," Jill said, rubbing her chin. "I'm more interested in learning how they *work*. Still, it could tell me something about how they function. Yes. How do you kill a vampire?"

"I am *so* glad you asked!" Selene said, heaving herself off the bed. "Okay, so first, beheading. In fact, *always* try beheading first. It pretty much works on anything. Unless it's a hydra and then you're totally screwed. But we don't get hydra in the Americas, so don't worry too much. Anyway, yeah. Okay, a stake through the heart *does* work. Sort of. But not as well as in the movies. See, they don't explode in dust or goo . . . the stake just sort of . . . I dunno . . . *stuns* them, I guess. Makes them *act* dead. But if you take it out then up they get again. Also, you actually have to get it *through. The. Heart."* She emphasized this with prods of her finger against her own chest. "That means carefully angling it through the ribs or smashing them open. Not easy to do in a hurry. Oh, but you don't have to use a *wooden* stake. Iron nails work just as well, and fit better too. Let's see . . . "

"Silver," Clara said.

"Right, silver!" Selene grinned. "Silver is a good vampire deterrent. Works against a lot of magical stuff, actually. Kind of like beheading. What else . . . oh yeah. Fire."

"Fire?" said Jill.

"Fire," said Clara.

"When in doubt," Selene said, miming a flicking motion with her hand. *"Burn 'em."*

"Well," said Jill after a thoughtful silence. "That is very interesting. But how do they *work* exactly?"

Selene and Clara exchanged a look. It was a look Jill was becoming used to. It seemed to mean: "How are we putting up with this woman? Oh right, she's *paying us* . . . "

Clara said:

"We don't know for certain."

Jill nodded to herself, went back to her computer. "But you are certain Johnny Bathory is a real vampire?"

"Yes," said both the other women in unison.

"Okay," said Jill. "I'm gonna need to talk to him."

They stared at her. She looked up, her expression open and innocent. She adjusted her glasses. "According to his website, his band is playing in Las Vegas for the next week. We could be there by tonight. Or tomorrow morning, if we don't want to leave right away."

Las Vegas sits like a glittering jewel in the middle of a vast, dusty desert. It is only a glass gem—not real diamond—but it is set about with such lights and sounds that it appears more brilliant than any precious stone. Dive beneath the city, beneath the neon-lit strip with its hustlers and tipsy tourists, and you enter an altogether different world, one built out of concrete and flooded with cast-off water, decorated with graffiti and the furnishings scrounged from the dumpsters and back alleys of the city.

Getting water in the desert is a trick, but what do you do with the water when you're done with it? Hence the extensive system of flood drains and sewers that stretch out beneath the famous city. Unseen, unthought-of, but certainly not uninhabited.

People live there, just as they do in the city above. People die there, just as in the city above. And there are other people— people you won't find in the city above—and what they do down there is debatable. You could call it living, but—as Jill would be quick to point out—to live first you must *be alive*.

Currently, two such people stood in the bright strip where the sewer opened to the sky and cattails grew thick in the mucky water, which reflected the vivid yellow light from the street-lamps. They were arguing.

It was nearly midnight, but you wouldn't have guessed it from the noise filtering down from above. Not unless you were experienced in the nightlife of Las Vegas.

This noise was what allowed the two people to argue freely.

One of them, who was smaller and vaguely female shaped, stood with her knees locked and one hand on her hip, while she used the other to jab an accusing finger into the chest of her opponent. He was bigger, leaner, but he cowered away from her nonetheless.

"What were you *thinking*, Darryl?" the smaller one was saying in a harsh rasp of a voice. "What is the first rule of the clan? If *they* find out about us where does your protection go then, Darryl?"

"That's why I *called* you," Darryl wailed, cringing. "We can hide the body. No one has to know!"

"Do. Not. Feed. On. Surface people!" the woman yelled. "You were told when you joined us!"

"But her kind disappear all the time!" snapped Darryl. "They overdose, or they get lost. Sometimes . . . *they just die*, okay?"

"This isn't any *ordinary* surface girl, she was one of *his*," hissed the woman. "But you knew that, Darryl. And you drained her anyway. You're gonna get *his* attention this time, and I won't take the fall for you. This is *your mess,* and you can clean it up or take your chances upstairs."

"That will *kill* me, Martha!" Darryl pleaded, then burst out, as the woman—Martha—turned to walk away, "You leave me here, you've as good as killed me!"

Martha paused, the line of her back tense in the artificial light. Then she was a blur, a darting shape lost in the confusion of water reflections.

"You had to ask," said a hoarse voice by Darryl's ear.

There was a small *snick,* and Darryl opened his mouth to scream.

Nothing came out.

He heard, somewhere below him, the sound of his body falling into the water. Then Martha's face came into view, hard and jagged. His mouth moved open and shut; he tried to yell.

"G'bye, Darryl," she said, and dropped the head.

Darryl saw the water rushing toward his head—and then nothing. Whatever had kept him going, it was gone by the time he hit the surface.

Martha walked back into the sewer, disappearing into the shadow.

"It's an *amazing* experience!" said the girl, her eyes like stars inside the black splotches of makeup decorating her face. "They make you promise not to say, of course—I mean *really* promise— but it is *so* worth it, you know. He is *such* a generous artist!"

The video showed a crowd of people, all dressed in varying amounts of black leather and fishnets, lined up in the sun outside the back door of a theater. The narrator's voice, calm and cultured, spoke over them: "It is the hope of sharing the experience of fans like Belinda that keeps these devotees of Johnny Bathory standing in line outside the stage door for upward of twelve hours. Some fans arrive days in advance, bringing supplies of food and toiletries. Local authorities have since required Bathory to restrict the amount of time they may spend waiting in line for safety reasons. Now any backstage ticket hopeful may arrive twelve hours before curtains up at the earliest . . . "

"Are you watching *videos?*" Selene said incredulously. "How can you *do* that?"

Jill paused and looked up from her computer.   Arcana swooped and dipped as they ran over a rough patch on 95 South. "I have a strong stomach," she said. "I loaded these up before we left. I'm trying to figure out the best way to actually *talk* to him."

Selene laughed. "It won't be easy. Bathory's the most famous vampire for a *reason.*"

"He's the only one on MTV?" Jill guessed.

"*That,*" Selene admitted. "And he's the best protected. Not a hunter in the Americas doesn't know Bathory's a vampire, but I don't think a single one has gotten within shooting distance. *Think* about it: he's got bouncers, he's got agents, and he's got an army of fans who would die for him if those fail. Perfect cover, when you think about it.   Honestly, I don't know why Clara said yes. My guess is she thinks she can sneak you backstage or whatever using her spirit ring. *Literally* going backstage," Selene chuckled.

Jill remembered Clara's rings: small, lumpy things made out of braided metal. Wearing them phased you out of the real world and into a sort of ghost land. Jill accepted the hypothesis of how they worked, but she still didn't understand the physics of it. Last time there had been other things on her mind. Now she began picking at the question in her usual way.

"So these two worlds," she said. "The ones we go between when Clara—or you—puts on one of those rings. There's our world—"

"And there's the spirit world," Selene said, nodding. "Which is where this world gets all its magic from. There's a certain amount of bleed-through between the two, from what I understand."

"Is it anything like the infinite multiverse?" Jill asked. "Like, where history could go two ways, so that means there's two universes, each with a different version of history? And it keeps splitting and splitting, because of all the little differences and variations. Instead of one universe, there's an infinite multiverse because of the infinite possibilities?"

Selene raised an eyebrow at her. "You know, for all you say *my* work is unbelievable, sometimes your science can sound just as crazy."

"My science is supported by demonstrable evidence and peer review," Jill said. "Your claims are just that—*claims*—until I can see some evidence."

"You mean there's *evidence* of multiple universes?" Selene nearly spat over the wheel.

"Not yet," Jill said calmly. "For now it's just a hypothesis."

"Ha. Okay," Selene gave herself a little shake. "All right, here's my . . . um . . . *hypothesis* about this world and the spirit world."

"I'm listening," Jill said.

"Well, *our* world is our world, right? It's made up of physics and stuff. Okay, well, the *spirit world* is the world for, well, the spirits. It's where your nightmares go to be real. That sort of thing. When you make up an imaginary friend, say, that friend only exists inside your head . . . but in the spirit world *they really do exist*. And I think the spirit world is a lot bigger than this one, with lots of little sub-worlds inside it."

Jill nodded. "Like dark matter and energy."

"Sorry?"

"Dark matter and dark energy," Jill said, "are just names for all the matter and energy in the universe that we can't directly observe. They aren't necessarily *one* thing—more likely they are many things, it's just we haven't been able to figure out what they are. But we know *something's* there, and so we call it dark matter, or dark energy."

Selene shrugged. "Maybe they're the same things?" she suggested.

Jill leaned back in her seat and stared out at the road, which was currently stretching on and on through nothing much of anything. "That would be . . . convenient," she admitted. "But not likely."

Selene hummed, and drummed her fingers on the steering wheel. A little frown that had come to rest on her forehead put down roots and grew until she was scowling at the road.

"Something wrong?" Jill asked.

Selene grimaced. "Ah, it's just—I dunno. Makes me uncomfortable the way you're so cool about all this."

Jill raised an eyebrow at that.

"*You* know," Selene said, sparing a hand from the steering wheel to flap it expressively. "The way you don't *reject* these things, but you don't accept them either. I show you a dead unicorn, you don't say: 'this is fake; this is impossible' you say: 'I've never seen anything like this before . . . *I'm gonna poke it until I find out how it works.*'"

Jill frowned and blinked. "Why should that make you uncomfortable?" she asked.

Selene groaned.

"I'm gonna regret saying this, but . . . well. This stuff. It's been around a while. No one's ever *really* studied it before. Not the way you're going at it."

"Your point?"

"Maybe there's a *reason* no one's studied it? What if there are things out there that aren't *supposed* to be studied? From my experience, there are things that really don't want you to know about them. What if you run into something that *you're just not meant to understand?*"

Jill was already shaking her head. "That has never been *my* experience. Humanity has never improved itself or the world through ignorance and apathy. We *must* question, we must continue to study, to explore, to further our understanding of the world—or *worlds*. It is only through knowledge and discovery and understanding that we can hope to survive."

Selene glanced at her out of the corner of her eye, then rolled it skywards. Jill didn't see; she had gone back to her computer. She took out a pair of headphones on thin white cords from her pocket and stuck the buds into her ears as she plugged them in and went to the next video.

Selene drove, and after a while the nothingness around them was gradually replaced by the suburbs, the sprawl, and finally the towers of Las Vegas.

"Johnny Bathory, now, that can't be your real name, can it, sir?" The talk show host with the plasticky hair had an air of cordial superiority as he leaned back behind his desk and folded his hands.

Sitting on the couch next to his desk, lounging on the con-servative navy fabric like some exotic and deadly animal, was a man wearing tight leather jeans, boots with four-inch soles, and a studded leather jacket. His bare chest underneath was lean and pale and crisscrossed with delicate silver chains. He wore a leather collar as high as his neck, which forced him to keep his chin up. His hair was a wild, black bush and the face underneath it was powder white. He wore heavy black lipstick and heavier black eyeliner, and contacts that made his eyes appear yellow.

"Of course it's my real name, Gerry," this person said. He had a hoarse, quiet voice, at odds with his striking appearance.

"But according to your biography your legal name is Douglas Reed," said the host coaxingly.

"Yes, yes," said the man. "That's the name my parents gave me. But it's not my real name."

"But you picked your stage name?"

"That's correct."

"What was the reasoning behind your choice?"

"Well, when I was growing up there was this kid, see, and his name was Johnny. And when I was nine years old he cut his own throat—"

"Oh my goodness!"

"—and in the note they found with his body it just said 'don't forget me.' And I felt real bad, because he was my age, see? And so I thought: *I'll* be Johnny, that way Johnny won't ever be forgotten. And I've been Johnny ever since. And Bathory, that's easy. That's my family name. I'm descended from Eliza-beth Báthory."

"The Hungarian countess?"

"The Hungarian vampire. When I say she is my ancestor I mean my maker line descends from her."

"Ah. Of course. Yes. Now, let's talk about this vampire per-sona of yours . . . "

"It's not too hard to believe, is it?" Johnny Bathory said with a grin, showing off his fangs. "I mean, I'm a rock star. We're practically nocturnal. We take way too many drugs, have way too much sex, and play way too much loud music. Any rock star that makes it past twenty-seven, I assure you, is actually a vampire. I'm just the only one who's open about it."

*   *   *

Clara was waiting for them outside a modest motel just off High-way 95. It had slot machines in the lobby, only one of which was unoccupied, and it smelled of cigarettes.

"Why not stay on the Strip?" Jill asked, poking her head out. "I'm sure we can get a room for the week."

"This is cheaper," Clara said.

"You let me worry about that," said Jill, with the confidence of one whose escrow payment just came through.

Selene gazed at Clara imploringly. "Come *on*," she said. "How often do you get to stay at a four star Las Vegas hotel?"

"The last time I was here I stayed at the Venetian," Clara said. "I was not impressed."

"Technically, Strip hotels aren't *in* Las Vegas," Jill pointed out. "Most of the Strip is actually in the unincorporated community of—"

"But that's the one with the *canal*," Selene sputtered. "And . . . how did *you*?"

"I did them a favor," Clara said shortly.

Jill sighed. "Staying at the Castle gives us much better access to Johnny Bathory. It makes *sense*."

Although Clara looked unconvinced, and Selene seemed less than enthusiastic to be staying in close proximity to a vampire ("Why not the Bellagio? It has this *great* fountain!") eventually Jill and her all-powerful credit card won out, and they continued south, out of Las Vegas proper, until the looming replica of the Eiffel Tower announced they had arrived at the resort capital of the new world.

Arcana, woefully out of place among the sleek limousines, cabs, and billboard trucks, lumbered down the Strip like a dusty cowboy through a fancy club. After a certain amount of con-fusion Jill got them pulled into the entrance to the Castle, which sat at the south end of the Strip, its fake stone ram-parts in sharp contrast to the otherwise modern-style build-ings. The jarring transition was exacerbated by the enormous LCD screen over the portcullis entrance showing a looping video of Johnny Bathory—wearing a pair of devil horns and a leather speedo, prancing about with a microphone practically in his mouth—with flashing words running across the bottom proclaiming, "JOHNNY BATHORY, LIVE IN CONCERT—THIS WEEK ONLY."

Arcana pulled up behind a Las Vegas Metro squad car, which Jill barely glanced at as she jumped down and hurried inside, Selene on her heels. Clara parked her bike behind Arcana and waited there, her arms folded in silent disapproval.

The lobby of the Castle, in keeping with the overall theme, was built after the design of a medieval keep, with shields bearing coats of arms lining the high walls. There was also a huge fireplace set behind the check-in desk, with roaring fake flames projected in it. As a result, the clerks looked as though they were standing in an inferno. A large sign at the end announced "ALL BATHORY SHOWS SOLD OUT. STAND-BY TICKETS ONLY."

The place was filled with a milling crowd: middle-aged white men in T-shirts and shorts, middle-aged women in obnoxious print dresses, and between the adults, dozens of children from toddlers to teens, some of them wearing princess tiaras, others carrying fake swords. Many of them (young and old) carried huge paper bags stamped with the Castle's emblem (a large stylized C with little turrets woven into the design). Luggage trollies wheeled this way and that, maneuvered by porters dressed as pages.

Jill stared at the scene, and glanced at Selene a little skeptically.

"And he's a *real* vampire?" she asked, just to be sure.

Selene actually buried her face in her hands. "*Yes.* Okay? *Yes.* Check us in for three nights, would you?"

While Jill did this Selene surreptitiously checked the exits. It was a habit.

When they emerged it was to find Clara bracketed by two police officers. Selene froze in the doorway, hands automatically going for her guns—which were at Jill's insistence safely locked in Arcana—while Jill frowned and strode toward the group purposefully.

Yet as she approached it appeared Clara was not in any sort of trouble. She looked resigned and long-suffering, but the officers were smiling and laughing. Almost *relieved*, Jill thought. She cleared her throat.

One of the officers, a jovial, overweight man with a red face and yellow hair, turned to her and schooled his expression.

"Clara?" Jill asked, trying to convey in a single word the questions, "What is going on? Are you in trouble? Are *we* in trouble? How much do they know?"

Clara just looked at her impassively and said: "We have a case."

They turned out to be Officers Nescal and Dunes. Nescal was olive skinned with lank dark hair, while Dunes was the blond one. He gave Jill a hard look, and Selene a harder one when she shifted uneasily.

"Officer Dunes," Clara finished, "this Jill Hamilton and Selene Shields. They are friends of mine."

"Friends?" said Officer Dunes, and threw a look at Clara which implied more than his spoken question. In answer, Clara nodded sharply.

Officer Dunes heaved a sigh like a horse, his great frame swelling and relaxing with a shudder. "Well I suppose you'd better come along. I expect you'll find out on your own anyway."

"I'm sorry . . . *what?*" Jill said, making a slicing motion with her arms as the officers moved toward their squad car. "What *case* Clara? What's going on?"

Clara's shoulders sagged. "There have been . . . complications," she said. "Officer Dunes is requesting our . . . expert opinion on a. . . . " She looking questioningly at the officer.

For answer, Dunes held the door to the nearest squad car open. "I'll explain when we get to the morgue," he said.

"Riiiight," said Selene, drawing the syllable out in her sarcasm. "We'll be taking our *own* car, thanks very much."

Officer Dunes shrugged. "Suit yourself." He climbed into the car, and Nescal slid into the driver's seat, and they pulled out into the road. Clara followed at a sedate pace on Unicorn, while Selene and Jill sat in Arcana and waited. When the squad car noticed Arcana was still sitting in the parking lot, it calmly pulled over to the curb and waited. Selene cursed and started the engine.

"What's going on?" Jill asked.

"Ask the giant," Selene scowled, pulling out of the hotel's driveway.

Following on the heels of the cruiser and the motorbike, Arcana made its way back out onto the Strip, turning north toward downtown.

"You don't work with local law enforcement?" Jill asked as they stopped at a light.

"Nngh," said Selene. "Try not to. Ask too many questions. Usually try to arrest me."

"For carrying unlicensed firearms?" Jill suggested innocently.

"*Those* are easy enough to hide," Selene said. "If you know how. If you see 'em coming. Which I do. No . . . I think it has more to do with *this*," she waved a hand in front of her face.

"What . . . because you're African-American?" Jill asked, surprised.

"Because I'm *black*," Selene corrected testily.

Jill blinked at her. "Really?" she said incredulously.

Selene nodded.

The light turned green.

"*Really?*"

"You know," Selene said, easing Arcana forward. "I read in one o' them crap mags this column where it said *everyone* should try having gay sex at least once in their life, just to see what it's like, y'know? Well, *I* think it'd be better if we could change skins. And everyone had to spend at least *one day* with a different skin color. Just to *see what it's like.*"

Jill fell silent at that, shrinking back into her seat.

Arcana chugged through the city, following the police cruiser and the black figure on the motorcycle.

"I just hope Clara knows what she's doing," Selene grumbled, shifting into fourth.

Jill didn't answer.

The city morgue turned out to be a gray, humorless building with half-washed-out graffiti on one side. They parked Arcana out front, a tactful distance from Officer Dune's cruiser, and piled out. Selene grabbed Clara by the elbow as soon as she had dismounted and dragged her around to the back of the truck.

"*Tell me,*" she hissed, viciously prodding the larger woman's chest, "what [prod] is [prod] going *on?*"

Clara looked over to where Officer Dunes had gotten out of his car and was waiting, leaning his forearms on the hood. She looked back down at Selene.

"I saved his life the last time I was here," she said. "Helped him with a possession case. He knows enough to be afraid."

"And now . . . what?"

"He has something he wants me to see. I thought Jill would appreciate being able to contribute. Why did you come?"

Selene punched her lightly in the arm. "You know why," she growled. "Come on, let's get this over with."

The body of a woman lay on the cold, stainless-steel table. She was remarkably pale, even for a corpse, almost gray as a stone. She looked like she had been fairly young in life, with dyed black hair and a lot of piercings—now empty. Officer Dunes took a tray from a nearby table and handed it to Clara.

"We had to remove her jewelry, but you can take a look if it helps."

Clara brushed the tray aside; Selene took it instead. The taller woman stalked around the body, her head cocked to one side, frowning. She came to a stop beside the corpse's head and held out two fingers over her neck. Coming around the bulk of the officer, Jill saw that there was an ugly wound there, as though something had bitten into her neck above the right carotid artery. Jill looked up at Clara, her eyes very wide.

"Don't tell me . . . " she whispered.

"Was this woman exsanguinated when you found her?" Clara asked.

"It was actually Nescal who found her," Dunes said, jerking his head toward the dour-faced officer. "But yeah, the coroner determined that she died from loss of blood. And that's the thing: there is *no* blood in her, and I mean *nothing*. She's not drained, she's *dry.*"

Selene, who'd been idly going through the contents of the tray, froze. Clara nodded, as if this was what she expected to hear. Jill looked between them, her eyes narrowed.

"Most of the department thinks it's some sick joke," Nescal said, his voice a little hoarse. "What with that vampire rocker in town, they think maybe some psycho got it into his head to dress up a kill—make it *look* like a vampire. But Dunes told me about the case you helped him with in Henderson, and we got to thinking . . . "

Clara straightened up. "You thought right," she said.

"This . . . " Jill said, coming forward to get a better look at the body. "This is a victim of a *vampire* attack?" She froze, her hands outstretched. "Gloves," she said sharply. "I need gloves. And a rubber apron." She looked around hurriedly.

Dunes provided both gloves and apron with amusement in his face, while Clara looked across the body at Nescal and asked: "Where did you find her?"

"Outside a storm drain in Winchester," the officer replied, shying away slightly as Jill dove at the corpse with surprising enthusiasm. "Your friend, is she a doctor?"

"Not yet," Jill answered. She was palpating the wound, peeling away layers of skin and muscle. "This is *fascinating*," she murmured. "Selene, can you take notes?"

But Selene had begun laying out all the ornaments collected from the corpse on a nearby table. Dunes obligingly brought down the morgue's microphone and hit record.

"This too," Jill said, handing him her phone. "I can't work it through my gloves—thanks."

She leaned forward again and pointed excitedly at the wound.

"It's not a sucking wound," she said. "Well, that's inaccurate. What I mean is, whatever drained her, it didn't *suck* the blood out. It opened her carotid artery and let her heart pump the blood out. Probably had an anticoagulant agent to help the flow. Do you have any swabs? I need swabs. And tweezers."

When these were provided she used the tweezers to prop the wound open—Nescal suddenly became very interested in what Selene was doing—and swabbed the inside.

"Not that I'll get anything," Jill muttered. "She's dry as a mummy. But look! You can see where the first incisions were made. I make that two teeth, very long and sharp—possibly with a slight curve. They were inserted once, here, where they missed the artery, and then again, here, where they punctured it. Then the owner of the teeth pulled back, rupturing the artery and doing significant damage to the soft tissue of the neck. There's some additional damage that suggests the victim struggled. I don't suppose you found any bruising? No, of course you didn't."

Clara left Jill to her study of the corpse and went over to Selene. After seeing a few dozen vampire victims, they all started to look the same, and while Jill was obsessed with the minutiae, to Clara it had long since congealed into a single picture that screamed "vampire attack!"

"What have you found?" she asked, leaning down to get a better look at Selene's array of rings and studs.

Shooting Nescal an unloving glance, Selene pointed to the little piles of black and silver jewelry.

"I got them sorted," she said. "Earrings, nose stud, lip ring, tongue stud, finger rings, something that *could* be an ear stud but might be a belly button stud. Nipple rings . . . "

Nescal coughed and turned away.

"Lot of metal," Clara remarked. "Any silver?"

"Not that I can see," Selene said. "Stainless steel all the way. But look at this." She had arranged the finger rings in a line along the bottom of the pan. These ranged from thin silver bands to thick ones with huge stones set in them. One which held a large black stone had a frame in the shape of an open mouth with elongated canines. Another was a signet-style ring bearing an upside-down cross with a crescent moon at its head.

With hardly a pause Clara singled this one out. She picked it up carefully and held it up to the light.

"'I am no Christ but which Christ do you know?'" she whispered under her breath.

"Say what?" said Selene.

"Johnny Bathory. That song's been going through my head. And this is his emblem."

"You got that right," said Selene. "And here, look: a bat pendant, fang pendant; the skull has little fangs too."

"So?" said Nescal. "She was some goth-punk JB fan. They're pretty thick on the ground these days."

"Yeah, *exactly,*" Selene said, giving the officer a hard gaze. "She was a Johnny Bathory fan."

Nescal's lined face twisted in thought. "So?" he said.

"She was killed by a vampire," Clara announced. "Johnny Bathory is a vampire."

The tightness in Nescal's face dissipated like a cloud in the desert. "Oh," he smiled. "*Everybody* knows that. It's part of his act."

Clara and Selene just stared at him.

"I mean . . . uh . . . it *is* part of his act. Isn't it?"

"What have you got, Jill?" Selene asked, turning away from the tray of jewelry.

"We-ell," said Jill, still bent over the body. "Her neck was brutalized. And the loss of blood is the most complete I've ever seen. There is a partial dislocation of her right shoulder, which suggests she was forcibly restrained. There is damage to her fingers and nails which seems to indicate she clawed at her at-tacker, but I can't find any trace of skin or tissue under her nails. I don't suppose your forensics cleaned them out?" she asked Of-ficer Dunes.

The man coughed uncomfortably.

"To tell the truth, forensics haven't *seen* this body," he said. "Junkie groupies go missing all the time. Sometimes they turn up alive . . . sometimes not. We're working on getting a positive ID on her—she didn't have a wallet—but the Sergeant didn't think we needed forensics. I wasn't going to pursue the matter, but then we were called in to break up an altercation at the Castle and up came Clara on that bike of hers and I thought—*well damn,* she'll know what to do with this." He shrugged expressively. "And now you're telling me it's *vampires*?"

"*A* vampire," said Clara. "I cannot be sure if there are more."

"With the flood drainage system Las Vegas has got?" Selene said. "You'll be lucky if you haven't got a *colony* living down there."

"But," said Nescal, who was still grappling with events. "The drains are full of people."

Jill stared at him.

"*Normal* people," he said. "Homeless people, that is. We would have heard—"

"They wouldda *told* you if they thought there was a colony of vampires living in the dark and selectively feeding on them?" Selene said, every word dripping sarcasm.

Nescal folded his arms defensively. "We would have heard something, I'm sure."

"Vampires do not need to breathe," Clara said quietly. "They do not eat or drink—they feed on blood, that is their only sustenance. They can live in places humans cannot. They can feed on people and *not* kill them. They are very good at hiding themselves. They have to be; for although they are powerful at night, day is anathema to them, and all an enemy need do is discover their location during daylight hours and they are as good as destroyed."

A respectful silence followed this speech, until Dunes broke it by coughing. "So . . . what do we do with this?" He waved a hand at the body on the table.

Clara dipped and raised her shoulders. "Identify her. Notify her family. Leave the vampires to us."

"We'll need to search the area where she was found," Selene muttered into Clara's arm. "Someone messed up here. There's bound to be . . . other evidence."

"Yes," agreed Clara. "We will need access to the storm drain in which you found her. Preferably soon, while it's still light."

The mouth of the drain yawned before them in the form of three gaping black holes, each separated by a concrete pillar. A smell of pungent pond weed wafted out at them.

"We found the body just here," Dunes explained, politely lifting the police tape and unlocking the metal gate. "Scrub crews have already been through, I'm afraid."

Clara nodded, as if this did not surprise her. "You will leave us here," she told the officer.

"Like hell we will," Nescal protested, almost laughing. He stopped immediately when his partner put a hand on his arm.

"You weren't around for the Henderson case," Dunes said. "When Nordstern says leave her to it, you're better off as far away as possible." He gave Clara an apologetic look. "It's safer for everyone that way."

"What about *her*," Nescal said, pointing at Jill.

Jill, who was trying on a pair of Selene's combat boots, looked up and raised an eyebrow.

"What?" she said. "I could be a tracker."

"Hunter," Selene corrected out of the corner of her mouth. "And no, sweetie, you couldn't."

"We have a . . . an *arrangement* with Jill," Clara said stiffly.

"I will attempt to document what we find in full detail, and report back," Jill offered.

The other two women glared at her, but this seemed to mollify Nescal.

They entered the drain with the afternoon sun at their backs, their long shadows stretching out to meet the imposing blackness of the cavern. Selene, who had strapped a flashlight to her gun Freddie, took the lead, while Clara walked behind Jill, casting her beam side to side and behind them.

The drain went down a ways, and the water rose to mid-calf. The temperature dropped dramatically, and the darkness pressed in on all sides.

Then they rounded a corner, and daylight streamed in; about twenty yards along, the drain ran out under the sky. There, in response to the sun, reeds and rushes and other plants grew in thick bunches from the ripe water. Insects hummed and a startled bird rose up in surprise, its wingbeats cutting through the air until it disappeared beyond the concrete lip above.

Selene paused in the shadow just before the open space. The rushes had clearly been trampled recently, with two discernible tracks of bent and broken stalks. In one patch, it looked like something had been burned right off the water's surface.

Jill tried to make a beeline for it, but found the back of her jacket held in Clara's iron grip.

"Let me sweep it first," said the tall woman, and stepped out into the sun.

Jill waited in the shadows with Selene as Clara crossed the strip of sunlight, carefully hugging one side of the channel, and disappeared into the darkness beyond. They could still see her as a black shape silhouetted against the erratic beam of her flashlight.

She reappeared a moment later, having crossed over and now walking back along the other wall. She put her flashlight away and beckoned to them.

"Stay away from the middle," she said.

"Why?" asked Jill, but she obediently veered away from the strange, burned patch and came to stand next to Clara. Carefully she pulled out her phone and began taking pictures.

"Because that is where he died," the woman answered.

"He died?" Jill echoed. "*He* died? *Who* died?"

"The vampire," said Selene, and pointed at the burned patch. The rushes there were crumpled and singed, and there was a thick bed of ash floating on the surface of the water.

"Wait," said Jill. "A vampire died? I thought the vampire killed that girl!"

"Yes, one did," said Clara, moving out toward the patch of ashes like it was a skittish cat she was trying to capture. "*And* one died here."

Jill frowned, then predictably latched on to the one thing that did not make sense in her mind.

"Why do you think it was male?"

Selene rolled her eyes.

"It is a statistical probability," Clara said, but she sounded distracted. She bent over the bed of ash and carefully lowered her arms into it. Her face crunched into an expression of the utmost concentration as she felt about under the surface.

"A lotta vampires tend to prey on people who resemble the class of person they felt the most resentful of in life," Selene explained dryly while they waited. "So you get a lot of male vampires hunting human women. And vice versa. White supremacist vampires are the *worst*. Also the most satisfying to kill."

"Ah," Jill said, and found nothing else to say.

Out in the center of the channel, Clara made a small noise of satisfaction.

"You found something, girlfriend?" Selene called out.

Clara grunted in response, both hands sunk elbow-deep in ashy water, but she did not straighten up. "I think," she said, still feeling around under the surface. "I think I've got his head."

Selene straightened up and Jill surged forward, saying, "Really? Bring it up, let's see!"

The two hunters gave her exasperated looks.

"It's a *vampire* head," Selene said tiredly.

Jill thought about this.

"But you said they don't burst into flames when exposed to sunlight," she said.

"Yeah, doesn't mean that sunlight don't do bad things to their bodies. As is exemplified by Clara currently standing in the middle of one. You better roll it, honey, I'll cover you."

So as Clara began the odd-looking task of rolling the unseen object along the bottom of the channel, dragging it through rushes and weeds, Selene took out her gun again and stood above her, sweeping the area.

"Why so cautious?" Jill asked, ducking to keep out of the gun's line of sight.

"To say vampires are helpless during the day is an over simplification," Selene said. "Technically, they're powerless against *sunlight*. These drains are *perfect* for them for more than one reason. You get complete darkness even during daytime." This last was spoken as Clara reached the edge of the shadow of the nearby drain and stepped inside.

Jill hesitated for a moment, but only a moment. She came up next to Clara's side and got out her flashlight and her phone.

"Well, come on," she said. "Let's see it."

Water streaming from her leather sleeves and gauntlets, Clara slowly raised her find up out of the muck. It was grayish in color, with pale splotches and bits of green algae sticking to it. The top was a mess of limp, gray-brown hair, and the rest . . .

"Well, what do you know," said Jill. "It *is* male."

"Was," Clara corrected mildly.

It was not a pleasant face. The features were twisted, and the open eyes, though covered in a thin whitish film, were stained red underneath. But by the width of the jaw and the stubble on the chin, it was recognizably male.

Handing Selene her phone, Jill stuck the flashlight between her teeth and pulled on a pair of latex gloves. Gingerly she took the grisly specimen from Clara and turned it over, examining the mouth, nose, ears and eyes. She lifted a lip and looked in perplexity at the more or less ordinary (if badly maintained) set of teeth.

"Here," said Clara, and deftly pushed up against one of the canines. It slid back easily, and from the opening a long, curving fang descended into view. Delicate and graceful as a cat's claw, it was half covered with membrane with only the pearly tip visible at the end.

"Well I'll be . . . " Jill murmured around the flashlight. She mimicked Clara's motion with the other canine, producing the same result. "Fascinating," she said. "Selene, take pictures of these."

With a sigh Selene obediently began taking pictures.

"There's no sign of putrefaction," Jill went on.

"What?" said Clara.

Balancing the head on one hand, Jill took the flashlight out of her mouth. "No putrefaction," she said. "Which is strange. Even if he was killed recently, there should be some signs of animal activity—considering he was lying in a veritable haven for microbes, worms, and other scavengers."

"Vampire flesh is toxic to most creatures," Clara announced. "Werewolves are the only ones who can eat them, but I hear they don't taste very good."

"Werewolves, huh?" Jill said, and Selene shut her eyes as if bracing for a physical blow. Glancing up, Jill saw her expression and relented. "We'll save them for another day. Hold him, Clara, I want to try something."

With Clara holding the remains firmly in both hands, Jill borrowed one of Selene's knives and cut a small piece of tissue from the vampire's neck—near where it had evidently been severed with a meat cleaver.

"Uh, Jill?" Selene said uncertainly as Jill, holding the piece of flesh at the end of her finger, inched toward the strip of blinding sunlight.

"I just need to see—oh, whoa."

As soon as Jill's finger, with the piece of dead vampire at the tip of it, emerged into direct sunlight, the piece of flesh began to smoke and sizzle. It bubbled, boiled, and finally ignited in a brief flash. Then there was nothing but a thin layer of pale gray ash.

Jill raised an eyebrow.

"They don't burst into flames?" she asked sarcastically.

"Living ones, no," Selene said. "Dead ones? It's pretty much like, y'know, what's that stuff that blows up when you put it in water?"

"Alkali metals," Jill murmured, pulling back into the shadow. Taking a vial from a pocket she carefully shook the ash into it. She took further samples from the head's hair and neck tissue, storing them similarly. Finally she took another strip of flesh and, holding it between two fingers, plunged her hand into the water.

A foot below the water's surface, invisible in the murk, there was no reaction when exposed to sunlight. Slowly raising her hand, however, caused the strip to warm gradually, and by the time Jill could see her own hand (barely an inch from the surface) the piece of flesh ignited, very much like a chunk of sodium in water, and flared brightly for a moment. Jill felt it, like the scorching of a candle flame, and then the coolness of the water rushed in; the fire had punctured her glove.

"Well, *that's* interesting," she said, straightening up and stripping off the glove.

"Yes," said Clara impassively. "May I burn this now?" she asked, indicating the head.

Jill's eyes veritably bugged out in horror. "Absolutely *not*," she said, snatching the head out of Clara's grip, heedless of her bare hand. "This is the most valuable specimen we've found yet. You *will not* destroy it. Now lend me your coat."

"What?" Clara's tone was chill.

"Lend me your *coat*," Jill insisted. "We need something to keep the sun off him until we get him a light-tight box"

"That won't matter in a few days," Selene said, even as Clara recoiled backwards. "Vampire decomposition—"

"He's *not* decomposing," Jill snapped, tugging at Clara's sleeve.

"—doesn't work like human decomposition," Selene finished. "He'll be dust in forty or so hours, no matter what you do."

"Well, then I *want to see that*," Jill insisted.

In the end it was Selene who sacrificed her work shirt to form a makeshift shroud, wrapping the head up in an awkward bundle, which Jill carried protectively clutched to her chest the rest of the way back.

Dunes was waiting for them at the exit of the drain.

"You found something?" he asked with barely concealed surprise as he let them out.

"It's not conclusive," Jill said. "Open up your car. I'll show you."

Dunes, to his credit, only whistled at the sight of the vampire head, unwrapped on the back seat.

"And you found this?" he said, turning to Clara.

"I expected to," she said.

"I can't be positive," Jill said. "But if you compare his bite to the wound on your victim's neck, that should be enough to identify him as her killer."

Officer Dunes rubbed the back of his neck unhappily. "Yes," he admitted. "It could. But you see our problem now, don't you?"

Clara and Selene exchanged bewildered glances, but Jill frowned thoughtfully.

"We don't have just *one* victim anymore," Dunes said, and the two hunters groaned. "We have a dead girl, and maybe this is the head of her killer. *But he's dead too.* Which sorta demands the question: *who killed him?* I don't think it was the lady we got back in the morgue."

"He was decapitated cleanly," Jill offered. "Some irregularity in the soft tissue suggests his assailant used a knife—a small but sharp one—as you can see that, although the spine has been severed, there is some tearing around his trachea and skin."

"Must have been a strong someone," Nescal, who'd been lingering by Dunes's elbow, pointed out. "Exceptionally strong." He shot a glance at Clara.

"Given the weapon used," Jill said. "I doubt it was someone with less than supernatural strength. I'm sure Clara could do this, but she uses a *sword*."

"There would be no tearing," Clara announced. "And I would not have left the head for someone to find." She sniffed disdainfully.

"*And* we only got here this morning," Selene pointed out, a little defensively.

"You said vampires were strong," Jill said. "Strong enough to do this?"

"Oh, *easily,*" Selene assured her.

"But why—*sorry* if this is a stupid question," Dunes said. "*Why* would a vampire kill *another* vampire? *If* this thing *is* a vampire head . . . "

"Why would a human kill another human?" Clara countered. "Vampires are by nature a proud and violent race—much like humans. Just because they prey on us does not mean they do not attack each other."

Officer Dunes rubbed his eyes.

"Yes, of course. *Thank you,* Clara. And thank you, Miss, er . . . "

"Hamilton," Jill provided.

"Miss Hamilton. And I'm sorry about this, but I really do need to take your . . . um . . . *find.* For evidence."

Selene and Clara sighed, but they seemed resigned.

"*What?*" said Jill. "Oh no, I found him. I haven't properly studied him yet. You'll give me copies of the necropsy report *at least* . . . "

"Now, you know I can't answer that," Officer Dunes said, reaching to re-wrap the head. Selene snatched her shirt back before he could grab it.

"At *least* check his bite," Jill insisted, even as the head was carefully boxed up. "And keep him out of the sun, and record his rate of decomposition, and . . . "

"*Thank you,* Clara," Dunes said, lowering himself into his cruiser. "I'll call if something comes up."

Clara just gave one of her inverted shrugs.

The three women watched as the police cruiser pulled out into the evening traffic and disappeared into the hoard of cars, glimmering in the last rays of the sinking sun.

"Well *crud,*" said Jill, putting her hands on her hips.

"Ah, don't you worry," Selene said, patting her on the shoulder. "We'll get you another vampire, I promise."

"Honestly, I'd prefer to *talk* to one," Jill admitted as they walked back to Arcana. "The wealth of information we could gain . . . if like you said, there are vampires around who are hundreds of years old. It could revolutionize our history. Not to mention our understanding of biology."

"Yeah, yeah," said Selene, getting into the driver's seat. "The *trick* would be finding a vampire who's *actually willing* to talk to you."

"There's still that Bathory guy," Jill pointed out. "I'll ask Clara about getting me an interview with him."

"An interview with a vampire," Selene said, grinning humorlessly as she followed Clara back toward the Strip. "We all know how well *that* goes."

"Ha ha," said Jill.

Getting at Johnny Bathory, however, proved to be more or less impossible. Aside from the practical roadblocks put in place to keep the ordinary masses out of his hair before, during, and after the show ("It really is an ingenious defense system," Selene admitted with grudging admiration. "What will protect you from a deranged fan also goes a long way to protecting you from a determined hunter.") Clara's attempt to scope out the landscape using her spirit ring proved equally fruitless.

"He has *wards,*" she said disgustedly, after disappearing for a mere fifteen minutes. "It would take a magician to get through them."

"A magician," said Jill. "There are *magicians?*"

"It's a general term for someone who studies or practices magic," Clara sighed.

"Oh. Can we hire one? I mean, this *is* Las Vegas . . . "

Selene laughed at that. "Sorry, they don't have *our kind* of magician here."

And there it rested. Jill dejectedly ordered room service and sat up late entering her notes from the day into her laptop while Clara and Selene slept in shifts.

"The vampire this . . . it's sort of a metaphor for life, you know," said the man with spiky, bleached-blond hair and heavy eye shadow. The tag at the bottom of the screen identified him as Clark Wuornos, the keyboardist for *Johnny Bathory.* "Because . . . like . . . vampires are *dead.* But they're also alive. That's sort of the act we have going on with Johnny B. Life and death go together. So we're celebrating death, this thing that's going to happen to all of us eventually. But we're also celebrating the fact that we're alive to have all this. Sex, blood, rock n' roll and all that."

"Don't you mean drugs?"

"Sorry?"

"Isn't it sex, *drugs* and rock n' roll."

"Oh, yeah. Ha ha. But blood works too . . . because—you know—*vampire!*"

"The vampire thing is pretty exciting."

"Well, yeah. I mean a vampire is basically the ultimate combination of life and death. They're scary and attractive at the same time. It's really the sexiest thing in the world to be a vampire . . . "

"I have an idea," Jill said as they gathered for breakfast in the Castle's main cafeteria—a restaurant made to look like the banquet hall of a medieval keep. "You think it was another vampire who killed the vampire whose head we found yesterday, right?"

Selene, stooped over a monstrous cup of coffee, silently covered her eyes with her hand. Clara, who had a bit more self control, nodded.

"Well," said Jill, neatly folding her napkin. "Then why don't we go find *that* vampire? Should be easier to get into those drains than past Bathory's bodyguards.

Selene actually put her head on the table at that.

"Not a good idea," Clara said.

"Why not?"

"Vampires are fast. Dangerous. Unpredictable. We would not be able to adequately protect you."

"Not even if we went down there during the day? I mean, I know it's dark so they can get about. But wouldn't just the fact that it *was* daytime sort of . . . um . . . slow them down?"

Clara frowned, considering this.

Selene's head rose up off the table.

"You got a death wish, girl?"

"I want to *learn*," Jill insisted. "I mean, it's not like I want to *kill* them. I just want to talk."

Selene laughed humorlessly, stuttering to a stop when she caught sight of Clara's expression.

"No," she said. "You can't be seriously . . . "

Clara gave one of her inverted shrugs. "If we put her in enough armor . . . I think my gauntlets might fit if we cinch them down all the way."

"But . . . "

"What—armor?"

"They *are* slower during the day. And I have flares."

"*What armor?*" Jill insisted.

The armor turned out to be leather. Mostly. When it was laid out on the hotel bed it looked rather like a particularly hard-core outfit worn by a fantasy role-playing actor. It was odd, however, in that it seemed designed to protect the joints and the interior of the arms and legs more than the knees, elbows, chest, and other places usually covered by such things. It wasn't until Jill realized that it had been designed to protect the wearer's *arteries* that it began to make sense.

The leather was hard and shiny, scuffed in places and clearly well used.

"You'll want to wear comfortable clothes underneath," Clara said. "Otherwise it chafes."

"I'll bet," said Jill, gingerly picking up a thigh guard. It looked almost like a piece of a robot's exoskeleton, save for the enormous buckles on the outside. "Where do you *keep* all this?" she asked.

"Usually I'm wearing it," Clara said mildly. At their surprised looks she just shrugged. "I've been ambushed enough times."

The armor turned out to be mostly too big all over. The legs were too long to be any use, but Jill found the upper-arm guards fit around her thighs almost perfectly.

"Go figure," Selene said with a wry smile.

They used the forearm guards for Jill's upper arms, and wrapped her legs from the knees down with strips of what Clara called "kevleather." They did the same with her arms. Finally, after some fiddling, Clara got the neck guard carefully buckled on. This piece stretched down over Jill's collar bones and up to her chin. With it on it was impossible to look down, and nearly as difficult to turn her head.

"Will this actually work?" she asked, pulling at the neck piece. "Isn't there more to protecting yourself against vampires?"

"Not really," Selene said. "I told you, religious paraphernalia isn't always effective, garlic just makes them sneeze, and silver is only a minor deterrent. If you want to use magic against a vampire, you need a real magician who really knows her stuff. Pretty much, your best bet is a good physical barrier between their teeth and your soft bits."

Jill tapped at the leather gauntlet on her arm. "And this will stop them?"

"Stop a determined vampire?" Selene said. "Nyah, but it *will* slow them down. That's all we need."

"What about you?"

Clara sighed. "With vampires the best strategy is to kill them before they attack you. That's what we'll do."

"Don't you *dare*," said Jill. "I want to *talk* to them, remember?"

"I will keep that in mind," Clara said gravely, even as Selene rolled her eyes.

The armor was stiff and uncomfortable and made Jill feel like she was in a robot costume. It was also hot, and she was sweating before they got to the sewer.

"How do you *stand* this?" she asked Clara while they waited for Selene to pick the lock on the gate.

Clara, who was wearing her thick leather biking pants and padded leather jacket, lowered and raised her shoulders. "I got used to it," she said.

"What about in the summer?" Jill persisted. "Don't you get heatstroke?"

Clara's face took on a vacant, closed-off expression.

"No," she said.

There was a clink of chains, and to her evident relief Selene announced the gate was open.

This time, without the overbearing presence of the police officers, Selene had opted to bring out what she termed "the big guns." These included her trench gun, Freddie, her sawn-off shotgun, Elvis, and a strange tubular contraption she called "The Sparkler."

Clara drew her sword as they descended into the drain, out of the light, and Selene switched on the flashlight she had attached beneath Freddie's barrel. The beam, bright in comparison to the inky dark, illuminated a wide swath of graffiti on the wall, and reflected from the ripples on the surface of the water in dancing patterns above them.

Selene led the way, keeping her gun poised but her hands relaxed, her footsteps measured, with every so often a hitch in her stride as sore joints and bruised muscles—left over from their previous misadventure—protested the use. She was also, Jill noticed now, protecting her right side, where there was a cracked rib barely two weeks healed.

"Will you be all right?" Jill asked her.

Selene paused so she could peer around in the darkness at the smaller woman.

"You're asking me this . . . *now*?" she growled.

"Um . . . yes?" Jill mumbled, embarrassed.

Selene shook her head and kept walking. "Don't you worry about *me*, once the adrenaline kicks in I won't feel a thing."

They progressed slowly further into the drain, through the patch of sunlight, back into the shadow, and on and on. The ground rose and fell in smooth inclines which were strangely awkward to navigate on foot. They passed out into open air channels more than once, where Jill could hear the noise of traffic just beyond the concrete lip above them, and then back down beneath the streets and buildings.

Deep into one of these tunnels Selene paused. Three giant, circular apertures opened up high along the side of the channel they were currently in, out of which drifted thick, tepid air.

Selene and Jill waited, ankle deep in water, while Clara climbed up and investigated. After due inspection she sheathed her sword and crawled bodily into the middle one. Turning around and poking her head out, she said: "This one," and extended an arm.

Selene helped Jill up, then climbed Clara's arm as if it were a tree branch, slithering past Jill to take the lead once more.

Now they crawled, or walked bent over when the tunnel expanded, and soon Jill's back and knees began to complain. But neither Selene, with her injuries, nor Clara, who was almost a foot taller than either of them, complained, and so Jill remained silent, grimly pushing herself along.

Eventually the tunnel opened onto a wide cistern with several more tunnels (blessedly large) leading off from the other side.

There was a scuffle in the dark, and Selene swung her light—and her gun—around to a low ledge that jutted out into the shallow water. There a jumble of cardboard boxes had been arranged, and as they watched, a disheveled head appeared, its eyes bloodshot and the pupils tiny pricks in the middle of washed-out, hazel irises. A tangle of white hair drifted like spiderwebs against the dark backdrop.

"Hello," said Jill. "Sorry to bother you."

The man stared at them sullenly. He didn't seem to notice that Selene had a gun, or that Clara had a large sword.

"They don't like light," the man mumbled, retreating back into the shell of cardboard that served as his home. "They'll get you if you don't turn off your light."

"Who will get us?" Selene asked sharply.

"Nngh," was all the man said, and they saw no more of him. After a while they moved on.

They did, however, see more evidence of human habitation: they crossed the cistern on a path of wooden pallets which led out to the center where a wall of plastic crates gave some privacy to what looked like an improvised bedroom: a rocking chair, mattress, and bedside table were set out (also on pallets, to keep them out of the water). A few stray splashes and a knocked over crate suggested it had been vacated in a hurry.

"Sewer people," Jill remarked. "I remember reading about this once. They have them in New York City and Paris, too."

"Homeless buggers, drunks and junkies," Selene said. "Perfect for vampire fodder."

"But wouldn't they . . . um . . . *notice?*" Jill asked, carefully stepping around the bed.

"Surprisingly, a lot of people don't." Selene checked behind a wall made of flattened cardboard boxes. "This way."

"Sorry, *what?*"

"Vampires have ways of . . . altering a person's conscious state," Clara said. "We don't fully understand it."

"For obvious reasons," Selene added dryly.

A part of her, Jill realized, was becoming more and more alarmed at their situation. It was pointing out how they were walking into the territory of an unknown entity, whose powers she did not fully comprehend. But it was drowned out by the rest of her, which was so skeptical that she dearly wanted to prove Selene and Clara's outrageous claims false—or, excitingly, *true*. This part was having such a difficult time grasping the idea of vampires—as Selene and Clara described them—as real things, that the idea of being attacked by one registered as a probability of something like getting hit by lightning or eaten by a shark. It could happen, sure, but it was so unlikely she was having a hard time taking her fears seriously.

Mostly, she was so very curious.

There was a wide streak of wetness coming out of a tunnel that opened some three feet above the cistern's floor. This was not running water, but merely wet concrete where water had been left by the passage of someone with wet feet. After examination, Selene announced they had been coming *out* of the tunnel—the opposite direction from which Jill's group was headed.

"We go in," Clara said, sounding resigned.

They did, and encountered more water on the floor. It smelled old and stale, but not particularly vile. Some of it had been splashed along the tunnel walls, as if someone had run down the tunnel in a hurry.

They found the remains of another homestead about thirty yards in. This one had been merely a collection of blankets and old cushions on cinderblocks, but now they were scattered and soaked in the water.

"Where did everyone go?" Jill wondered aloud.

"Better question," said Selene. "*Why* did everyone leave?"

They continued up the tunnel in close formation, Clara walking sideways so she could keep an eye out behind them. She was so near that her left elbow kept bumping into Jill's back. For her part, Jill kept stepping on Selene's heels. She stopped apologizing after it appeared the hunter was more annoyed by her whispered *Sorry*'s than she was by the physical distraction.

Then, quite abruptly, Selene stopped. A moment later she shut off her light.

They stood perfectly still, and in the dark they heard it.

Voices, raised in argument.

Too faint for the words to be made out, the tones spoke clearly enough on their own. They echoed so it was almost impossible to tell where one voice ended and another began, and as the group inched closer it became apparent that there were, in fact, *many* voices all raised in protest.

Words solidified out of the chaos of sound. Someone said:

"We outnumber *and* outgun him—we could just—"

Someone else said:

"Have you *seen* his guards?"

"*Yeah,* but he's not gonna be stupid enough to come down here on his own. Besides, they're *human!*"

"The brothers *Gunn* were human," said a sharp and scratchy voice, cutting through the others with an ease born of absolute authority.

"Only *one* of them," mumbled a voice, quickly hushed.

"What I am trying to make you dead-brainers understand is that the fight for our rightful place—not least our *continued existence*—has been brought to a head by the unacceptably rash actions of a *certain individual,* and unless you get your acts in line we are *all . . .* "

The speaker trailed off. There was a sound of many voices speaking in undertones together.

Jill felt Selene, who was in front of her, reach past her in the dark. She must have given some physical signal to Clara, because all of a sudden Jill felt large, strong hands on her shoulders, and she was being gently dragged backwards.

And because Jill had never received any sort of combat training, and because she was mostly thinking about setting eyes on the owners of the voices, she said out loud:

"What are you *doing?*"

Only the first three words got out properly because Clara clapped a hand over her mouth and it came out more like:

"What are you *doimph*—"

Something big dropped from the ceiling of the tunnel between Jill and Selene. It made a splash as its feet hit the water, and she felt something cold, very much like a hand, land on her face.

The fingers tightened.

Selene's flashlight, when it went on, nearly blinded her. It *did* blind the person who had a grip on her face that was quickly becoming painful.

With a slither of metal against leather and then a dull *thunk,* the hand came away at once.

By the slanting light of the torch Jill saw a man in a black, button-down shirt and tight leather-looking pants. He had skin so pale it was almost greenish in places, and currently he had Clara's sword sticking out of his chest.

It looked *wrong* somehow. Jill's mind told her it must be a trick—like those fake swords that are broken off halfway down the blade so actors can hold them against their bodies and make it *look* like they'd been stabbed. But she knew Clara had a real, long, and very sharp sword—not to mention she was certainly strong enough to drive it into someone's chest.

Then it clicked: the man was not bleeding. There was a sword driven clean through his sternum and his shirt was torn, but he was not bleeding.

In fact, he was hardly moving either. He stared at them blankly. Then Selene stepped up and, taking out a huge knife—almost like a meat cleaver—swung it at his neck.

The knife met the spine and stopped. Selene yanked it out and struck again. And again. On the fourth stroke the man's head sort of lolled off to the side, and Selene grabbed it by the hair and tore it away.

Clara removed her sword, and the body crumpled into the water.

Jill found her heart was pounding, her head felt like she'd done a dozen somersaults in a row, and she'd forgotten to inhale.

She took a deep breath. The first words out of her mouth were:

"But I wanted to *talk* to a vampire!"

Clara gave her a look like she wasn't certain she didn't want to stab Jill next, and Selene rolled her eyes.

"He tried to bite your head off," she said. "I don't think he'd have talked to you even if we asked nicely."

"Retreating," said Clara.

"What?" said Jill.

"That's what we're doing," Clara said. "We're *retreating*. Now come, the others will have heard us."

They ran. They only got about twenty feet before another dark shape lunged at them from out of what Jill had thought was a sheer wall.

"Ass *hat!*" Selene screamed, firing her gun in the direction of the body even as Jill and Clara dove for the ground. "Clara, we got a shifter!"

"Not for long," Clara growled through gritted teeth.

Jill knew better than to ask what a shifter was. She huddled on the ground, the water seeping up the back of her jeans, with her knees in her chest, while the fight went on above and around her. The tunnel suddenly filled with smoke, cold and smelling of stone tombs. It was such a different smell than the dull musk of the drains that for a moment it was almost refreshing. Then it abruptly solidified into a human shape, and the next moment the sharp end of Clara's sword exploded from its chest.

This time the vampire was not paralyzed. It struggled, kicked, and nearly writhed itself off the sword. Before it could break free, however, Clara's other hand, which now held a wicked-looking knife, appeared by its face and stabbed repeatedly into its throat.

Clara did not so much cut the creature's head off as shred its neck, and it wobbled sickly for a while, before with a rip and a crunch, Clara managed to tear the head off.

Jill found herself bracketed closely by the two women, each with their back to her and retreating slowly down the tunnel. Jill tripped and crawled as best she could, trying to ignore the echoing gunfire that Selene was using to cover their retreat, but every shot sent a shudder through her body and made her ears ring.

Clara said something, but it was lost in a bang from Freddie.

"Say what?" said Selene as she reloaded.

"Hold your fire," Clara said. "They aren't following us."

"H-how do you know that?" Jill gasped.

"Because they are in front of us," Clara said.

They had reached the end of the tunnel and emerged into the wide cistern where they had met the sewer dweller before. Now, as Selene shined her beam around the vast cavern, it illuminated a crowd of pale-faced people. They ranged in age from late teens to early forties, but few of them had graying hair or showed signs of extreme age. They were dressed in a variety of clothes, some of them rather old fashioned, but mostly in dark combinations of black and blue. They were predominantly white, Jill noted with interest, though there were a few people whose whiteness was tinged with a warmer green, whom she guessed might have been Latino or Asian, judging by their features.

They were, as one, staring at them with eyes that glinted red in the beam of the flashlight. In their center was a small woman with a mess of auburn hair. Unlike the majority, she showed noticeable signs of age in her withered face, and though she was barely taller than Jill, she stood in such a powerful way (legs apart with her hands on her hips) that it was clear she was the most important individual present.

"*Now* can I t-talk to them?" Jill stuttered.

"I think the time for your kind of talking is past, hon," Selene said, putting a firm hand on Jill's shoulder. Leaning in she whispered: "Keep your back to the wall and your head down. There is a chance we might not all die here."

"But—" Jill began.

"Either you two are the *dumbest* hunters I've ever met," said the withered woman with auburn hair. "Or that mundane is paying you *way* too much."

"I am Claymore Nordstern," Clara said, and Jill, despite her growing horror, started at the use of her real name. The large woman gestured casually with her knife hand at Selene, who was holding Freddie under the crook of her arm and the cleaver knife in the other. "This is Selene Shields."

The lead vampire twitched her head to the side and back again, her wire-thin mouth cracked into a sort of grimace. "Oh, so you want to do this the *old fashioned* way," she said with a sneer. "Well, you can call me Martha, and these here . . . " she nodded at the assembled crowd around her. *"These* are my babies."

"Very well," Clara said. It sounded like she was passing sentence. "Martha. We did not come here hunting. We will leave in peace if you allow us."

Martha shook her head, sending her hair tossing. "Too late for that. You've already killed two of my brood."

"Because they *attacked* me!" Jill gasped. "We're *very* sorry!"

Selene groaned.

Martha laughed.

"Funny kid you've got there," she said. "Thanks for giving me the only good laugh I've had all week." She made a clicking noise in the back of her throat, and jerked a thumb in Clara's direction. "Get 'em," she said, her grating voice a low rasp.

The vampires moved so fast they blurred around the edges. Jill saw one come practically flying at Clara, and the big woman went over sideways under the force of the impact. She was up again in an instant and beating the thing back with her sword, but by that time they were already encircled in a ring of sneering white faces. Selene and Clara closed, back to back around Jill, their weapons at the ready.

There was a flurry of action: Freddie went off practically in Jill's ear, and Clara grunted under the force of a vampire slamming into her. Jill had the sense to duck down, covering her ears with her hands, even as a vampire went sailing above her head. This one landed on Clara's shoulders, and she saw the vampire, his mouth opened wide, and there was a strange, gleaming fluid dripping from his snakelike fangs.

Something thick and dark ripped through the air. It cleaved the head off the vampire that was menacing Selene, and neatly bisected the one riding on Clara's shoulders. As always there was no blood, but Jill still felt her stomach give a little turn at the sight of the upper half of the vampire, his eyes still blinking in confusion, as the pale gray innards slowly distended from his severed waist.

Clara didn't hesitate. She brought her sword around in a clean arc and mercilessly hacked his head off.

And then there was a strange silence. Selene swept her light over the room, only to discover a wide swath of headless vampire corpses where before a small army had stood.

The only one still standing was the auburn-haired vampire, Martha, and she was held in the firm grip of a tall, pale man with lank, black hair. He wore sagging, worn-out jeans and a threadbare t-shirt.

The two exchanged words, too quiet for Jill to make out, and then with a neat flick of his wrist the man decapitated the auburn-haired woman with his fingernails. Her body fell to the ground, but her head remained, hanging by its hair from the man's other hand. He appeared to study it thoughtfully, and then tossed it aside with an uncaring shrug. He glanced at them, and gave them a rueful sort of smile.

"Sorry," he said. "I had to wait for them to be distracted. Thank you for that."

And, though his eyes were red now instead of yellow, and his fangs were much smaller and infinitely more wicked, Jill recognized him.

As one Clara and Selene moved to close in on him, weapons at the ready.

"Stop that *at once!*" Jill screamed, and they froze out of pure surprise.

The man, whom Jill was increasingly certain was actually Johnny Bathory, dusted vampire corpse off his hands and turned to leave.

"Wait!" Jill cried, running after him. She avoided Selene's grasping hands and made it a few more feet before Clara caught her in an iron grip.

Johnny Bathory—it really *was* him—paused and turned back to look at her quizzically.

"*What?*" he asked.

"You—" Jill found she had to gasp rather hard to force the words out. "Why did *you* kill them?"

Johnny Bathory looked around at the mayhem of corpses as if surprised to see them there. "Do I need to give you a reason?" he asked. His voice was deeper than Jill remembered from the interviews. Richer and fuller, with a slight twist to the ends of

his words that suggested a foreign accent heavily diluted by use
of American English.

"Why did you kill *them* and not *us?*" Jill forged on.

"What, do you *want* me to?" Johnny Bathory pivoted on one
heel and began to saunter toward them.

Clara's hold on Jill's arm tightened, and she raised her sword.

Johnny Bathory gave the weapon a disdainful look, and
sneered so that one fang was clearly visible against his red
tongue.

"No, *no,*" Jill said. "I just—I want to *understand* . . . uh . . . you.
Vampires. I . . . I just have some questions."

Johnny Bathory came up to the very edge of Clara's sword
range, and then leaned in.

"Are you asking me for an *interview?*" he asked, a sly smile
creeping up his face. Up close Jill could see his skin was pock-
marked with old acne scars, and there was a thin line of perfectly
white tissue running up from the neckline of his shirt and over
his chin.

"I . . . guess?" Jill said uncertainly.

Johnny Bathory straightened up, turned, and began walking
away again.

"Three p.m.," he said. "Today. The backstage-pass signup
area. Come *alone,*" he added, flashing a grin over his shoulder at
Selene and Clara. "Wear something *nice.*"

He disappeared into the shadows, melting away like ink into
dark water, and then they were alone in the field of dead vampires.

Jill was shaken. She insisted she was shaken, and Selene believed her. She had a little difficulty believing Jill was not in
shock as well as she coolly went over all the vampire bodies,
measuring and tagging them and taking clippings of their hair
and fingernails—even scrapings of their skin.

But for once she was not interested in taking any actual dead
bodies with them.

"We will notify Officer Dunes," she said with grim satisfaction. "He should know about this." And she would not stop
badgering Clara until she gave her the policeman's direct num-

ber. Jill called him as soon as they got out of the drain and left a terse message. Then she had Selene drive her back to the hotel where she took a very long shower.

When she finally emerged, dripping but clean and wrapped in one of the Castle's princess-style bathrobes, there was a hard glint in her eye that set off warning bells inside Selene's head.

"You can't be seriously considering that psycho's offer?" she blurted out.

Jill looked up and frowned at her.

"I asked him for an interview," she said with a shrug. "He said *yes*. I *finally* have a shot at interviewing a vampire. I *have* to go . . . " She gave a little start, as if coming out of a daze. "I have to go *alone*," she finished.

Selene slowly raised her eyebrows, in the manner of one watching someone realize the obvious.

"*Ye*-ah," she said. "That's *kind* of a deal breaker."

"No," said Jill, going over to her suitcase and fishing through its contents. "No, no. I have to go anyway. I may never get a better chance."

"Your life will be *filled* with better chances!" Selene assured her. "Clara," she tried, turning to the large woman who had been sitting, silent, in a corner. "*Talk* to her. You tell her!"

Clara chewed thoughtfully on her lower lip.

"Clara . . . " Selene said in a warning tone.

Clara shifted uncomfortably. "Johnny Bathory is unusual in many respects," she said.

Jill paused. "You don't think he's a good example?" she said with a frown.

Clara seemed confused by this. "Not at all. What I mean is . . . there *is* a chance he will not kill you on principle, as any other vampire would."

"Oh, so there's a *small* chance?" Selene said, covering her face in her hands. "Well, *that* makes it all right. Look, Jill, I won't stop you doing what you feel you need to do. I'm your bodyguard, not your babysitter, but I'm telling you girl, it's gonna be a lot harder to keep you alive if you don't even let us *do our jobs*."

"I understand," Jill said, pulling out a black sweater, holding it up, frowning, and then tossing it aside. "And I am open to any pieces of *practical* advice you may have to offer."

Selene threw her hands in the air, in the imitation of an explosion, and stomped off into the bathroom. Clara did one of her inverted shrugs.

"Wear white," she said.

"What?" said Jill.

"Wear white," said Clara.

"I don't think I even *own* any white clothes that aren't *underwear . . .*" Jill began.

"It doesn't have to be clothes," Clara allowed. "But Johnny Bathory is granting you a truce. You should show that you are conscious of the honor."

"You've been accused by members of the Christian church of being . . . well, basically of being the spawn of the devil. That you're intentionally corrupting today's young people into being . . . what did that one fellow say?"

"Minions of Satan," Johnny Bathory said with a wry smile.

"That's right," said the interviewer. "What do you have to say in response to that?"

"I really don't know, actually. I mean, what *can* you say to that? Do they want me to say sorry or something? I mean, I guess I could say that, but I wouldn't mean it. I'd keep on doing what I'm doing. And being a minion of Satan, I think, really isn't so bad. I mean, you read the Bible, look at all the horrible things God has done, all the horrible things *His* minions have done, and you compare that to Satan . . . I dunno, I almost feel like the Devil is the better one. At least he's *honest* about being evil."

The interviewer laughed nervously. "But what do you say to people who accuse you of corrupting today's youth? Of introducing them to the sex, drugs and rock 'n' roll lifestyle?"

"Look," said Johnny Bathory, adjusting himself in his chair. "I'm not corrupting or introducing anyone to anything. What I try to do with my music—what I've always tried to do—is to give a voice to the people who have no voices, or who haven't been heard. When I'm up there performing, I'm not just performing for . . . *at* the audience. I really am performing *for* them. I think every one of my fans would do what I do if they could, but they can't, so *I* do it *for* them. I do it for all of us. And if that looks ugly or scary, well, maybe you should worry more about what's being done to these kids in school or at church or at their jobs than the stupid stuff that's coming out of my mouth."

Jill stood in the baking hot afternoon Nevada sun and felt horribly out of place. She'd ended up digging out her last remaining pair of jeans that didn't have rips, tears or stains on them, and pulled on the most edgy top she owned. This was a black, strappy, spandex exercise top with a shelf bra that never failed to make Jill feel like a flat-chested boy. Tied around her waist with the ends hanging to her knees was a strip of white cloth— actually torn from one of the Castle's bedsheets. She wore a pair of running shoes (Selene had insisted) and no makeup.

She stood in line with hundreds of other young women in sheer black outfits and elaborate face paint, and felt more and more uncomfortable. Like the rest of them she'd been given a yellow wristband with a number on it as soon as she arrived and said she wanted to enter for a backstage pass, but aside from that she could not have looked more different.

They all wore heels, for a start, and most of them were in strategically ripped pantyhose. Many were in corsets—black shiny ones or velvet red—and they all had heavily decorated faces. Some of these designs were clearly modeled after Johnny Bathory, others were more standard Goth, while others seemed to have tried to come up with designs of their own, with more or less success.

They were all very excited and intent, and talked among one another in cliques of threes and fours. Jill caught snatches of conversation like . . .

"This is my fifth concert . . . "

"You lucky cow!"

"Is it true he picks the winners *personally?*"

"You mean we actually get to *see* him? *Eee!*"

Jill stood alone, letting the motion of the crowd push and pull at her, felt hotter and hotter, and wondered if this had been one great setup. The vampires in the sewers seemed a long way away now she was in the hot sun surrounded by ordinary (if extraordinarily dressed) humans. She was glad Selene and Clara had been made to wait out front, where they couldn't see her.

Slowly the sun went down and the pavement cooled. It cooled so much Jill was glad Selene had made her bring a coat. She put it on.

A little before seven, after she had been standing on increasingly sore feet for almost four hours, there was a hum of excited conversation near the front of the crowd, and slowly the line of people began to move. They shuffled forward and down a side street and finally filed into the back lot of the hotel. Just after Jill passed under the archway sign—"Castle Back Lot, registered vehicles only"—there was a commotion behind her, and she looked back to find a couple of burly men in black t-shirts rolling the gate closed, much to the consternation of those shut out. Then she slammed into the person in front of her and stopped. The lot was packed beyond capacity, with people pressed in and up against one another. Jill, wedged against a woman in a corset and a feathered headdress on one side and the cool metal of the gate on the other, was comparatively lucky.

In the harsh yellow floodlights, she saw a little stage at the other end of the lot, up against the side of the hotel. High enough to be visible above the heads of the crowd, it stood below a rusty and battered iron door onto which had peen painted "PRIVATE" in big letters. Two more burly and humorless men in black t-shirts stood flanking it, and more were arranged in a human barricade around the base of the stage.

There was an excited hum as a small man in ripped jeans and a dirty t-shirt stepped out of the door. He wore a backwards baseball cap with his plain sandy hair sticking out beneath it. He held a clipboard, and as Jill watched, he took a cordless microphone out of his back pocket and tapped it.

There was a dull *pthud pthud* sound from all the speakers arrayed around the parking lot.

"Good evening ladies," he said in a pleasant and surprisingly British voice. He squinted into the crowd. "And . . . gentlemen. Yes, there are some gentlemen here, lovely, how nice to see you all. So, as you can probably tell I . . . am not Johnny Bathory. In fact, it's not at all important who I am, just what I'm about to tell you. Now, as some of you have doubtless done this before . . . "

There was scattered laughter from the crowd.

" . . . you are probably already aware of the rules. But I must ask you to please be quiet and listen, as we may have some backstage virgins and we want them to understand this, don't we?"

The crowd mumbled assent. Jill rose on tiptoe for a better look.

The man with the microphone held up the clipboard with a flourish and began to read dramatically.

"In order to qualify for a backstage pass, you *must* be wearing that little yellow wristband we gave you when you arrived. You must also step up onto the stage if you are chosen. We have some kind men to help you do this if you require assistance.

"You must *not* scream too loudly, since I need to hear what Johnny tells me and 'sides it hurts me ears. You must also not rush this little stage area, or throw anything—including yourself—at Mr. Bathory. As soon as you rush the stage or toss *anything* toward it he goes back inside and *no one* gets to come backstage.

"There will be five *and only five* backstagers chosen. You cannot bring a plus one, you cannot bring cameras or phones or any recording devices. We will hold these items in a secure place if you are chosen, don't worry, but you *cannot* bring them with you backstage.

"You *may* give gifts . . . to one of the nice gentlemen down here. Because Johnny goes straight from here to his warm up he cannot accept gifts. If you are chosen, and you have a gift that is small, you may present it to him after the show. If he does not pick his five from you lot here, you will be dismissed and a new batch shown in.

"Now, are there any questions?" the man asked.

Jill put her hand up immediately, to ask if having a notebook and pen was also not allowed. She'd thought ahead and brought one, in case they did take her phone.

It seemed, however, that questions were answered based on how loudly they were shouted. Near the front someone screamed: "When do we get to see Johnny?!"

"That's a very good question," said the man, grinning. "I'm so glad you asked that. Because the answer is . . . you get to see him . . . *now!*"

The roar was so loud Jill had to clap her hands over her ears, and she winced, looking down. Because of this she missed the moment when Johnny Bathory actually appeared, but she assumed he'd come through the same battered old door as the man, because when she looked up there he was.

He was wearing a pair of tight-fitting black underwear, black leather chaps, boots with one-inch soles and four-inch heels, a lot of makeup and a long leather coat with a collar that stuck up behind his head. His hair stood wildly on end, and the deep black rings around his eyes made the yellow irises stand out in a ghoulish way. Or made him look a little like a raccoon, Jill thought.

He looked exactly like he did in interviews and performances, and nothing like the man Jill had seen earlier in the drains. It was only his body language—the set of his shoulders and the careful way he walked in those ridiculous shoes—and the particular shape of his chin and nose under all that paint that convinced her this was the same person.

Johnny Bathory did not speak; he walked from one end of the little stage to the other, one hand resting contemplatively on his chin.

The attention of the crowd went with him; Jill felt the other people sway around her as they leaned toward the man on the stage with every fiber of their being. She wondered how he would do the picking. Would she have to wait until the last name was called? Was this whole thing a setup?

Johnny Bathory looked out over the crowd, but Jill could not tell whether he was looking at them or merely gazing off over their heads.

Then he raised a hand and pointed one black-painted nail into the crowd.

The girl next to Jill screamed. It was a scream of excitement and exultation, and Jill felt as though her eardrums might have ruptured.

As suddenly as the scream came, it cut off abruptly; Johnny Bathory was shaking his head, *and still pointing.*

In a daze Jill realized he was pointing at her.

Cautiously she raised her hand and waved.

Johnny Bathory nodded.

The crowd around her erupted in cheers, and the girl who had screamed before turned to Jill and gave her a wet-faced hug. In the way of crowds they opened before her and pushed from behind, forcing her to the front where one of the humorless men gave her a leg up on stage.

Jill scrambled to her feet, glad of her sensible shoes, and stood in a daze. She was aware of Johnny Bathory standing mere feet from her, and of the thick crowd of faces below, but only in the most general sense. She realized now the reason they could see Bathory so easily in the dim twilight was because there was a spotlight pointed at the stage, and now it was shining right in her face. How Bathory could see to pick his backstagers was beyond her.

One of the men by the door led her helpfully to a white line painted on the stage, and put her at one end of it. There she stood while Johnny Bathory picked his remaining four. These were in turn cheered, pushed up to the stage, and came to stand next to Jill.

They were an odd assortment. One was a lovely, teenaged girl dressed in a lacy black short skirt and corset, striped stockings and a tiny hat affixed to her head with numerous pins. She was also, Jill noted with distant surprise, an amputee; her left arm ended in a stump just below her elbow. She'd decorated it with red paint so for a moment it looked as though her arm had just been bitten off. She was quivering with excitement when she came to stand on the line, and kept whispering, *"Oh my god. Oh my god. Ohmygod . . ."* under her breath.

The third to be chosen Jill thought was an especially tall woman, until she got up to the stage and turned out to be a tall, fine-boned man in remarkably good drag. He wore an over-bust corset and fishnet tights and improbably red pumps. He was laughing deliriously and hugged the one-armed girl when he came to join them.

The fourth was a punkish young woman covered in tattoos with a fluffy bleached mohawk. The fifth was a comparatively ordinary woman in ripped jeans and a Johnny Bathory t-shirt. She had a nose piercing and wore horn-rimmed glasses.

When they were all assembled, Johnny Bathory walked up and down in front of them, as if surveying stock he was about to take home from market.

Jill kept thinking about how he'd decapitated the vampire in the sewer. *With a flick of his wrist.*

Then he smiled at them, a leering grin so over the top Jill went back to feeling this was just a show, something exciting and fun for the fans of a rock star.

"See you later," he whispered in his weak, hoarse voice, and exited the stage.

They did not follow him. They waited on the stage while the lot slowly emptied, and then they were led around to the side and taken in through a door marked Staff Entrance Only.

Somehow Jill had forgotten about the concert. Between what had happened in the drain and the shock of being physically pulled up on stage, she had wanted the whole ordeal to be over with so much that she'd assumed they'd be taken straight to the dressing room or something.

But no. They were led through a narrow corridor with naked pipes running overhead, up some stairs and then through another door marked Stage Mait. Here a friendly tech came up and collected their phones and cameras into a little black lockbox, and they were shown to a set of five folding chairs that looked out on a strange landscape of boxes, cables and platforms constructed of pipe and black-painted wood.

It took Jill a moment to realize they were looking at the stage—from the *side.*

"Wouldn't want you to miss the show," their guide said with a chuckle as they took their seats.

Jill sank gratefully into the nearest chair available, while her fellow backstagers squealed with excitement and fairly shivered into their seats.

The pre-show started not long after that. It was all very loud, even though they sat behind the biggest speakers and so were not subjected to the full blast of sound the regular audience received. If she craned her neck Jill could just see them: a crowd of people pressed against the human wall of security down at the foot of the stage, and more in the boxes above her head.

Then the band came onstage and the noise fairly doubled. It was hard to see the band from this angle—Johnny Bathory was mostly eclipsed by his guitarist, and the keyboardist was half hidden behind the drummer's stand. The other backstagers didn't seem to mind this: they whooped and hollered with the rest of the audience, and Jill joined in. At first she did it so that she would not raise suspicion, but after a while she began to actually *listen* to the music, and found herself genuinely applauding after every song.

It was not pleasant music. It was dramatic music. It was not relaxing or soothing: it was hard-edged and heart pounding. But the songs, as they were arranged, seemed to have some internal narrative and kept Jill's attention, ever after she had to cover her ears from the sheer volume.

Johnny Bathory did not just sing: he danced, he kicked and strutted. After a while his jacket came off, and then his chaps. He danced around in just the underwear for a while (extra loud screaming from the contingent backstage) before he disappeared down a trapdoor in the stage floor.

The next time he appeared he was wearing what looked like a ragged evening dress with shreds of cloth hanging down below his feet, and he was being lowered by wires out of the rafters from the ceiling. He held his arms out stiffly to either side, looking like a well-used children's doll.

As soon as he hit the stage a grip in black ran up and unhooked something from his back, and he began to dance and sing once more.

The dress came off him in pieces over the course of the next few songs. Jill wondered if they had to get a new dress every night, or if it was a special one that you could take apart and put back together again. Underneath it he wore a corset that seemed to be mostly made of belts, tight black underwear, and thigh-high leather boots with stiletto heels.

He finished the performance in those heels, something Jill watched with numb fascination, her feet hurting just to look at the way he jumped and slid around.

After a particularly long and rambling song, the show ended. The audience roared. The curtain came down, and in the dark there was a muddled thumping and the sound of a person in high heels staggering past them.

"For the love of all hell," someone said. "Turn on the stupid light, Jerry."

The light came on, and there was the band. Jill got one glimpse of the five men in various stages of makeup and undress before the other backstagers mobbed them.

She stood awkwardly on the edge of the crowd, uncertain what to do. Fortunately a couple of burly stage hands intervened and herded them all down some stairs and along a corridor.

Someone was fairly shrieking "Johnny, Johnny, *Johnny!*" and there was the sound of laughing and giggling. Then they were bundled into a huge lift.

"Is this the *service* elevator?" someone asked.

One of the band members—the keyboardist, Jill thought—huffed a laugh and said: "Believe it or not, it's the best ride in the place. No one else gets to use this lift!"

It was a large elevator, but Jill was crammed into a corner by the crowd. It also moved incredibly slowly: there was no feeling of being pulled upward, and the only assurance she had that they were moving at all was the lighted display that told them they were on Floor 5 . . . Floor 6 . . . Floor 7 . . .

Jill sank to a crouch in her corner, concentrating on watching the progression of floors, and trying to ignore the increasing ruckus of the band and their fans.

It was at Floor 38—the very top of the building—that the elevator finally stopped and the doors opened. The whole crowd tumbled out, leaving Jill to drift in their wake.

This floor was even more opulent than the others, with tapestries on the wall and a thick, soft carpet. The window at the far end of the corridor showed a glimpse of the lights of the Strip.

"You Miss Hamilton?" a deep voice asked from several feet above her. She turned to find a dour black man in modest jeans and a black t-shirt with "MINION" in big white letters waiting patiently beside the elevator.

"Um . . . yes?" she said.

"You go this way," he said, and led her down the corridor, turning at the window, to where it dead ended in a door. Using a card key on a chain he unlocked it and held it open while she drifted inside. The door shut with a soft *click* behind her.

Jill found herself alone then, in what must have been the Castle's Presidential Suite.

It was enormous, with steps leading down from the door and out into a spacious lounge area. There was a wet bar beside a floor-to-ceiling window, and plump, fluffy couches and chairs set out around a heavy wooden table. There was a display of waxily perfect dahlias there, the color of dark red wine.

As Jill wandered further out into the room she noted several other doors leading off it. One was left ajar and through it she glimpsed a room with an enormous four-poster bed in the center of it. Around a corner where the wall protruded into the room she saw there was a kitchenette, with a bowl of fruit set out on the counter. The bowl had little lion feet on it, like the ones sometimes found on old-fashioned bathtubs.

"It is a bit contrived, isn't it?" said a hoarse voice from behind her.

She turned, and found Johnny Bathory just shutting the door to the bedroom. He was still mostly in costume: leather underwear and thigh-high, stiletto-heeled boots. The corset he'd been wearing at the end of the show was unlaced but still clung resolutely around his waist. His makeup—white with heavy, dark eyeliner and a black stripe that covered his chin and lower lip—looked a bit smudged. Unless that was intentional. Jill couldn't tell.

"I'm sorry?" she said, finding her voice at last.

Johnny Bathory gestured at the room.

"It's typical Las Vegas, isn't it? Trying to be like something else, only entertaining. So it winds up being *nothing like* what it's trying to imitate."

His voice had dropped. Now it sounded more like it had earlier, in the sewer: deeper, rougher, and with a slight twinge to the ends of his words that suggested some well-smothered accent, too faint for Jill to recognize. She thought it suited him much better.

"I guess," she said, backing and turning as the man advanced into the room. He fumbled with something behind his back and then pulled the corset off, tossing it onto a nearby chair. Then he went and sat in it and began un-strapping his boots.

"It's sort of tragic, I think. I mean, spending all this time trying to remind people of something real, when the real thing is so much better you couldn't possibly hope to top it. Best they do is *remind* people of the real thing, and all those people think is how crappy their model is."

He kicked his boots off and stood up, rolling down the fishnet stockings that were revealed beneath them. Jill wondered if she should look away.

Johnny Bathory didn't seem to care. He stripped off the stockings, draping them over the back of the chair, and walked past her in nothing but his underwear to another door, which turned out to lead to a bathroom. He left it open behind him, and a few seconds later the leather underwear sailed out of it and landed next to the boots. Then there was the sound of running water and some splashing.

"Have you eaten yet?" he asked from the bathroom.

Jill was at this point so nervous the very thought of food made her feel like vomiting. But she hadn't eaten all afternoon, and was feeling a little shaky. Unless that was the nerves, too.

"No ... er ... but I'm not hungry," she said.

The water shut off. Johnny Bathory came out wearing a towel and nothing else. He had a damp cloth in one hand, and was scraping makeup out from behind his ears. His wet hair hung limply at his shoulders. He had an odd sort of tattoo above his left bicep. It looked like it had once been a circle with something inside, but it was ripped and scarred, black around the edges. It reminded Jill a little of the death marks the unicorns had used, only rougher and older.

"I only asked," he said, "because the Castle caters dinner for us every night. I usually give my share to the bouncers, but I figured ... " He made a shrugging motion at Jill. "It's not like *I* can eat it."

Casually he reached into his mouth and, with a small popping noise, took out a set of dentures. Underneath them his teeth appeared a little crooked and yellow, but not otherwise extraordinary. He put the discarded dentures on the coffee table— Jill saw they were indeed the oversized vampire fangs he displayed in interviews—and wandered off into the master bedroom.

"What . . . er . . . *do* you eat?" Jill asked quaveringly.

The rummaging sounds from the bedroom stopped, and Johnny Bathory stuck his head back out. Without the makeup his face looked astonishingly plain, apart from the prominent acne pockmarks and pale scar. He was not a particularly handsome man—his face was a little too long, his eyes a little too deep set—but without the radical face paint he didn't look like someone Jill would have paid any notice to on the street.

Now one eyebrow was raised in surprise.

"You really need to ask *me?*" he said. "Surely your sword and shield could have told you *that* at least."

"They are secondary sources," Jill said. "And I meant . . . specifics. Like . . . how do you . . . *feed?*"

Johnny Bathory's whole face seemed to droop in disappointment. "You don't have to talk about it like it's something *dirty,*" he said, a little reproachfully. "We all do it."

His head disappeared into the bedroom and Jill was left standing awkwardly in the main room. Belatedly she remembered her pen and notepad, and got them out and wrote down a heading.

Interview w/ J Bathory, vampire

Notes . . .

She was chewing on the end of her pen when Johnny Bathory came out of the bedroom. He was wearing a pair of frayed, brown corduroy pants and a t-shirt with a faded print of a dragon's head on it. His hair, neatly combed, was pulled back into a ponytail, and he was barefoot. He looked . . . well, he looked a little nerdy, Jill thought.

Except for the eyes. He had taken out the yellow contacts, and now his irises were vibrantly red, and even more unnerving.

In long, loose strides he crossed the room to the kitchenette. He took two glasses from a cupboard above the sink, then paused.

"Just water for me," Jill said hastily.

Bathory shrugged, filled one glass with water from the tap, then opened the freezer and took out some ice.

"Usually, I don't," he said.

At Jill's befuddled expression he smiled a little and added: "Feed, I mean. On blood, anyway. I don't need much anymore. But as tonight is a special occasion . . . " He opened the refrigerator, and there was a clink of glass as he pulled out a bottle of dark, viscous liquid. Twisting the lid off he poured himself half a glass and stuck it in the microwave.

"I love these things," he said, tapping the humming machine. "Time was I had to re-heat the stuff over a fire. It's not bad chilled," he allowed. "But room temperature?" he made a face Jill recognized from the show, twisting his mouth and sticking his tongue out so that the tip nearly touched his chin.

"You don't . . . um . . . prefer it . . . fresh?" Jill asked in a small voice.

"Of course," Bathory said with a shrug. "But fresh as in spurting from someone's neck?" He shuddered. "That's just . . . rude. And a bit sloppy, between you and me."

"Ah," said Jill, making a note in her book. Now that they were talking and she had so far not been attacked, she was beginning to get her confidence back. "There are some sources that imply there is a . . . um . . . *sexual* connotation to your method of feeding, is that true at all?"

Johnny Bathory made a stifled choking noise, and his shoulders shook. He shot Jill a deprecating grin.

"That, I can only imagine, is entirely a *human* invention," he said. "From my experience, vampires don't fetishize their feeding habits any more than humans do. I'm not saying there aren't vampires who *do* but . . . if there *is* a sexual connotation, it's mostly in *your* heads, not ours."

"Interesting," muttered Jill, writing this down. "And can you subsist on the blood of other organisms?"

"Okay, first, it's not the blood." The microwave beeped and Johnny Bathory took his glass out. He stirred the contents with a spoon and blew on it. "Not . . . in the nutritional sense. We *are* technically dead. We don't have a pulse. We don't have an active digestive system. We don't even need to *breathe*. I only got into a habit of it because it's hard to sing otherwise. And it helps to suspend people's disbelief."

"That . . . you're a vampire?" Jill asked.

"That I'm a human *pretending* to be a vampire," Johnny Bathory said. He held out the glass of water and ice.

Forcing her legs to work, Jill walked stiffly over. She took the glass, trying to avoid touching him without looking like it. Bathory just grinned at her with his yellow, crooked teeth, his red eyes gleaming, and raised his own glass.

"Cheers," he said, and knocked back the contents in a single gulp.

Jill sipped her water thoughtfully. The coolness in her mouth was a pleasant physical anchor.

"How *does* it work, then?" she asked.

Johnny Bathory laughed, but he looked a little sad. "That's the . . . what do you call it? Sixty-four thousand dollar question." He moved past Jill and back out into the living room, where he sat down in the biggest chair, folding one leg comfortably beneath him. He gestured to the couch opposite. "Please sit down," he said. "You look like a stiff breeze could knock you over."

Reluctantly Jill came and sat down on the edge of the couch, putting her glass on the table next to Bathory's discarded dentures. She held her pad and pen protectively in front of her chest.

"As best I can tell," Bathory said after thinking a minute, "it's about the energy. Blood carries life: living cells and with them the means to keep the body to which it belongs alive. *That's* what we feed on; that pure life force. Does that answer your question?"

"It is useful information," Jill said, scribbling on her pad. She glanced up to find Johnny Bathory looking at her with an odd, intent expression. She couldn't tell if it was more like the way a cat watches a bird in the grass, or the way a horse freezes at the sight of a potential predator.

"What else," Bathory said—and this time Jill noticed how he had to inhale before he spoke—"what else did you want to know?"

Jill tapped the end of her pen against her pad of paper. "As much as you can tell me," she said frankly. "I'd also like to take some . . . um . . . physical measurements."

Johnny Bathory seemed amused at that. "If I'd known I wouldn't have bothered to get dressed—" he began.

"Nothing like *that*," Jill cut in, flapping her free hand. "I just . . . well, I'd like to get a good look at your fangs."

"Most people do," Johnny Bathory said with a grin.

"Your *real* ones," Jill insisted. "It's for science," she added.

Bathory made a facial motion that suggested an eye roll without any actual eye movement. But he leaned forward obligingly and opened his mouth. With a flick his yellow human canines popped back up against the roof of his mouth and in one slow, smooth movement the long, sharp fangs descended from the gaping holes in his gums. They were a little longer than the ones Jill had observed on the dead vampire, but otherwise identical: narrow and slightly curved. The thin membrane that covered them was pinkish and transparent.

"May I?" she asked, holding up a fresh piece of paper.

Johnny Bathory shrugged. Taking this as a yes, Jill placed the paper carefully behind the left fang and made a quick trace. By the time she had finished it was already leaking a pale, transparent liquid, which dripped on the paper, threatening the ink.

"Sorry," Bathory said as soon as Jill snatched the paper away. "It's a reflex, like drool."

"Is it toxic?" Jill asked, holding the paper awkwardly away from her.

"Not particularly. It's an anticoagulant and a sedative."

"That makes sense," Jill said, feeling about on her person for a spare cloth. She ended up using the white sash Clara had made for her to wipe the paper down. "Could I take a sample?" she asked.

"No," Johnny Bathory said, quite pleasantly. "You can ask more questions, though."

"Oh," said Jill, momentarily deflating as she realized she had left the list of questions on her phone . . . which was down in a locker somewhere. After some thought she decided to go with:

"How . . . er . . . how did you become a vampire? The mechanics of it, I mean."

Johnny Bathory leaned back in his seat and folded his arms. "I don't feel like talking about that," he said quietly.

Jill sighed and made a mark on her paper. "How dangerous is sunlight to you, really?"

"Pass," said Johnny Bathory, a small smile tugging at the side of his mouth.

"You know," Jill said, a little frustrated. "There's a lot of information *about* vampires out there in the world already. *Fictional* vampires. Some of it is *misinformation,* as I have learned— but I have no way of knowing which is true or false unless *you* tell me."

"Most of it is inaccurate," Johnny Bathory allowed. "Though you have to understand, all vampires are individuals. We're all a little different from one another in our abilities and . . . tastes."

"Like you're different from that vampire in the drain?"

"Yes."

"Why did you kill her, anyway?"

Johnny Bathory put his head on one side to look at Jill piercingly. "Why should it matter to you if one vampire kills another? I would think, from your point of view, the less of us the better."

"I don't know," Jill said. "I'm not a hunter. I just want to *understand.* For all I know vampires fulfill some obscure but important biological niche."

Bathory gave her a critical stare. Then he leaned forward (Jill instinctively leaned away) and inspected her closely. His eyes were more than just red, she noticed; they were so vivid they almost appeared to glow.

"Great Hecate," he murmured. "You really mean it."

He got up and paced around the chair, leaning his arms on the back. Nervously he flicked at a piece of invisible dust on his shoulder.

"Vampires are made . . . " he began, "by the exsanguination of a living human by another vampire, and then the addition of that vampire's blood. It's all very . . . messy. But that is how I— and every other vampire you meet—were made. More or less." He swallowed. Inhaled.

"Sunlight. That's different. It depends on the vampire; how strong the blood is and of what lineage they are."

"Does moonlight affect you adversely?" Jill asked.

"What?"

"Moonlight is just sunlight," Jill explained. "Reflecting off the moon and back to earth. Same thing. Does it bother you?"

Johnny Bathory gave her a funny look, as if he didn't know whether to be amused or annoyed. "No," he said at length. "Neither does starlight, before you ask."

"Interesting," said Jill, making a note. "And, getting back to an earlier question, can you survive on the blood of other organisms?"

"If it's red," Bathory said. "It works for us."

"What do *you* usually feed on?"

Johnny Bathory grinned. He had pulled his fangs in and snapped his canines back, but the smile was still off-putting. "Donations," he said.

"So . . . you prefer to feed on human blood?" Jill prodded.

"Most of us do."

"And these feedings . . . how often do they result in the death of the human involved?"

"Sometimes," Johnny Bathory said calmly. "Depends on the vampire."

Jill looked up at him and frowned. "That doesn't bother you?" she asked.

Johnny Bathory shrugged. "If I make an effort, it does."

"What does *that* mean?"

Bathory straightened up and looked at her with a sort of intense interest. Definitely catlike now. A cat who sees a mouse wander out of its hole, oblivious to all danger.

"Something you must understand about us," he said quietly. "As a human, you are *alive*. As such, you can *die*. You do not know what death *is*. And so you fear it, like you fear everything that is unknown and unknowable. You build imaginative castles all around it, to protect your delicate psyche. As a vampire . . . I know death. I *have* died. It holds no mystery for me or for any vampire. As a result we have, as a group, lost some respect for it. We think that because we have died once we cannot die again. We have no sympathy for things, such as you, who have yet to experience it and so hold death in a higher regard. In short, we do not feel it is such a big *deal* to die, or to cause the death of another . . . whether they are vampire or human."

Silence stretched on after this as Jill digested what had just been said. During this time Bathory seemed to consider his words, and added:

"Of course it is a false security; we *can* die . . . again and again and again. But it is still an effort for me to remember that; to remember what death looks like from your side of the wall. It is an effort that most of us do not bother to make. Does that answer your question?"

Jill nodded stiffly.

"How old are you?" she asked.

"Older than you."

Jill snorted in annoyance.

Johnny Bathory folded his arms over the back of the chair and gave her half a grin. "In all honesty, I'm not exactly sure anymore. They changed the calendars a couple times, and I lost track. I did tally it up once, but that was a while ago."

"Can you give me an estimate at least?" Jill asked. "It would be helpful."

Johnny Bathory got a distant look on his face, staring off into space over Jill's shoulder. He frowned. "I remember when there were still packs of werewolves in the forests of Deutschland," he said softly. "I remember when a Sami witch was something to be feared. I remember when the world was quiet and the skies were dark." He sounded a little wistful. Jill listened with what she felt was commendable patience, and then scribbled *pre-industrial revolution?* in the margin of her paper.

"Do you sleep?" she asked.

"Sleep?" Bathory seemed surprised by the question, or perhaps the change of subject. "No, not exactly. I can hibernate. I used to suffer from loss of consciousness during the day, but I grew out of that."

"Do most vampires . . . uh . . . lose consciousness during the day?"

"Only the young ones. It depends on how strong their blood is."

"You've mentioned this 'blood' before," Jill pointed out, flipping to a new page. "What exactly is that?"

She looked up to find Bathory examining her with marked interest. She raised her eyebrows at him.

"It's *our* blood. The essence of a vampire," he said simply. "My blood is my maker's blood, which in turn was *her* maker's blood. All the way back to the first vampire. Or one of the first vampires, depending on who you ask."

"Explain," Jill said.

Bathory inhaled. "There are some," he said, "who believe that all vampires can trace their blood back to a single, original vampire. Like the way your navel orange trees are all just shoots of that one navel orange tree some medieval monks managed to splice together. The same way all navel oranges are, in essence, the original navel orange tree, so all vampires are just branches off the original vampire."

"And what do *you* believe?" Jill prodded.

"I make a practice of not *believing* things," Johnny Bathory said. "What I *think* is that there was not one, but several proto-vampires, if you will. You will find many variations in ability and power among us, and because we cannot breed, cannot *evolve*, it means there are different *lineages* of vampire. It looks to me as though there are several strains, each with its own unique subset of strengths and weaknesses. For example, many of the vampires you will find in the Americas have the same blood as those from central and eastern Europe. However, a small number of them have blood—and therefore powers—which are completely different. *Ethiopian* vampires are so different they're hardly recognizable. There's a lineage of vampires from Russia who are almost entirely immune to the adverse effects of sunlight, though they are so mentally unstable they don't last very long."

"Fascinating," said Jill, writing industriously. "How many different strains are you aware of?"

"About seven," Bathory said. "It averages out to one per continent. Though most of the vampires you'll meet will be of the European lineage, like myself."

"And . . . what do you think these proto-vampires *were*?" she asked.

"I'm sorry?"

"Where did *they* come from?" Jill pressed on. "Were they just bigger, badder versions of vampire, or were they something else entirely?"

Johnny Bathory grinned at her. "That's where *you* come in," he said.

"What?"

"You're the one who's studying us." He raised his hands and slowly extended and contracted his index and middle fingers. "For *science*. Did it ever occur to you that the only reason you're *here*, talking to *me*, is that I'm *also* curious? That I'm tired of just accepting the world for what it is and I'd also like to understand *why* it is? And for once, I'm taking a stake in this game. Because I want to know just as much as you do."

"What do you mean by that . . . taking a stake in this game?"

Bathory cast a look of cheerful pity at her. "Come now, you don't think you're the first person to wonder: 'hey, what's up with all these hauntings and curses and angelic interference?' The reason your world doesn't know about us is not because no one's ever thought to *study* us . . . but because no one's lived long enough to tell their tale."

Jill felt a deep stillness settle in her stomach. It was not exactly like ice; more like a glacier covered in snow that spread out to the tips of her fingers. She clutched her notepad tightly.

"So why . . . " she began, but her voice caught in her throat and she had to cough a little before she could continue. "Why did you pick me? Why help *me*?"

Johnny Bathory stood up and moved out from behind the chair. He did not approach, but Jill was suddenly conscious of the fact that there was nothing between them now. He put his hands in his pockets and smiled blandly.

"Because, despite all appearance of a complete lack of self-preservation," he said, "you're not entirely stupid. Because you actually *do* have a chance. You have the tools and the talent to uncover things I couldn't, not in five hundred years. You, unlike your predecessors, have arms and armor. You have a sword and shield."

"Not right now," Jill pointed out, drawing her knees up into her chest and resting the pad on top of them.

"True," Bathory allowed. "And that's why I knew it had to be *me*. Before you tried to pull a stunt like this with someone like *Martha* again."

"Because you also want to understand the supernatural?"

"Because I want to understand why I'm here. Why do I burn in sunlight? Why don't I dream? Where do I come from? Where did *everyone else* come from?" Johnny Bathory said. "For a time there it seemed like all the old powers had gone to sleep. Every year there were fewer and fewer of us. But now things are changing. Old shadows are creeping back in around the edges of the world. Unicorns have been seen in the wild again. I know I'm part of a bigger, more mysterious world, but I really have hardly more knowledge of how it actually works than you do. And I hate that."

"So why don't you come out?" Jill asked. "Tell the truth about being a vampire—not just this mocked up version you do for show?"

Johnny Bathory folded his arms defensively. "Because I don't want things to go back to the way they were. Back to the days when people were more superstitious; when ordinary people would hunt and kill my kind if they knew what we were—would even hunt their own kind, if they thought they were vampires. Now that it's just die-hard fanatics like your sword and shield, things are much easier. A part of me doesn't want that to change. A bigger part of me wants to understand."

"Even though the prospect scares you?" Jill pointed out.

Johnny Bathory shrugged and smiled, putting his hands back in his pockets. "It's been a long time since anything scared me," he said. "Honestly, I kind of enjoy it."

He glanced sideways, at the clock in the kitchenette. It was now almost midnight. "One more question," he said, and there was a tightness in his shoulders and in his voice that put Jill on edge.

"Oh," she said, dismayed. Her mind was suddenly flooded with questions. *Why exactly is sunlight so destructive? Discuss effects of religious paraphernalia? Racial demographics among vampires? Extent and limits of various abilities? Are the other members of your band vampires as well?* With an effort she shut her eyes and closed her notebook. When she opened them again it was to the sight of Johnny Bathory gazing at her from out of his blood-red ones.

"Any advice for me?" she asked.

Bathory looked pleasantly surprised at this. "Oh yes," he said, his voice dropping to a growl. "Don't do anything this stupid ever again."

There was a flickering around his feet, and he glanced down. Jill saw his shadow, which by rights should have been pooled beneath him from the overhead light, was instead stretched out—*toward her*—and it was the silhouette of a thin, ragged man, the arms thrashing and grasping silently against the carpet.

Slowly, Johnny Bathory took his hands out of his pockets to let them hang at his sides. They were clenched in tight fists, which made the contrast with the wild, thrashing, clawing hands and arms of his shadow even more disturbing.

"It's time for you to go," he said.

"Why is that?" Jill couldn't help asking, even as she slowly unfolded her legs.

Johnny Bathory looked resigned. "It's been a long day and I'm *tired*," he said. "The longer you sit there, unthreatening and unguarded, the harder it is for me to remember that you are a *person*, and not some animal to string up and drain in the bathroom."

"Is that what you do to the others?" Jill asked in a small voice.

Bathory snorted in disdain. His shadow *writhed*. "Nothing so radical," he said. "There's a reason I pick *five*. Split between them and under the influence of my venom they don't even notice the loss. I told you, I don't need much these days."

He took a step forward. (His shadow leapt across the floor, nearly reaching Jill's feet.)

"What I *need* and what I *want*, however, are two very different things."

Jill stood up.

"Don't run," Bathory said. He words were a little slurred now, and Jill saw it was because his fangs—his real ones—were extended again. "Don't turn around. I told you, it's an effort—and I'm *tired*."

Pushing her notebook into her pocket Jill felt around for the back of the couch, stepped up onto it, and then lifted one leg over the back and gently lowered herself to the floor, pulling her other leg after her. Trying not to scramble, she walked backward in the direction of the door, all the while keeping her eyes locked on the vampire.

"Thank you," she said, proud of how she kept the wobble out of her voice. "You've been *very* helpful, and I appreciate it."

"Thank me when it's over," Bathory said, his voice a low growl.

Jill's searching fingers met the cool metal of the door handle. She glanced around the suite, and confirmed that this must be the door she came in by. A deep sense of calm settled on her, and with it a realization dawned.

"It'll never be over," she said.

Johnny Bathory nodded.

"Good-bye," said Jill, and let herself out. She held his gaze until the door shut between them.

The large black man was waiting for her out in the hall. From two doors down came the raucous sound of partying.

"Ready to leave, miss?" he asked.

"Yes, please," said Jill.

The man nodded. "Good," he said, and presented her with a tray holding her phone. "There are two women waiting for you outside the stage. They've been getting impatient."

Clara and Selene seemed both pleased and surprised to find Jill alive and in one piece. Jill didn't know whether to be amused or offended. She was beginning to shake, a deep trembling that started in her hands and knees and traveled upward and inward. Clara ended up more or less carrying her back to their room.

They wanted to know what had happened, but after everything, Jill found it difficult to speak. Thinking was becoming more difficult too, as fatigue and hunger began to catch up with her. What she did know was that she could not spend another night in the Castle. Not with Johnny Bathory and his wild shadow there. She made them pack up and check out, though Selene insisted she eat while they did so.

Then, having eaten, and safely tucked in the passenger seat of Arcana, she promptly passed out.

She was woken almost immediately when Selene pulled into the parking lot of a motel at the edge of the city and Clara carried her to bed, but her eyelids felt like they were made of lead and her body like a limp noodle, and she was barely coherent enough to hear Selene say, "I'll take the first watch . . . " and thus assured, she went straight back to sleep.

She did not sleep well. It was a restless, fitful slumber, and lurking in the back of her mind was the feeling that *something* was watching her. Waiting. And if she drifted too deep it would open wide jaws and snap her up. More than once she woke with a start to find her heart pounding, and each time it was harder and harder to go back to sleep. Then at last she opened her eyes to find it was light outside, and got up with relief to go get break-fast.

When she returned Clara was on the phone looking an-noyed.

"Officer *Dunes,*" Selene mouthed, taking a box of food.

"I can only tell you how it was when we left it," Clara said stoically.

"What's happened?" Jill asked.

Clara took the phone from her ear. "The vampires, the dead ones in the sewer: his men didn't find any bodies."

A deep confusion settled on Jill's mind, and she stared at Clara blankly until something Johnny Bathory had said the night before rose to the surface.

The reason your world doesn't know about us is not because no one's ever thought to study us . . . but because no one's lived long enough to tell their tale.

"Oh," she said heavily, and touched Clara's sleeve. "Tell him . . . tell him there was one more vampire. He was the one who killed them. He cleaned up after we'd gone. I think he doesn't want people to know; he's protecting himself. And Of-ficer Dunes."

Clara frowned, but repeated the words into the phone.

More indistinct, fuzzy voice. It sounded angry.

"You can tell him we are confident there will be no more vampire murders," Jill offered. Her voice must have come through loud enough for Dunes to hear, for the chattering stopped.

"I am sorry," said Clara into the phone. "That is all I can tell you."

She hung up.

"I think it's time we left," she said, slipping her phone into her pocket.

Jill, her mouth full of breakfast, silently agreed.

They decided to go north, on the grounds that Selene was driving, and Selene had driven through Arizona enough times already, and the only other two directions were southwest toward Los Angeles or northwest, back the way they had come. Jill didn't much care at this point. She had never been to Utah or Arizona before, so it was all new to her. It was just a relief to be *moving on.* She was so tired from the restless night before that as soon as they were clear of Las Vegas, tearing north along Interstate 15, she leaned back and let her eyes drift shut.

At last, she thought. *I can sleep.*

And then she did. Deeply and soundly.

And then . . .

Then she *dreamed.*

It was one of those horribly realistic dreams. At first she thought she was back in the hotel, that it was still night and they had yet to leave the city. She could see the silhouette of Selene in the window against the curtains, and by that filtered light she could make out the mountainous hump that was Clara slumped on the other bed. But there was a thick, white fog drifting through the room that she did not remember, and she opened her mouth to ask Selene about it; Selene would know what to do.

She couldn't speak.

And, now that she tried, she couldn't move either. She was stuck, lying on her back, as the mist swirled up and around her, engulfing her.

It was cold. *Cold like six feet underground on a snowy night* she knew, and didn't know how.

She could not shut her eyes. Then again, in the convenient way of dreams, she didn't need to blink either.

The fog was thickening before her, twining together into a shape roughly man-sized.

It was terrifying to watch, and yet Jill felt no surprise when the form of Johnny Bathory solidified out of the mist.

He looked a little different in her dream; his hair was down, hanging loosely around his shoulders, and he wore a simple black cloak which faded into the mist.

Jill tried to sit up (she couldn't); she tried to call for help (no sound came out). She wasn't sure if she was even breathing anymore, but in the dream she didn't need to.

She could hold her breath forever, lie silent in the ground, safe under the snow.

"You'll have to forgive me," the vampire said, coming forward to stand at her bedside. "It's been a while since I had such a frank conversation with anyone. It was more unsettling than I expected."

Jill didn't answer. She couldn't.

Johnny Bathory seemed to withdraw into his cape. He hovered at the edge of Jill's bed and looked down at her thoughtfully. Slowly, a smile crept up and out of his mouth, leaving his face like some distorted mask.

"You asked for the wrong thing," the vampire said. "Considering your age, it was an understandable oversight." A hand emerged from his cape, ivory white and thin. Jill felt something she thought were bones close around her wrist, and realized it was his other hand.

Gently he lifted her arm, turned her hand palm up, and pressed something hard and cold into it with his other hand, curling her fingers to close around it.

"You should not fear the dark, Jill Hamilton," he said. "But you should show it some respect."

He lowered her hand back onto the bed and took a step back.

Then he dissolved, melting back into the cold, white mist, like a tumble of water in slow motion.

At last, Jill screamed.

The world suddenly got a lot brighter. It was also a good deal warmer; sweltering, in fact, and Jill felt sticky with sweat.

There was a sickening swerve as Selene jumped in the driver's seat.

"*Jesus* woman are you okay?"

Jill's eyes came all the way open as she realized she was not in bed, but in Arcana. That it was *daytime,* and they were traveling almost seventy miles per hour.

Jill gasped, breathing in large, life-affirming gulps. "Just . . . a dream. Bad one. It's nothing."

"Didn't *sound* like nothing," Selene said, signaling to exit the highway. Clara, riding ahead on her motorcycle, noticed and began drifting to the right.

They pulled off onto a lonely desert road, raising a cloud of dust as Arcana rolled over to the shoulder and jerked to a halt. Clara kicked the stand down on her bike and walked over.

"Jill had a bad dream," Selene said, by way of explanation, as she came around the front and pulled the passenger door open.

"Can you remember it?" Clara asked practically as Jill climbed out.

Jill was feeling rather silly by this time. She'd just had a nightmare. Not surprising, all things considered. And here were Clara and Selene, acting as if she'd been assaulted or something.

She shook her head and managed a weak laugh. "Not really," she said. "It was just a stupid dream."

Selene patted her gently on the shoulder. "Sometimes stupid dreams *ain't* 'just' stupid dreams, hon."

Jill frowned at her, feeling suddenly cold in the bright desert sun.

"Jill," said Clara, looking seriously at Jill's right hand, which was curled into a tight fist, "What have you got in your *hand*?"

It took a surprising amount of effort for Jill uncurl her fingers. They felt so cold and stiff, she had to use her other hand to force them open in the end. There in her palm was a small bottle, full to the brim with a thick, dark liquid.

Jill wanted to scream and hurl it into the desert.

She didn't. Instead she handed it to Selene, who inspected it closely, then abruptly cupped her hands around it.

"This is *vampire blood,*" she practically yelped. "Jill, where did you *get* this?"

"Bathory . . . gave it to me," Jill said, pressing herself back against Arcana's side.

"Bathory?" Selene looked around sharply. "*When?*"

"Just now," Jill said quietly. "In my dream. He was here. There. He came in mist. He . . . he put that in my hand."

Selene stared at her, eyes bulging.

"He is a dream-walker," Clara said.

"Is that a bad thing?" Jill asked.

"It's a ghost skill," Clara said. "Not many vampires can do it, let alone to the extent that they can transfer physical objects from one realm to the other."

"Forget vampires," said Selene. "Not even many *ghosts* can do that." She shook herself. "Wait, you said he *gave* this to you?" She indicated the bottle still cupped in her hands.

Jill nodded, suppressing a shudder.

"He gave you his blood," Clara said, her voice a dull monotone. Then she gave a low whistle.

"I don't understand," Jill said. "What does that mean?"

Selene shook her head, carefully wrapping the bottle in her bandana and passing it back to Jill. "I've got no idea," she said. "This one's all you, girlfriend: you always did want *samples*."

Jill, still feeling cold and shaken, looked out at the bleached desert surrounding them, and found she couldn't argue.

"A lot of people say you're only in it for the money and the sex," the interviewer said. "What do you say to those who insist you're just a shallow rock 'n' roll star?"

The man in makeup and yellow contacts shrugged. "Well I think that's an over simplification," he said mildly. "I mean, I'm also in it for the *blood*."

"Is there a message you'd like to send to your fans?"

Johnny Bathory laughed, and for a moment his hoarse, weak voice dropped and filled. It was a rich, dark laugh, with an undertone like a growl.

"Well, my fans . . . you know my whole work is my message. If I could say something in particular, I suppose I'd say *thanks*. You know I get to do what I love because of you, so I love you guys, I really do. You people make me feel alive."

"Any parting words for your critics?"

"Not really," Johnny Bathory said with a wide grin. "I don't pay them much attention. It's all for my fans, you see. I'd do anything for those guys. Seriously, anytime someone mistreats a JB fan I'm like . . . I kinda want to hunt them down and eat them."

"You look after your own, eh?"

"I try, Jenny. I do try."

"Well, that's all the time we have. Once again, *thank you* Johnny Bathory for coming on the show. That's *Johnny Bathory*, ladies and gentlemen. You can buy his music from retailers worldwide and on the internet, and he's playing live at the Castle, Las Vegas, for the next week. It's a mind-blowing show, and you should *definitely* go check it out."

*

Well I'm a jack ripper
And I'm a greedy god
I'm an idol for the opiate masses
Maybe I'm not your savior
But I'll still have your
Love and lust and guts and blood.

Sex, blood
Rock and roll
Sex, blood
Rock and roll

You wanna give me life
Well I will give you death
I will give you all the things that you want to fear
In return I ask for your worshipful heart
And the hearts of the gods you created!

You say you'll give me devotion
You want a Christ for your night
But all you get is revulsion, sin
And you'll go down without a fight.

Wait 'til you see my teeth
Wait 'til you see my teeth
Wait 'til you see my TEETH
Wait 'til you see me.

You say you'll give me devotion
Let it go without a fight.
But all you get is revulsion, sin
You're gonna give me your life's light.

Sex, blood
Rock and roll
Sex, blood
Rock and roll

The more that you fear me
the stronger I grow
The more that you love me
the stronger I grow
Well I am no Christ, oh, I am no Christ
I'm no Christ but which Christ do you know?

Sex, blood
Rock and roll
Sex, blood
Rock and roll

You say you'll give me devotion
A way to get through the night.
But all you get is revulsion, sin
And you'll go down without a fight.

Sex, blood
Rock and roll

Wait 'til you see my teeth
Wait 'til you see my teeth
Wait 'til you see my TEETH
Wait 'til you see my TEETH
Wait 'til you see me.

—See My Teeth, *Johnny Bathory*

In November of 2013 I decided to undertake a modified version of the NaNoWriMo challenge, and made it my goal to write 50,000 words period. I achieved this mainly by writing many stories at once, so if one line of inspiration ran dry I could just jump to another. "How Riding Got Her Red Hood" came in the middle of all this, and served as a welcome distraction from the complicated plots I was wrestling with. Simply put, it is a retelling of "Little Red Riding Hood," though I used the general principles of that story as inspiration, rather than any particular version. It can be considered a sister tale to "Sandals and Sword," which appeared in the collection Fiddler's Dream and Other Stories *(Goldeen Ogawa, 2011).*

HOW RIDING GOT HER RED HOOD

LONG AGO at the edge of a dark, wild wood there lived a girl named Riding. You may think that is a strange name for a young girl, but you must remember that this was a very long time ago, and names were different back then. Riding lived alone, her mother and father being dead, and her only relation was her old grandmother who lived deep in the wood. Riding was a resourceful girl, however, and knew how to cook and clean and sew clothes. She had sewn herself a cape of white deerskin, with a matching white hood, of which she was very proud. Deciding it was time to pay her grandmother a visit, and wanting to show off her handiwork, she packed a basket of fresh buns and jam and set off into the forest, wearing her white cape and hood.

Now as it happened, in this forest there also lived an evil old man. He was no danger to Riding's grandmother, for she was old and wrinkled and not at all attractive to him. He liked young girls, as young as Riding or younger, whom he would trap and kill and eat, and do all sorts of other horrible things to. He was such an evil man that it was easy to see from looking at his face; his eyes would stare and his mouth would snap open and closed as he spoke, making a horrible *cloppering* sound. He was so recognizable that he fled into the forest to escape the families of his previous victims. Still fearful of being discovered, he went out and killed one of the wolves who also lived in the forest, skinned it, and ever after wore the skin as a disguise.

A fine disguise it was, too, as the man was a good hand with a knife and had done an excellent job of preserving the hide. He perfected a way of walking silently on all fours, just like a wolf, and wore specially padded shoes and gloves so he left pawprints instead of footprints.

So when he saw young Riding tripping happily through the forest in her bright white cape with the white hood up over her head he hurried home and put on his wolfsuit and then waited on the road for her.

Now when Riding saw what appeared to be a wolf standing in the road she stopped. She knew that wolves were wild and vicious creatures, but also that they were not inherently evil. If one was willing to stop and talk with her, then she thought she should treat it with respect.

"Hello," said Riding, greeting the wolf with a short bow.

"Hello little girl," said the wolf. "Where are you going?"

"I am going to visit my gran," said Riding, for if all the wolf wanted to know was where she was going she saw no harm in that.

"Where does your gran live?" asked the wolf.

"Why, she lives at the end of this road," said Riding, wondering why a wolf, who lived in the forest, had not noticed her gran's house yet.

"I see," said the wolf (who, it must be remembered, was not really a wolf but the evil man pretending to be a wolf). "I shall go ahead and tell her you are coming, shall I? Take your time. Maybe you can pick her a bouquet of flowers on the way . . . "

"Why, that is very kind of you," said Riding, who knew it was in her best interest to be polite to the wolf. "Thank you, I will."

"Good-bye," said the wolf, and sprang off down the road.

Now it must be said that the evil man was also clever, and fond of elaborate plans. So while Riding dillied and dallied, picking daisies and clover by the wayside, he ran as fast as he could to Riding's grandmother's house. He knocked on the door, and when the old woman opened it, he forced his way inside and killed her with a single blow. Then, even though she was old and stringy and didn't look very good tasting, he cut up her body and baked it into a pie, and poured her blood into a wine jar and hid her bones under the bed. He hid the wolfsuit under the bed as well and then climbed under the blankets, tied on the grandmother's bonnet, and waited.

Meanwhile, Riding, picking flowers and not suspecting a thing, heard an animal growling in the bushes.

"Who is there?" she asked.

"I am wolf," said the growls.

"The one from before?" asked Riding, hopefully.

"That was no wolf," said the growling voice, and Riding thought she saw a four-legged shadow creeping between the trees. "That was an abomination. A man who takes pleasure in torturing and killing his own pups. He slew my brother and now uses his skin as a disguise. His disguise is that of a wolf, but he is something much, much worse, and more dangerous to you."

"Oh dear," said Riding.

"I will accompany you to your grandmother's house," said the growling wolf. "If your grandmother is safe within, I will leave you there. But if things seem wrong, rap three times and I will come in."

"That is very kind of you," said Riding.

"Not at all," growled the wolf. "I long to avenge my brother."

So Riding went the rest of the way to her grandmother's house, now very nervous and not a little frightened. She was quite relieved when, in response to her knock on the door she heard her grandmother's voice call:

"Come in, my dear, come in. Don't mind me. I've a bit of a cold and I'm stuck in bed."

Poor Gran! thought Riding, letting herself in. *Good thing I have brought her buns and jam. That should make her feel better.*

She peered into the bedroom and saw what she thought was her gran lying in the bed, wearing the little bonnet Riding had made for her last winter.

"Here Gran, I've made you buns and jam," said Riding, offering her the basket.

"How very kind of you dear," said her gran (who, you must remember, was not really her gran but the evil man pretending to be her gran). "Just leave it by the foot of the bed. I've baked you a pie and there's some wine in the kitchen for you. Go eat and drink, you must be hungry and thirsty."

And Riding, seeing nothing wrong with this, went into the kitchen. But when she took the pie out she found it was a meat pie—not the fruity kind she liked—and the wine was not wine, but blood! With a horrible turning in her stomach she realized something was very wrong, and she ran and rapped, as hard and loud as she could, on the front door.

"What is wrong, my dear?" called her grandmother—but *not* her grandmother, for now Riding could tell that the difference in the voice was not from a cold.

"Nothing, dear Gran," she said, trying to keep her voice calm. If she screamed and let the evil man know she'd caught on he might run away, and then the wolf would not have his vengeance. So she went back into the bedroom and took up her basket. "Here," she said, "let me feed you some buns."

"I'm not hungry for buns," said the person in her grand-mother's bed. "I am hungry for YOU!"

And the man sprang out of the bed, wearing only her grand-mother's bonnet, and grabbed at Riding, who scrambled back-ward and tripped over the end of the bed. She fell on the floor, and the man would have had her then, except at that moment the wolf (who'd been having some trouble with the handle of the front door) leapt clean over her into the room and sank his fangs into the evil man's throat.

After the wolf had made sure the evil man was dead, Riding took off her white cape and hood and dyed them red in his blood. They burned the rest of the man in a great fire, but they buried the remains of her grandmother and the wolf's brother side by side under a great oak tree in the middle of the forest.

Riding no longer lives in the house by the wood, but in her grandmother's cottage. There she cooks and cleans and sews, and when bad men stumble into the wood seeking a place to hide, she puts on her blood-red cape and hood and goes and finds her friend the wolf, and together they go hunting.

I have chosen to close this issue of Apsis Fiction *with a story that should, I hope, echo the one which started it. "The Dragons of Geda" is the fifth story in the* Professor Odd *series, being preceded by "The Elder Machine" (Heliopause, 2014). It was begun at the tail end of 2012, and is notable for being the story I was writing when I went to Death Valley in February 2013 to research the* Driving Arcana *episode "Shadows in the Valley of Death." This has no relevance to the story itself, but it's a fun little fact you won't learn anywhere else. The cast of Professor Odd's party of multiversal travelers will return in the Season 1 two-part finale:* The Monster's Daughter, *coming in* Apsis Fiction *2.2:* Perihelion 2015.

THE DRAGONS OF GEDA

Prologue

THERE WAS A CAVE BENEATH THE CITY, and in it a thing with many teeth. Kilni knew about it because of the stories her *korkéna* had told her when she was young, before she went away. She had even pointed out the entrance to the cave, beside the drain that led from the palace to the main canal. As a child Kilni had been terrified of it: it was so big and dark, like a yawning mouth. Studs of quartz like jagged teeth framed the aperture, and by its side was a marble panel with gashes upon its surface; a tally of all those who had entered the cavern—and never returned.

Now Kilni flew through it, hurling herself into the dark and unknown with a sense of relief—for what was dark and unknown and likely fully of teeth was still preferable to what was known and immediate: that they would take her and they would kill her—cut out her heart and burn it—for what she had overheard by accident.

The Ronduath, the Cavern of Shadows, was the one place they might not follow her.

Immediately within, her foot slipped in slime and muck, and Kilni fell hard onto the stone. She slid, unable to find a handhold, until she plunged into icy, dark waters.

Elves cannot freeze, but Kilni still had to stifle a yell of surprise as the cold water closed over her chest.

She flung out her arms to swim, and her hands collided with stone walls on either side. She was not in open water then, but in a narrow canal. Kicking herself forward she moved right up next to the nearer precipice, and stretched her hand up, up, up... until the very tips of her fingers closed over the top of the ledge. Too high to pull herself out, the other wall too far away to be useful as a foothold. Kilni settled for moving along in the water, dragging a hand along each wall, hoping to feel a step or handle carved into the stone.

She heard voices behind her. She had not realized she was still so close to the entrance. She tried again to reach the top of the wall, and found it lower here. Gripping the ledge with both hands she pushed herself under the water until her arms were completely straight, and then with a furious kicking of her legs she drove herself up, pulling with her arms and jack-knifing her body until she managed to get her shoulders over the edge. Then it was only a matter of some frantic wriggling and she rolled forward, pushing herself, dripping, onto the stone.

She felt herself to be on a ledge maybe three feet wide. Now that she had been in the dark a while, the faint glow of the phosphorescent algae began to prick out in weak greens and blues against the pervading black. It outlined the way of the ledge, and at the sound of footsteps behind her she took off at a run—careful to keep one hand on the wall for balance and to make sure she did not miss any branching paths.

Light bloomed behind her, and with a shout the sound of footsteps increased. She had been spotted.

Almost at the same time the wall disappeared from under her fingertips, and she found herself able to dart sideways around a bend.

She was lost to her pursuers' sight, but they had seen her turn and would be upon her in an instant.

Then her hand brushed something that was not stone but wood. The panels of a door. Kilni felt for the latch, lifted it, and with as much quiet dexterity as she could manage, slipped around and closed it quickly behind her.

There was a moment of complete silence, of utter darkness, while Kilni waited with held breath for the sound of the pursuit to pass her by.

It never came.

Instead she became aware that the air here was warm and dry, that she stood not on stone tile but on a soft, springy carpet.

There was a bizarre humming sound, like a thousand voices moaning at once, and lights rose into being above her.

They were dim and many-colored, but after the pitch black of the cavern Kilni had to blink several times to make sense of what she saw.

She was standing in a low stairwell, and above her there ran racks of pulsing lights, like soft glowing gems. Tubes and wires ran between them in a complicated maze, and as she ascended the stairs in wonder she saw more: an oval room mostly filled by a giant wooden table, which in turn was piled with strange objects.

The lights were concentrated around two chairs, one on either side of the stairway that led back down to the door . . .

. . . only there was no door anymore. Now it was merely a blank, black rectangle, so empty and void it frightened her.

In shock, Kilni turned herself around slowly.

She appeared to be in someone's house, not unlike the sort used by the Low Elves. There were cosy little alcoves punched into the walls, one with a window seat, another with a basin and taps and a strange sort of stove. A ladder led up to a catwalk that ran the circumference of the room, beyond which Kilni could glimpse more doors. The walls were lined with windows, but they all had their blinds—lacey, pink things—drawn closed.

Strange to have windows in a room in a cave under the earth, Kilni thought, and went toward one with the intention of flicking the curtain aside.

There was another hum, like a million voices shouting *"welcome!"* and the lights flashed.

Startled, Kilni jerked back from the windows and turned toward the door, ready to take flight again, until she saw what stood at the top of the stairs.

There was only one of it, and it was certainly no elf.

It was covered in soft, short golden hair, and it had a blue scarf tied loosely around its neck. Aside from that it wore nothing else, but carried a huge sphere of striped red and white, which must have been quite light judging by the way the creature held it loosely under one arm.

It had a long, pointed snout with a soft, wet, dark nose, two triangular ears that stuck up on either side of its head, and soft brown eyes.

It was maybe five feet tall, and Kilni glimpsed a fluffy cream and gold tail held stiffly behind it.

"Oh *bother,*" said the creature in heavily accented, but recognizable Common Tongue. Then it turned and called back over its shoulder: "*Pro-FES-sor!* The Oddity's picked up a stray *again!*"

Part One

I T HAD BEEN a wonderful day.

"Let's go somewhere *nice,*" Professor Odd had said, flipping switches and sending cascades of blinking lights across the cockpit of the Oddity.

"Define 'nice,'" Alister said warily.

"Warm," said the Professor, winding a hand crank. There was a sound like *bonnnng* from deep within the Oddity. "Sunny, breezy, white sand, blue water—the beach, Mister Alister, we're going to the *beach!* Go look in the laundry room, would you? The Oddity's probably given us some towels."

Alister didn't budge.

"Which beach?" he insisted. It sounded innocent enough, but ever since their trip for pizza had turned into a desperate battle to save a planet from hordes of destructive robots, he would never underestimate how wildly events could escalate once Professor Odd got involved.

Professor Odd pressed a finger against her thin, pale lips, considering.

"I was thinking somewhere on Geda," she said. "A tropical island, away from the big cities. No one will bother us. You'll like it; the atmosphere is compatible, and they have dinosaurs."

Alister blinked. He knew that different universes ran at different times relative to each other, but he hadn't expected to visit one in the middle of the Jurassic period.

"It's a . . . what, then?" he asked, intrigued in spite of himself. "One of those temporally retarded universes?"

"Not at all," Professor Odd said, flipping a line of switches. "Geda is a planet in a temporally average universe. And they're not technically dinosaurs; not as you would think of them. Put simply, Alister, Geda is a planet where the vast array of species you humans have grouped under the term 'dinosaur' *never went extinct.* They continued to evolve, of course, so some of them no longer look much like they did back when their ancestors were making fossils. Some of them do, though."

"Don't worry, Alister, Geda is a *fun* world." Elo said, appearing at his elbow. She was even more golden and furry than usual, as she had taken off her jumpsuit and was wearing nothing but a utility belt and a blue scarf tied around her neck. She carried a pile of towels in her arms, and Alister noted with resignation that they were all combinations of the most glaring colors. One of them was even pink with purple polka-dots.

"GEDA'S ATMOSPHERE HAS A HIGHER PERCENTAGE OF OXYGEN RELATIVE TO YOUR NATIVE VERSION OF EARTH," Dave added, rolling around the cluttered table. His panvironment suit had a ridiculous sun hat tied to the blue glass dome, and three of his tentacle arms, encased in jointed exoskeletal sleeves, were wrapped around a wicker picnic basket. "HOWEVER, IT ALSO RECEIVES MORE SOLAR RADIATION."

"What does that mean?" Alister asked.

"It means," said Professor Odd, pushing herself away from the console. "That you'll have more energy, but you'll get heatstroke and sunburn easier. So drink lots of water and wear sunscreen."

There was a humming sound, and brilliant sunlight flooded the stairwell. Alister had to squint, shading his face with one hand, until his eyes adjusted.

The Oddity's portal had opened onto a bright, pristine white beach, curving in a graceful arc to a distant headland, green with forest and jutting with sharp, spire-like stones. Out across an impossibly blue ocean he could make out an arm of rock, which shielded much of the beach from the pounding white breakers.

A warm breeze blew into the Oddity, filling it with the smell of sun-warmed rocks, salt, and a distant pungent odor of blossoming trees.

Alister felt a cool tube pressed into his hand, and he looked down to find Elo handing him a bottle of cream.

"Dave's right about the radiation," she said, rubbing some of the white cream over her nose. "You and the Professor especially, you're both so pale."

Wordlessly, Alister took the bottle. Back home, he had only ever been to the beach a handful of times, and had found it to be a disappointment: overcast, cold, and too windy, sand got everywhere, and the ocean too big and fierce to swim in. But this looked nothing like the beaches of the Old Country; it looked like something off a postcard.

It was *wonderful*. Even though all he had for swimwear was a pair of lemon yellow and pink zebra-striped shorts thanks to the Oddity, Alister soon forgot any misgivings he had about his attire.

The air on Geda was astonishing. Alister had read about athletes who trained at altitude, so their bodies produced more red blood cells and made their circulation more efficient. Alister's body, which was adjusted to the relatively oxygen-weak atmosphere of his earth, felt like someone had replaced his blood with happy juice. He also wondered if Geda's gravity was weaker; he felt like he could run and jump faster, farther, in addition to not having to breathe as hard.

He and Elo chased each other up and down the beach, occasionally diving into the surf when they got too hot. Professor Odd, wearing a sun hat almost as ridiculous as Dave's (it was a pinwheel of purple and orange, with a matching purple fringe), inflated a red-and-white beach ball and lobbed it at them the next time they raced past.

For his part, Dave drove his suit over to the rocky lagoon nearby and slithered out, splashing around in the shallow pools. Professor Odd rolled up the legs of her trousers to her knees and waded around, taking notes on the flora and fauna she found— sometimes extricating the latter from Dave's arms.

"Stop scaring the octopi," she chided.

When Alister and Elo had exhausted themselves on the beach they staggered up onto the soft dry sand and Alister laid out the towels while Elo unpacked the picnic basket. Whatever he felt about the Oddity's taste in clothes, Alister had to admit it more than made up for that with its food: there were cucumber and cream cheese sandwiches on soft white bread for him, along with crispy chips and three different kinds of sauces. For Elo there was a whole chicken, and lots and lots of water.

Pleasantly warm, tired, and full of sandwich, Alister stretched out on the polka-dot towel, Dave's hat over his head, and went to sleep.

The last thing he heard was Elo muttering something about going back to the Oddity to see if she could find an umbrella, and then he was sinking fast into a pleasant golden slumber.

It lasted for what felt like only ten seconds, though in reality it had probably been a few minutes. He heard Elo shouting something about the Oddity having picked up a "stray," and a distant splashing following by the soft pounding of bare feet on sand coming closer as the Professor ran over.

Reluctantly Alister sat up, removing Dave's sun hat and blinking at the bright, washed-out blue world that confronted him. It took a few moments for his pupils to constrict, and then he saw Elo, still with the beach ball under one arm, leading someone down the bank from the tangle of driftwood that hid the Oddity's portal.

Alister then had to blink fiercely to make sure he saw the figure right, for she looked exactly like an alien he had seen on television once. Very tall and slender with coppery skin, she had a long, straight nose and dark, strong eyebrows that instead of curving down to frame her eye sockets, flew up and away on either side of her face, like the wings of a falcon. Like the alien from the telly she also had long, delicate pointed ears—though Alister could see hers were not made of plaster and tape from the way they caught the light and went slightly transparent.

She had a bemused look on her face; her black hair was a mess, pulling free from the braids running down from either temple; there was a smudge of something dark and greenish on one cheek, and she was sopping wet. She stared out at the beach

with wide eyes so dark Alister had to look twice before he realized they were blue.

Professor Odd arrived in a scatter of sand, digging deep
trenches in the white beach. She was in her shirtsleeves and
trousers, which were rolled up to her knees, dark glasses and her
ridiculous sun hat—she hadn't bothered with a wig. Her flesh-
colored tentacle with green leopard spots came to rest curled
on one shoulder like a curious parrot, its pink tip flicking with
interest.

The alien really stared then, and made an involuntary jerk
as if she were thinking about running away, but Elo's paw on
her arm stilled her. Instead she looked around, her apparent
bewilderment increasing until Alister felt quite sorry for her.

Professor Odd was equally surprised.

"But you're a *native!*" she exclaimed, peering at the alien. Her
tentacle rose beside her head, its end wriggling back and forth,
as if it wanted to dart out and explore the newcomer. "But you're
not from the middle-lands, how did the Oddity find you?"

To Alister's surprise and relief, the alien actually understood
this, and replied in recognizable, if somewhat lisping English: "I
am Timantiel Tuvielstytar ya Suku Lohihuya, I come from Gilsufar," as if this explained everything. When they made it clear
by their expressions that it did not, she went on. "I ran into
the Ronduath, finding means to hide from mine enemy. I went
through a door and found myself . . . " she trailed off, spreading
her hands wide.

"She was in the Oddity when I went to get an umbrella," Elo
offered helpfully.

"Yes . . . " said Professor Odd, rubbing her chin and walking
in a slow circle around the alien—native—whatever. "Yes, of
course you were. *Well,* better come sit down and tell us all about
it. Timantiel Tuvielstytar *ya* . . . " she trailed off, frowning.

"Suku Lohihuya," finished the native. She gave a little shrug
and added, "You may call me Kilni." She kept looking around her,
as if worried she would be followed. Alister noticed she had a
strand of limp algae caught in her hair.

"Kilni," said Professor Odd, like she was getting the shape of
the word comfortable in her mouth. "Kilni, Kilni, Kilni-Kilni.
Well then, *Kilni,* that is Elo, *he* is Alister, and *I* am Professor

Odd—and you needn't worry about being followed, the Oddity won't have let anyone in after you, and if my memory serves we are almost exactly on the far side of the world from Gilsufar—as far as you *can get* on a globular world."

She might have gone on, but Alister had come to tug insistently at her sleeve—as he had seen Elo do many times before. Not wanting to be too offensive he spoke in a whisper:

"Professor, who is she? And by that I mean, *what* is she? And why does she look like a Vulcan?"

Professor Odd turned to him in surprise. "Why, she's not a Vulcan at all, Mr. Alister," she exclaimed, making him wince in embarrassment. "Vulcans are a fictional race. *She* is one of the *Luiniset,* an elf of Geda."

Alister sat cross-legged on the sand opposite from Kilni, who was wringing out her hair with the cleanest of the towels. From under the folds of cloth her dark blue eyes regarded him steadily, calculating. Alister returned the gaze with matched gravity.

"So . . . you are a *Man,"* she said at length, shaking her long hair out. She somehow managed to make the word sound like an insult, and for that reason alone Alister found himself retorting, "I am *human,"* with a steely tone.

Elo elbowed him in the ribs. "But you're a *male* human," she reminded him.

"He is a *vérman,* I can see that," Kilni said, as though the fact was so obvious she found it painful.

Professor Odd groaned and massaged the base of her tentacle. "To the Luiniset, Alister, humans are mythological creatures, rather like elves are to you," she said. "They use the Old English words: *Man* is human, regardless of sex. *Vérman* is a male Man, *vifman* is a female." She pushed herself around so she was facing Kilni. "Humanity has continued to evolve since the last time your people had contact with them," she said. "Alister is no warrior; he is a scholar. He will not try to seduce you."

"I—*what?"* Alister said, choking on his own spit in surprise.

"The legends tell of *vérman* who steal away Luinisetia and tempt them into mortality," Kilni said accusingly. "But I shall believe the Professor when she tells me you are not like them. I certainly do not find you at all attractive."

Alister was so taken aback he could only stare in consternation. He could see, despite her bedraggled state, that Kilni was extremely beautiful; but it was that unreal kind of beauty that made him feel stupid and ugly by comparison, and so any attraction he might have felt was terminally deflated. Now that he was getting a better grasp of her personality, he decided he would rather attempt to seduce *Dave*, who at the very least would not sneer at him like he was some sort of pond weed.

"*Well,* now that we have that sorted out," said Professor Odd with a bright grin, "perhaps you could tell us your story, Kilni, and how you came to have *permocalculus* stuck in your hair?"

As it eventually came out, Kilni's story was this:

Some years ago she had been taken as a novice in the order of the Vesil Tarkaliya, the Watchers of the Water, whose duty it was to guard elven towns and cities against the terrible *orka* that lived at the bottom of pools and in the sea. There had been reports of some dragons (descendants of dinosaurs, Professor Odd hastily explained) joining with the *orka*. Since dragons had long been the elves' allies, the High Council (which Alister assumed was something like a parliament) decided that the Vesil Tarkaliya needed someone who could talk some sense into the dragons. The House of Lohihuya was the oldest clan of Dragonspeakers in the world. As the youngest member of the house, Kilni had been sent to the Vesil Tarkaliya to train as a novice.

"The Vesil Tarkaliya are the most honored of warriors," she said in disgust. Clearly she no longer thought so. "I thought it a great honor. It *was* a great honor. But they are weak, doublefaced. Traitors and cowards." She stared at them with wide, beseeching eyes. "By accident I came upon my elders in the water sanctuary, and I found them there in conference with an *orka*!" She spat the word as if it tasted terrible. "They were not interrogating him—they did not even have him chained! They called him *henkaveli*—that is, spirit-brother—and talked of *alliances* and *honors*." She hung her head, shuddering even in the warm sun.

"I ran," she continued at length. "But they heard me. They chased me. I knew they would kill me for having uncovered their plot. So I ran into the Ronduath—that is the Dome of Shadows, the oldest part of Gilsufar. It is a sacred place, but no one dares tread there because of the Creature of a Thousand Teeth. But I dared. I was followed. I slipped into a channel— that is how I became so filthy—and when I found a wooden door under my hands I went inside, thinking to hide. And instead I find myself . . . " she gestured toward the portal to the Oddity.

She took a deep breath, as if the telling of her story had lifted a great weight from her shoulders. Then her blue eyes narrowed sharply at her assembled audience.

"That is the story of Timantiel Tuvielstytar ya Suku Lohi-huya," she said with formal regality. "Now I wonder what is yours? I have not seen creatures such as you in all the Seven Lands."

Alister looked questioningly at Professor Odd, who never seemed willing to discuss precisely who she was or what she did—even with the crew of the Oddity. But now she was smiling sunnily, and she said with no reservation whatsoever:

"Oh, us? We're simple trans-universal travelers. As I said: I am Professor Odd, and these are my . . . er . . . *students*, Alister Bane and Marhütz Elo."

"We're on vacation," Elo explained.

Alister had to choke back a grin at the expression of complete astonishment on Kilni's aristocratic face. He wondered, with a little glee, what her reaction to Dave would be.

"It seems to me," said Professor Odd, rubbing at her chin with the end of her tentacle, "that we have stumbled into some-thing of a political mess. Would you like to come back inside, Miss Kilni? And we'll see if we can't get it sorted out."

"Sort it . . . out?" Kilni said, slowly, as if the words were foreign to her. But Professor Odd, who was already on her way back to the Oddity, didn't answer.

"I expect she'll do something daft," Elo said pleasantly, rolling up towels and packing up the picnic basket. "Like, go *talk* to them, or something."

"Go talk . . . " Kilni's blue eyes opened wide in alarm. "But that is calamity! They will *kill* her!"

"Not if she gets the first word in," Elo said, with a wink at Alister. "You haven't seen our Professor at work. Have you got the towels then, Alister? Alister?"

Alister was looking around, first in casual curiosity, and then in increasing concern, for the beach and the sea were deserted. Dave's panvironment suit still sat by the edge of the rocky lagoon, its dome top cracked open; empty.

"Where's Dave?" he asked sharply.

"Dave?" Kilni repeated.

"Dave!" Elo called over her shoulder.

Nothing.

"We have a problem," Alister announced, hanging the towels over the butt of the time gun, which rested on the table. "Dave's missing."

Professor Odd turned slowly in her seat, a small frown crinkled between her smooth brows. "That's . . . inconvenient."

"Who is *Dave?*" Kilni wailed.

"He's this . . . brilliant creature," Alister said, distracted. "Bright green, one orange eye, ten arms . . . not much else. His suit's still there, Professor, but no sign of him."

"He went into the lagoon," Elo offered, bounding up the steps. "Can't find any trace of him coming out again."

Professor Odd cocked her head to one side, as if she had just been presented with a particularly difficult word puzzle. Rising from her seat she went to the door to go look for herself.

Yet on the threshold she stopped, her tentacle curled into a tight knot at the base of her neck.

"Miss Kilni," she said, her voice harsh and alert.

"Yes, Professor?" Kilni said, unbalanced but still with her pride intact.

"You said you could speak to dragons, Miss Kilni?"

"That is correct."

"Then would you kindly come here and ask the ones hiding in the forest around us what they want?"

Hesitantly, Kilni crept to the door and stood behind Professor Odd's arm. Behind her, Alister and Elo crowded over, their concern for Dave forgotten in their excitement at seeing real dragons.

Kilni leaned forward and let out a long, low call—something that was not quite a wolf's howl, not quite a bird's cry, and not quite a long singing note. It appeared to have the effect of making the ground shake, and to cause a shower of sand to fall from the pile of driftwood currently serving as the Oddity's portal gate. But this was actually due to the pounding of many feet running down to the beach, and a moment later there appeared through the door such a sight as Alister never thought he'd see with his living eyes.

Creatures the size of horses, but on two legs, like those of an ostrich, with long necks and high, noble faces, crowded together on the beach. Like ostriches they were feathered, but in iridescent tones of blue and green, and their arms were not winglike at all: they emerged from their feathery bodies like naked, scaly talons. Instead of beaks they had long snouts, and mouths lined with small, sharp-looking teeth. They had long, whiplike tails that ended in tufts of feathers, and each toe on the giant feet sinking into the sand was tipped with a vicious-looking claw.

They peered in at the crew of the Oddity with hard, black little eyes. They seemed curious, but it was a curiosity, Alister thought, that could easily turn hostile. Behind him he felt Elo retreat back up the steps and knew she was going to the console in case they needed to make a quick getaway.

But the feathery dragons—evolved dinosaurs, Alister reminded himself—did not come within five feet of the Oddity's door. Rather they stood, peering, pushing at each other for better spots, bobbing their heads up and down and making soft clicking noises.

"They are . . . curious," Kilni said, uncertain. "They are talking amongst themselves. They are not sure what to do. They say they have been watching you . . . "

She trailed off, for there had been a disturbance in the back of the crowd, and now the tall, two-legged dragons were being pushed aside. By his view through the gap between Professor Odd and the elf, Alister was not able to see the new arrival until it stood squarely in front of them. Then his jaw dropped.

It was huge, easily the size of an elephant—if the size of its head, which was all Alister could see, was any indication— and this head was wide and triangular like a rhinoceros's, dry and scaly like a crocodile's. But the scales only extended over its snout, where a single, curving horn protruded, and around its little dark eyes, above which stretched two more horns, each easily a yard long. Beyond them grew a thick coat of feathers, mottled brown and blue, which faded to a cream color on the giant frill that rose behind its head, finally ending in tufts of drooping feathers, not unlike a rooster's tail, punctuated at intervals by short, curving horns that flared out on either side.

This huge, horned face pushed itself unceremoniously between the smaller dragons, who fell back respectfully, until it was inches from the door. It blew heavy, plant-scented breath on them.

"That's a *triceratops,*" Alister whispered, his voice catching in his throat.

Professor Odd heard. Tilting her head back she spoke, low and swift: "Technically, it's a descendant of the dinosaur humans called *chasmosaurus,* one of the few remaining of the *ceratopsids.* The Luiniset call them *kosarvi*—which means pretty much the same thing."

"And that is?"

"Horn-face," Professor Odd said, turning back to the dinosaur in the doorway.

The dinosaur—Alister couldn't stop thinking of it as a *triceratops*—made a low grumbling noise, too friendly to be a growl, too rocky to be a purr. Then it let out a string of low hoots and whistles; it sounded like a parrot would, if a parrot were the size of an elephant.

"He says," Kilni translated, haltingly, "he says he is Hard Edge, the elder of these dragons. He says . . . he says they *remember* you," she said, turning to Professor Odd with wide eyes. "He calls you *Friend Kumallinién,* he says that his Grand Father remembers and still tells of your deeds."

Professor Odd looked politely blank for a few moments, and then her face broke into a wide grin. "Oh, *that* time. Yes, I landed in the middle of an inheritance dispute. Quite a job talking sense into a couple of eight-ton animals when I had to communicate by throwing rocks at them. Wasn't sure I didn't do more harm than good, in the end. How is that old rock-head?"

But Kilni was still staring at her, the dragon in the doorway temporarily forgotten. "You! *You're* the *Kumallinién?*"

"Yes, that was what the elves called me," Professor Odd said, as if just remembering. "It's only their word for 'odd person,'" she added under her breath, for Alister's benefit. "What?" she asked, turning back to Kilni. "They've heard of me in Gilsufar?"

"*Heard* of you?" Kilni exclaimed. "You are named in the Scroll of the Departed Elders! 'Let no one take a stone that is not their own, for the earth cannot be owned.' The *Kumallinién!* But I always thought you were an *elf.*"

They might have gone on, but the dinosaur—Hard Edge—interrupted with a long, mellow hoot. Kilni jumped back to attention, and he rumbled on a bit more.

"Now he is saying, they have heard of the conspiracy in Gilsufar even here. He says the answer lies—no, no that's *impossible*—sorry, he says the answer lies in the Library of Amnós. But that was lost at the end of the Second Age. Do you tell us to seek answers in the House of Death, Lord Dragon? For that would be an easier task!"

Hard Edge growled and shook his head. He looked past Kilni, straight at Professor Odd, and spoke in a low, sweet whistle.

"He says," Kilni began, but the Professor cut her off.

"I got that last bit," she said, putting up a hand. "Of all people, I am the one who can find it. Thank you . . . er . . . is that all?"

The giant face looked down, then to either side, then finally pulled back to allow one of the smaller dragons—one that reminded Alister of an ostrich—to come forward. This one was unusual in that it had a strange contraption strapped to its face: a metal frame with plates of glass over its eyes—*glasses!* Alister realized with a start—and it carried in its hands a battered stone tablet with runes etched on the surface.

It leaned forward and spoke to Kilni in an earnest, hissing voice, then with an unmistakable bow it presented the tablet to Professor Odd.

The Professor took it with a matching bow, and turned to Kilni, puzzled.

"That," said the elf in a strangled voice, "is the Amnós Codex, or a very good copy of it." Then to the dinosaur she added: *"Keetos melon-minun, namarvasti."*

Having discharged its duty, the little speckled dinosaur retreated behind Hard Edge's frill, and the whole crowd slowly backed away, as if they thought the Oddity's portal might take them with it if they remained too close. When they were but a curious herd down on the beach, Professor Odd leaned up into the cockpit:

"Cast us off, Elo. It'll take some navigation to find our way to Amnós."

Without a sound, the sunny beach and the colorful feathered dragons clustered on its sand flicked out of sight, replaced by the matte black of the Oddity's closed door. Kilni started backward so suddenly she fell up the stairs.

Stepping neatly over the stricken elf, Professor Odd carried the tablet up into the ship like it was made of thin ice. With one elbow she roughly pushed aside a gutted computer monitor, which in turn knocked a few loose gears onto the floor, to make room for the tablet.

"What about Dave?" Alister exclaimed, almost in the woman's ear.

"He'll catch up to us later," the Professor said absently, but Elo took pity.

"I'm leaving a guideline on the old portal," she said. "It'll sense when Dave is near and we can go pick him up. I wouldn't worry too much about him," she added, giving Alister a knowing look. "This is *Dave* we're talking about."

Alister knew. He knew that, of all of them, Dave was probably the best able to take care of himself. It still didn't feel right, though, to leave him behind like that.

But here was Professor Odd, pouring over the tablet, running her fingers over the carved runes, even going so far as to lean in and smell it.

"A copy," she declared after a minute's examination. "An old one, but still a copy. We'll have to hope it's accurate."

Kilni was hovering, alternately peering over the Professor's shoulder, peering fearfully out the windows, and shooting furtive glances at Elo, who was making bonging noises over in the console.

"What am I looking for?" she asked, pounding buttons. The Oddity did not have a normal keyboard. Instead it had racks and racks of multi-colored circular buttons, each one making a different sound when pressed. As a result, piloting the Oddity sounded like very strange, off-kilter music. Alister wondered how it sounded to someone as aesthetically sensitive as Kilni plainly was.

"I've come up with several libraries," Elo continued, looking carefully at one of the wide, rectangular screens. Alister still found these gave him headaches, so he left the reading of their location to the others: to him it only looked like an amorphous swirl of colors and lights, constantly shifting, with little pinpricks of clarity showing through. Every time he managed to focus on one, it would disappear before he could figure out what it was.

("You have to sort of unhook your left hemisphere," Professor Odd had told him, the one time he'd agreed to being given a lesson. "Let your intuitive thinking interpret it." This had given Alister a splitting headache, and he had refused any further lessons in driving the Oddity.)

Kilni, however, seemed fascinated by the images on the screen. She came to stand behind Elo, and soon was pointing at vague shapes and points of light.

"There!" she cried. "There is Gilsufar! And there! My mother's haven! Can you really go to all these places?"

"More accurately, we bring *them* to *us*," Elo admitted. "But yeah, you could say that. We can go to a lot of other places, too. Though right now I'm looking for this Amnós library. Think you could recognize that?"

Kilni shook her head, awed. "The Library of Amnós was taken by the *orka* in the Second Age. I hear it was buried under a mountain and an ocean. No one has been there since."

"But it was the greatest archive of Luinisetian history on all of Geda," Professor Odd announced, taking up her position in the pilot's seat opposite Elo. "In fact, all sorts of history. It was the home of the Index, back in the day. Anything you wanted to know you could find in the Library of Amnós."

"It was the greatest loss of the Black Wars," Kilni said regretfully. "The *orka* overran Amnós and buried its library. They wanted us to forget our history, our Lineage."

Professor Odd swung around in her chair, fixing Kilni with a stare like a rivet. "And what is your *Lineage*?" she asked, placing careful emphasis on the word.

Kilni drew herself up, rather in the same way she had when she'd told them her name. Angling a stare of equal wattage down her perfect nose she said, proudly: "That elves are the First Peoples, that we taught the powers of speech and reason to the dragons. That we alone lived in the light of Erú, before Basamoranth rose from the deep and devoured the shining city. The *orka*, who were birthed from Basamoranth, wish us to forget. But it is our birthright, the light is in our blood, and we cannot forget."

Such a speech, so filled with strange names and allusions to events Alister did not know, might have left him floundering— had he not found the sentiment vaguely familiar.

For her part, Professor Odd returned the elf's gaze unflinchingly. She said, "Hmm . . . " and then turned back to her own console.

"I thought that knowledge would be known to you, Kumallinién," Kilni said, deflating a little at the Professor's disinterest.

"It is different from the story I was told the last time I was here," Professor Odd said without turning around. "I have no way of ascertaining which, if either, is the correct one, with the information currently available. Also, your story troubles me; I have met several of your *orka,* and they have shown me nothing but kindness—no, do not protest," she said, glancing over her shoulder. "You are clearly a product of your culture, and I don't expect you to understand my point of view right away. The only thing I need from you now . . . " and she turned around again so she could look at Kilni directly.

"I need to know: do you want the truth? Or another story? Stories are nice," she added, spreading her hands. "But they are not always the *truth*. The *truth* is messy and complicated and uncomfortable—but it has this: knowing the truth you can have a better understanding of how your world works, and therefore a better idea of how to handle it. But it's not always what you want it to be. Have I made myself clear?"

Kilni regarded her gravely. Elo even stopped banging away on the keys, and a sort of silence descended in the Oddity. Only it was never really silent there; always, behind everything, was the quiet hum from what Alister imagined was the Oddity's engine. Or heart. Or whatever it had.

"I understand the difference," Kilni said carefully, after a long pause. "And if it is knowable, I would know the truth. I would know why my elders conspired with the *orka,* and why the dragons wish us to find Amnós."

Professor Odd's face broke into a huge grin.

"Excellent, then we can work together! Fetch me that tablet, Alister, I'll need to cross-reference some of the symbols . . . "

The city was half flooded, all but the stone shells of buildings having long since washed away. Standing on a parapet of what had once been a mighty castle one could look down into clear, dark waters and see the streets and avenues laid out below the shimmering surface. Looking up, it appeared a forest of stone columns rose from the placid sea, with only the great dome of the library rising like the swell of a mountain to break the flat horizon. A single light glimmered at its peak, growing softly into a pale orange glow against the darkening sky.

Turning stiffly because of the heavy plates of its suit, the watcher on the parapet raised an arm and made a light, igniting the small pool of oil that lay in a bowl beside him. The flame raced up, a streak of red in the dark, and soon the answering light atop the tower of the castle ruins blazed into life.

The invaders who built the city had lit these lights, night after night, to honor the twin moons, which they called Elysar and Eloreth. Though the invaders were long gone from their sunken city of Amnós, the watcher's people still kept the lights, in part to honor the moons which ruled the upper levels of the sea, and in part to honor the invaders who had built the city, and then left it to them.

The watcher dismounted from the parapet, casually casting himself off the ledge, falling ten feet before plunging into the water with a great splash. Then he was moving swiftly, disen-tangling himself from his ungainly suit, and slipping gracefully away down the submerged street.

Behind him, above the spires of the ruined palace of the Lords of Amnós, Elysar hung in the full, casting the lost city in a pale, cream light. On the dark horizon, smaller Eloreth was a white disc, chasing her elder sister up the dome of the sky.

Alister stood and stared at the double moons, enchanted.

They had come through into a cool, humid, and impossibly bright night. Alister had seen full-moon nights on earth that rivaled daytime, but then the shadows had been so deep, so black, that half the world was invisible. Now with these double moons some of those shadows were filled, and the entire place had the eerie quality of being double-lit.

This allowed Alister to get a good look at Amnós—or what remained of it. Freestanding walls of stone, pillars, and broken off pieces of roof pierced a dark sea. Some ways off, a magnificent construction of piled domes, turrets and spires stood outlined in the larger moon's light. It looked like a fairy-tale palace, except it was clearly ruinous: patches of night sky could be glimpsed through the many gaping holes, and some of the towers looked lopsided from all the missing stones. Yet nothing seemed in immediate danger of slipping into the sea, and the parapet he stood on now—attached to a huge, swelling dome—appeared well maintained and solid.

Someone whispered at his side, and he saw it was Kilni, who had come to stand beside him.

"*Amnós was a blazing city,*" she said, in a tone of one reciting poetry. "*Its towers strong and fair; its might was of the might of the just, its wisdom beyond compare. How then did we lose our blazing city? Our bright and shining spire? It has fallen into darkness, child, and we have lost our fire.* We must go carefully here," she added, speaking more normally. "The *orka* have infested this place like a plague. But oh, to see it now, even as a blackened shell—this is a wonder I never thought to witness. No elf has set foot here since the Fall."

"You're wrong, you know," Elo said. "About the fire, I mean. Look, someone's made a light," and she pointed.

There, sure enough, atop the highest tower of the castle, a small light had blossomed.

Kilni jerked, her long back straightening like a rod, her eyes gone wide in shock—then narrow in suspicion.

"That is Isilbérath," Professor Odd said, sounding pleased. She had put on a wig, bright scarlet and orange, and had extracted a glass tablet with rubber-covered edges from the breast of her coat. A mapper, she had called it. Now she held it up so that she could look at the ruinous skyline through it. Alister saw it come alive with fine lines of light and little squiggles of writing, which moved and changed as the Professor panned it across the vista. "The royal palace of Amnós," she murmured. "Which means *this* should be . . . " she swung around, directing the mapper at the dome that rose behind them, and let out a little cry of satisfaction. "*Yes*, the library! Or . . . whatever's left of it."

"*Kiryasto Amnósin*," Kilni murmured.

"Lead the way, if you would, Elo," Professor Odd said, gesturing.

Nodding, Elo dropped to all fours and began trotting down the parapet, pausing now and then to scent the air.

"Beware of *orka*," Kilni whispered. "They will not let us explore unhindered."

"I don't know what they smell like," Elo pointed out.

Kilni wrinkled her nose in distaste. "Like filth and foul water. Like corruption."

Elo stopped to sniff intensely at the underside of the parapet's bannister. "Someone *has* been here," she admitted. "But not an *orka*, I think."

"Friend or foe?" Alister asked.

"Couldn't tell you that," Elo said, and went on.

They had just passed into the shadowed half of the dome, the only light coming from the readouts on the mapper, when Elo abruptly vanished.

Alister froze, afraid she had tumbled off the parapet, but a moment later her head reappeared, poking out of a hidden doorway.

"It's this way," she said in a husky whisper. "Go carefully, whatever's here uses this path regularly."

Behind him, Alister felt Kilni tense up and reach for the knife at her waist, but suddenly Professor Odd was there, sparing a hand from the mapper to gently push Kilni's away.

"That would be unwise," she said. "We do not know what's in there, and I don't want to antagonize them accidentally."

"You don't know they'll be friendly," Kilni hissed in reply. "If they are *orka* they won't give you a chance to talk." But she took her hand away.

Elo had taken a small headlight and strapped it to her head, between her ears, and now its beam was traveling across the interior, illuminating it in sharp bands.

Stepping into the drier, cooler air, Alister felt his way down a couple of steps, and saw a curving, tiled ceiling, streaked with water stains and algae. There appeared to be images picked out, mosaic-like, in the tiles, but Elo moved her beam on before he could make out what they were.

The steps continued down, turning sharply back and forth, and when Elo looked away from the wall, her beam only lit a dusty blackness; the far side of the dome was lost in shadows.

Abruptly the beam, and the feeling of a vast open space, were cut off by the rise of a stone wall. This was honeycombed with holes, some of which were stopped up with plaster, others black and empty. But as they continued down, Alister saw that some of them contained scrolls. Others held stacks of thick glass, not unlike the Professor's mapper. Glancing behind him he saw Kilni's face, illuminated briefly by a flash from Elo's headlamp, gazing with such humble amazement, her eyes wide and unguarded, that she almost looked human.

They reached a bottom, of sorts, and here it looked like the path dead ended in a flat block of stone. But the Professor came through, and producing a flashlight of her own she handed the mapper to Alister, before pulling out the Codex and running her finger down the line of sigils.

"It's a code book," Alister whispered, amazed.

"More like a password keychain," Professor Odd muttered. "Still hard to decipher. Here, Kilni, what's this one mean?"

Kilni pushed her way forward, bent over the Codex, and felt the carving with one graceful finger.

"Here," she said. "Here is the sequence for Doors and Apertures. We just need to know which door *this* is."

"Easy enough," said Elo, directing her beam upward, to the lintel. There, sure enough, was a single rune: a sideways crescent over a six-pointed star. Professor Odd quickly found the corresponding character on the Codex, and reached forward to touch the door.

There was, Alister saw, a grid carved on its face, and within each square was a sigil, like the ones on the Codex. A sort of strange keypad, he thought.

Quickly, Professor Odd pressed her hand against a series of the sigils on the door, checking the Codex between each press. Each sigil she touched glowed a faint red in the dark, but once the sequence was complete nothing happened.

"It needs an elf's touch," Kilni said, a little of her natural pride returning. She stepped forward, and after glancing once at the tablet, quickly entered the same sequence.

Under Kilni's touch, the sigils glowed bright blue, and the rock emitted a faint hum, not unlike the voice of the Oddity. Then, with a groan and a grind, the stone slab slid aside, and a pale cream light flooded out from beyond.

The flashlights were switched off, and as Alister passed under the lintel behind the others, he saw the reason for the light: they were in a dome within the great dome, and at its top a huge prism rested, angling a strong beam of moonlight into the room below.

And what a room! Towers of honeycombed rock ranged all around them, and rising in the center in a series of concentric steps was a dais of stone and glass topped with a small mirrored sphere, which scattered the moonbeam in all directions.

Professor Odd held up the mapper, but she needn't have bothered. Kilni whispered, but loud enough for all to hear:

"*Gil-hampat,* that is the *Index!*"

"The best invention of the old Luiniset," Professor Odd proclaimed, bounding up the steps.

Alister and Kilni followed more reverently: the space had an ancient dignity, and the cold and stillness seemed as natural here as the water and moonlight outside. It seemed wrong, somehow, to disturb them.

Elo was also quiet, but for more practical reasons. She skirted the edge of the steps, running on all fours with her nose to the ground, occasionally pausing to listen intently.

Securing the perimeter, Alister thought, and was glad for their canine companion.

Professor Odd was talking all this while; a stream of conscious thought, as she did when something excited her.

"It's the original searching engine," she was saying, running her hands gently over the angular structure. "All the knowledge contained within the library—all the knowledge contained within all the libraries in the *world,* in fact—easily accessible at a *single* point. The great treasure of the Library of Amnós was not its tomes, but *this:* the Index. The Searcher, the Finder. Someone with the Index could read anything, from any book or scroll in any library anywhere—no matter what restrictions or security was on that individual book."

Professor Odd paused to switch the mapper for the Codex, and leaned in to peer at a little glass plate on what Alister guessed was the Index's front.

"Sounds . . . dangerous," Alister said. "Like Google, if Google could look everywhere."

"What is a *goo-gull?*" Kilni asked, wrinkling her nose.

"An extremely large number," Professor Odd said absentmindedly. She was tracing sigils on the Codex again, comparing them to those on the front of the Index. "Ten thousand sexdecillion, by the standard long scale. Or, a one followed by one hundred zeroes . . . alternatively, a misspelling of it is the name of the closest thing the humans of Alister's world have yet come to the Index.

"And yes, it is very dangerous. The Luiniset took precautions, too. You need the Codex to open the Index, and the elves took that with them when they left Amnós. No one—" her hand fluttered over the Index, and she gazed at it in something close to awe "—has opened this in over eight thousand years. Local years," she amended, an afterthought. "Do come over here, Miss Kilni, it appears I need your hands again."

Like a pilgrim facing a divine oracle, Kilni mounted the dais next to the Professor, and looked carefully at the Codex. Taking a deep breath she reached out and traced her fingers across the bank of sigils on the Index's front.

It was dark, caked with dirt, and there was moss growing in many of the crevices. Even so, Alister could see the blue glow that followed Kilni's touch, like the stone of the door.

Another great hum, one that filled the dome and vibrated the mirror above, which shook and made the pale moonlight dance around them.

But aside from that, nothing happened at all.

"Perhaps you entered it wrong?" Elo suggested into the perplexed silence.

"I did it all the time on my old laptop," Alister said, comfortingly, for Kilni looked crushed.

"No," she hissed, pulling herself together. "No, that was correct—on my soul as a Lohihuya, I made no error."

Professor Odd had pressed her face right up against the Index. "No mistake," she said after a moment. Standing suddenly she pulled out her own flashlight and cast it up, into the dark recesses of the dome where the reflected moonlight did not reach. "Someone," she said, quiet but piercing. "Someone has *changed the password.*"

There was a scrabbling, swishing sound, like feet slipping on smooth stone, and the distant clatter of a loose pebble skidding down the stairs.

Alister felt all the hairs on his back stand up, and Kilni reached blindly for the dagger at her belt. Professor Odd straightened, and cast her light in the direction of the sound.

Elo had melted away on silent paws. Alister didn't notice until he looked around and found her gone.

"*Orka!*" hissed Kilni, and let out a string of what were likely expletives in her native language.

"Not necessarily," said the Professor, going to the edge of the dais and looking around.

"Hello?" she called. "*Kuka siéllúa?* We're not here to hurt anyone, won't you please come talk to us?"

She looked expectantly at Kilni, who pursed her lips but repeated the words in elvish.

A faint, keening whistle came at them out of the dark. It was so high and fragile that Alister thought it must be from some sort of bird—or dragon.

Then from the darkness there was a swishing, a snarl, and a surprised voice cried:

"*Oof!*"

And Elo growled: "You be a smart lad and don't move, I've had quite enough of your sneaking around."

"If he is *orka* do not give him the chance—kill him!" Kilni shouted.

"No, don't hurt him! He could be a friend!" Professor Odd added, rather before Kilni had finished.

There was more slipping and swishing in the darkness, the sound of four feet awkwardly moving over stone, and Elo reappeared into the pool of moonlight from between two shelves, marching in an armlock a most extraordinary creature.

"You're both right," she said. "It *is* a 'he,' but beyond that I have no idea."

Alister found he had to agree.

The man-shaped being would have easily been inches taller than Kilni, if he had not been doubled over by Elo's grip on his arms. He had a long beard of matted white hair that appeared to have fish bones and shells braided into it, and wore a thick coat that draped around him in tendrils, like seaweed. Upon his head was a massive, stove-pipe hat that looked like a tower of fungus, and its brim drooped so far down that his face was almost hidden. Almost; Alister could see a mustache, as long and tangled as the beard, and above that a fine, pointed nose. In the darkness beneath the brim, two bright and fearful eyes glinted.

Kilni took one look at him and threw her hands up. "*Not an orka!* He is a Low Elf," she cried, and then descended into a torrent of her native language that Alister couldn't follow, but by the way she waved her arms and pointed accusingly at their captive he guessed it was not complimentary.

The strange character only gazed at her, astonished, like one in a dream. He seemed to forget Elo holding him, and peered at Kilni curiously.

When the elf's tirade had dwindled Professor Odd put a gentle hand on her elbow and leaned toward the man, a concerned crinkle in her brow.

"Can you understand us at all?" she asked. "Who are you?" The "low elf" straightened up. The action tipped the brim of his hat back, and the moonlight fell full upon an astonished face.

"F-forgive me," he stammered, in otherwise clear and perfect English. "My lady," he nodded his head to Kilni, "my lord," he nodded to Alister, "my . . . " he trailed off, coming to Professor Odd.

"Professor," she said, but she was smiling now.

"My professor," he said, making a little bob of his head. "I am sorry if I alarmed you, but I don't have visitors here, apart from my native hosts, whom I all know by sight and name—and you, who come with a Luiniset lady, a *vérman*, and a . . . " he glanced helplessly between Professor Odd and Elo, and shrugged. "I did not know what to do!"

"How come you speak perfect English?" Elo asked, sharply curious.

"Oh, I've come to be more comfortable with the Low Tongue in recent centuries," their captive said cheerfully. "The natives found it easier to master, and since I usually speak with them I fell into the habit of it. No, I'm afraid I haven't heard my old language spoken since the Fall. It has been a *long time,* you must admit, long enough for even one such as myself to grow rusty in his mother's tongue."

"Yes, and who is 'one such as yourself?'" Professor Odd asked, raising a hand to silence Kilni's automatic reaction.

The man drew himself up, out of Elo's now lax grip, and in rather the same way Kilni had first introduced herself, he said:

"I am Metsäron Kyntilvalopoyan ya Suku Kiryastal." He smiled, as if there was some inside joke to this name. "I am the last librarian of Amnós. You could say, I am the *lost librarian.*"

Kilni let out a great breath, and it was as though all the air went out of her in one long whoosh, for she appeared to collapse in upon herself, slumping beside the Professor, arms hanging limp at her sides.

Professor Odd shot her a brief but intense look, as if to mark this reaction for later consideration, then turned her full attention back to the strange librarian. Questions danced like candlelight in her big, cat eyes, and for his part Metsäron met her gaze evenly and without fear.

"Natives," said Professor Odd at last, beginning to pace up and down in front of their captive. "Interesting. English as the Low Tongue. You've been here since the Fall—that is several thousand years. How is it you were not discovered? Hiding? No . . . are we truly the first to come here? No, never, I refuse to believe that even the Luiniset are uncreative enough not to go exploring . . . You said your house name was *Kiryastal?*" She rounded on the librarian, her coat flaring out around her.

The librarian hesitated, unsure whether he was actually expected to answer this time. When the silence stretched on, however, and Professor Odd raised an entreating hand, he cleared his throat and said:

"In your language, it means *library*. My family were the curators of Kiryasto Amnósin." He spoke frankly, but a shadow of sadness passed behind his dark eyes at the mention of his family.

Long ago dead and gone, Alister thought, and felt a pang of sympathy.

Professor Odd, who had paced to one side of the dais, took a step backward toward the center. Then she stopped and twisted her head so she could look directly at Metsäron.

"And you've kept the library," she said. "All through these years. No visitors?"

"No . . . *Luinisetian* visitors," Metsäron said carefully, with a nervous glance at Kilni. "Until now," he added.

Professor Odd took another step backward.

"But you've become proficient in English, what you call the *Low Tongue*. You need someone to *talk to* in order to do that, let alone to become *more comfortable* with it than your native language. Who . . . " and here she took a final pace backward, bringing her even with the lost librarian. She turned and bent forward, so that her brow nearly touched the brim of his hat. "*Who . . .* have *you* been *talking to?*"

Metsäron hung his head, shuffled his feet. "Natives," he said, almost inaudibly.

A small, triumphant smile began at the corners of Professor Odd's mouth, slowly spreading into an unmistakable grin.

"Natives," she repeated, putting her head on one side, like a bird regarding a puzzle. Then she kept turning, twisting around to pin Kilni with a piercing gaze. "You know the term?"

Disgust distorted the fine features of the elf, twisting her fair face into something broken and human.

"There was a cult, long ago," she said. "Dissidents who contended that the Luiniset were invaders of Geda, that we did not belong here. They said the world belonged to the natives . . . whoever they were. It was always thought they meant the dragons."

"But no dragon has been here in thousands of years," Professor Odd said.

"Two, actually," Metsäron said, almost apologetically. "I hid. They did not see me. They had the Codex, but they could not access the Index."

"Yes, because the code in the Codex *doesn't work*," said Professor Odd, her eyes blazing with excitement. "*Why* is that? Who changed the code?"

Metsäron gently extracted his sleeve from Elo's lax paws and went to sit on the steps of the dais. He seemed old and bent, withered by time and grief. Professor Odd strode up next to him, her arms folded.

"It was in the last hours of the Fall," Metsäron said quietly, forcing even the reluctant Kilni to draw close. "The Codex had already been evacuated, which I think was their plan. My Grand Father, who was at the time High Custodian of the library, ordered the release code for the Index changed. There was something in it he did not wish outsiders, let alone the natives, to know. But he was killed in the Fall, and I was left to guard a locked door."

"So . . . " Professor Odd frowned. "You don't know what's in there?"

Metsäron raised his head, and in the diffuse moonlight his face appeared as pale and chiseled as granite. Something like an apology lurked in his eyes as he glanced at Kilni, and then he allowed himself a half-smile. A resigned smile.

"At the time I didn't," he admitted. "I thought it was my duty to guard that knowledge, whatever it was. But the years have been long, and the natives are patient. First they came to talk to *me*, and once we found a common tongue I grew to appreciate their company more than I ever did that of my kin. I came to see things from their point of view. I found sympathy for their predicament.

"The code for the Index is the most delicate and complex of all. It took ten generations of natives, held together by my memory, to calculate the solution. But we did, at last. They learned what they came to learn, and since then they have left me more or less alone. Now they keep the beacons, and they wait."

"Wait?" Professor Odd said. "Wait for what?"

Metsäron grunted as he levered himself to his feet. He stood straighter now, and looked the Professor evenly in the eye.

"Many questions you have put me, Professor," he said. "And these I have answered, though some pained me to do so. Now I have some for you."

Professor Odd shrugged. "Yes?"

"To whom do you answer? Are you an agent of this Luiniset, here? Do you work for the dragons? To what end do you intend to put the knowledge you seek?"

Professor Odd nodded, as though this was what she hoped to be asked.

"I'm not an agent for anyone," she said. "I'm an explorer; a seeker. I want to learn the truth, so that I can understand what is going on, so that I can help find a solution to what I think is an unfair and dangerous misunderstanding."

"And your . . . companions?"

"Same," said Alister at once, before even Elo could respond. "We're her students."

"And you?" Metsäron rounded on Kilni.

Kilni looked like she was at war within herself. Put on the spot, Alister could almost see her being torn in half by her feelings. With a monumental effort she pulled herself together and managed a jerky nod. "Like . . . them," she said, letting the words out in bursts.

"Very well then," said the lost librarian, stepping forward toward the Index. "Then I suppose the answer to your question, Professor, is this: I believe they may have been waiting for you."

"Come," he said, reaching out to the Index's pale surface. "Allow me to show you."

The hands of the librarian—wider, knobbier, but no less fine-boned than Kilni's—spread out over the board of sigils. Swiftly he tapped out a code, far more complex than the one on the Codex, leaving a trail of glowing blue signs in his fingers' wake.

Professor Odd drew close to his side, and with a motion of her hand beckoned Kilni to stand by her. Alister and Elo contented themselves by crowding around Metsäron's left shoulder, and watched in fascination as the Index came to pieces.

That was really the best way to describe it: the smooth block split, then split again, and the pieces began to move, rearranging themselves from a short pillar to something like a table. A table with one, wide leg anchored to the ground, and instead of a square or round top, two flat arms that stretched out and forward on either side. Little lines of light flowed in the cracks between the blocks, then dimmed and were squeezed out as they fused together into this new shape.

They were left with something roughly the shape of a slingshot, six feet across at the widest point. The space between the two arms hummed, then was lit by a pale bluish light.

"It's a display screen," Alister whispered, before he could stop himself.

"*Very* good," Professor Odd said from the other side of the librarian. She reached around with one long arm and tapped the block of stone that sat at the joint between the two arms, where the board of sigils was still intact. "This is where we input instructions?" she asked.

"O-oh, yes," said Metsäron. He seemed suddenly unsure of himself, seeing the Index open and waiting. "The last person to access it was a native some two hundred years ago. It will still be set to his preferences . . . er . . . "

Professor Odd had put him gently aside and was now tapping furiously away at the board of sigils. They flashed less brightly than when Metsäron had touched them, but from the satisfied noises the Professor made Alister guessed it was doing what she wanted.

"Something that's been bothering me," she said as she typed, "ever since I first came here, actually. *Where* did the dragons *come from?*"

"They have always been," Kilni said, bewildered. "They were here to greet the Luiniset on the morning of the first day."

"Yes, but the first day of *what?*" Professor Odd insisted. Squares of light were now appearing across the screen, each containing neat little rows of sigils. "The first day of the *world?* Or just the first day the elves *were here?* And *orka!*" She pulled up another string of boxes, and these Alister saw had little pictures in them.

One was unmistakably an elf. Another, a dinosaur. And another . . .

"What is *that?*" he couldn't help exclaiming, for the image in the third box was unlike anything he had ever seen.

A domed head made of overlapping plates with no discernible neck, seven apertures across the top of what passed for a face that he had to assume were eyes, and below that curled little appendages, like the pedipalps of a spider, under which escaped a few tendrils of delicate tentacles, not unlike the ones on Dave's backside. The thing's front was all little legs, folded in on themselves.

"That's an *orka,* Mister Alister," said Professor Odd. "These are the anatomical records of the three predominant species on Geda—with a descendant of *deinonychus* representing the dragons. Elves," she pointed, and the picture containing an elf enlarged so the entire body was displayed. "Dragons," again she pointed, and again the image enlarged. "And what it pleases our friend Kilni to call *orka.*" The final box moved to align with the others, and Alister saw that the rest of the body matched the head: like a giant pill bug with a long, curling tail and many legs, feathered at the ends with delicate spikes.

"You see what's bothering me," Professor Odd said, gesturing at the screen as if it were obvious.

The two elves merely gazed at her in befuddlement, and Alister rubbed his chin, frowning. But Elo leaned in close, and then let out a little yelp of excitement as she said: "The *orka* are different! I mean, *really* different!"

"Yes, I can see that," Kilni said, a little of the old sneer back in her voice. But Metsäron was regarding the wolf with newfound respect, and Professor Odd said: "Care to explain, Elo?"

Elo pushed her way to the front of their group, and leaned forward to point at the pictures of the elf and the dinosaur.

"Look at the similarities between the elf and the dinosaur," she said, pointing. "Two eyes, a nose, mouth, four appendages—hey, can you switch it to show their skeletons? *Thanks!*" Now the pictures showed x-rays, revealing the bones beneath the flesh. "*Look,*" insisted Elo. "Four fingers and a thumb on the end of each appendage, though they're different shapes and sizes. They even both have tails, if you count the elf's tailbone."

"I fail to see your point," Kilni said.

"*Well,*" said Elo, sounding almost exactly like Professor Odd in her enthusiasm, "now look at your *orka.*"

They did. Alister had to admit, different though elves were from dragons, the *orka* was farther removed from either of them.

"One, two, three . . . *seven* eyes," Elo said. "No recognizable nose, pedipalps and tentacles instead of teeth, lips and tongue; one, two, three, four—*twelve* appendages, rather than four, and . . . " the picture switched back to x-ray vision. Elo smacked a paw against an arm of the Index for emphasis. "*A branching spine.*"

It was incredible to behold: instead of a single column of bone and nerve, the *orka's* spine looked like an upside-down tree, branching out to run boughs the length of each one of its twelve legs and down to the curling tip of its tail.

"Your point being?" Kilni asked.

Elo opened her mouth to respond, but Professor Odd jumped in first, unable to restrain herself.

"You," she said, pointing at Kilni, "Me, Elo, Alister, the *dragons,* we're all different species, but we all share certain characteristics. That's because we all evolved, in our own respective worlds, from the *same source.* We are *all* terrestrial vertebrates. *Those,*" she pointed at the *orka.* "Those are *not.* They evolved from a *completely* different source. The number of eyes *alone* is telling."

"What are you saying?" Alister said. "That the *orka* are like giant sea stars? Or arthropods?"

"Have you ever seen an arthropod with a *spine?*" Professor Odd said, rounding on him. "No, Mister Alister. The *orka* are not like us, they are like no creature that ever walked, or swam, or flew across any of *our* earths. They are . . . "

"Aliens?" he suggested.

"Perhaps," Professor Odd said, and added in an undertone: "Or . . . *we are.*" She turned back to Metsäron, who seemed to be trying to hide in the gathering shadows. "Who are the *natives?*" she asked. "How did the Luiniset come to Geda?"

"*No!*" cried Kilni, tugging at her hair. "The Luiniset were the first, we were! We left the Low Lands behind and came in a great fleet to the Blue Shores, and the dragons welcomed us and called us friend, and—"

"Stories," Professor Odd interrupted. "Though it may be telling the truth after a fashion. But I think Metsäron, you know the real truth. Why else would you call what Kilni thinks of as *orka* . . . the natives?"

Metsäron's shoulders slumped.

"They did not like the word *orka,*" he admitted. "I explained the meaning of different names . . . and they chose natives. They felt it best described what they were. They have another name for us, too," he said, raising a sad face to Kilni's white one. "They call us invaders."

"I . . . *cannot* believe that," she hissed.

Professor Odd laid a gentle hand on her shoulder, and with the other she tapped the Index. "You do not have to *believe* anything," she said kindly. "Just watch, and learn. There is a file here labeled 'The Complete History of Geda,' I want you to be the one to access it."

Kilni moved reluctantly to stand beside the Professor. She recoiled physically a moment later, exclaiming: "But it is in the *Low Tongue!*"

"That would be my fault," said Metsäron serenely. "I had to translate it for the sake of the native's leader. But it is accurate, go on."

For a moment Alister thought Kilni wouldn't do it. His mind scrambled to think of something he could say to change her mind—for he desperately wanted to know what was really going on. From the look on her face, Elo felt the same. But then Kilni's right hand came up, and with stiff, jerking motions, she opened the file indicated.

Immediately all the little squares of dialogue, the pictures and files that Professor Odd had made the Index display, vanished. It was replaced by a black slate, in the center of which a tiny light glimmered. A string of text appeared at the bottom, written in a strange alphabet, but Kilni read the words in clear, precise English.

"In the beginning," she said, "there was a star: the great *Salrei Salar*, and around Him were the Nine: *Medril, Lyrus, Geda, Reänen, Kovor, Euthura, Amaugsamid, Drimeldrik* and *Ochmanon* . . . "

As she read out these unusual names bright rings of light came into being around the star, with smaller points of light hung upon them, like gems on a human's ring. They began with Medril's ring, close in to the star, and from there spread outward, with a significant gap between Kovor and Euthura. These outer four, as Alister thought of them, appeared significantly larger, and all at once the picture became heart-wrenchingly familiar. It was a map of the Solar System. Or, to be correct, *a* solar system: clearly these were not the planets he knew: Euthura was blue and had rings like Saturn; Kovor had significant polar ice caps; and though Drimeldrik was tipped sideways like Uranus, it was pale yellow instead of green.

"Of the Five closest to Salrei Salar," Kilni continued, "first was Medril, the Planet of Fire; second was Lyrus, the Planet of Poison; third was Geda, Planet of Oceans; fourth was Reänen, Planet of Balance; and fifth was Kovor, the Planet of Earth. Of all these Geda and Reänen were the closest, and shared many things. When the dragons found they were no longer welcome on Reänen they . . . " Kilni had to pause and compose herself after a moment of shock. "They came to Geda. They found a world covered in oceans, with little land but enough to live on. The land was yet barren, life on Geda having not yet reached beyond the seas. So the dragons brought seeds and turned the land into forests and there they thrived for many ages.

"Now it happened that, on Reänen, there were many strange races of beings, but the most beautiful and honorable by far were the High Elves. But war had come to the other races, and after a terrible battle in which many innocents were killed the elves tired of that world. They built great ships, and set off to sail among the stars, searching for a new home. In this way they too came to Geda, and the dragons welcomed them and called them friends. The elves thought they had reached paradise, and soon they forgot the flawed and complex world of Reänen, and came to believe that they had always lived so, on Geda, at peace with the world . . . " Kilni's voice died in a low moan, and Alister thought she would tear herself away from the Index, but Professor Odd kept a firm hand on her back.

"Go on," she said. "This is where it gets interesting."

Kilni shook herself, and went on reading, almost robotically.

"Through all this time, though dragons and elves inhabited the land and flourished there, in the depths of the sea the *orka* dwelled. For they had come not from the world of elf or dragon, but from the heart of Geda herself . . . the only . . . true . . . natives."

Kilni trailed off into a groan. Professor Odd stepped up to the Index as the elf sank to her knees, and looked again at the writing displayed there. She started.

"Something has been *added,*" she exclaimed, turning halfway to Metsäron.

"Oh yes," said the librarian pleasantly. "The natives were unhappy with their description. They added some further details the last time they were here."

"*We are not your devils,*" Professor Odd read from the display. "*We are not your foes. You have cast us in this role out of arrogance and ignorance. Until you learn otherwise, we will keep Amnós; we will wait beneath the waves.*"

She leaned back, and Alister saw she was smiling faintly. "Well," she murmured to herself. "*That* explains a lot."

"It explains *nothing!*" cried Kilni, wretched, from the floor.

"It does leave something to be explained," Professor Odd admitted. "How did the dragons come to Geda in the first place?"

"Forget dragons, what about *elves?*" Alister pointed out.

Professor Odd waved a hand dismissively. "Elves are forever traveling between worlds, it is no surprise to me that they managed a hop between mere planets. But *dinosaurs?* They never had such technology. Besides, they would have arrived to find the land here barren and lifeless; native life hadn't made it out of the ocean yet. They would have had to *terraform* this place. How did *that* happen?"

"Professor," Elo hissed in a sharp voice, and Professor Odd broke off her diatribe. "We are in the process of being surrounded."

"By what?" Alister asked.

"What do you *think?*" Kilni snarled, leaping to her feet, her dagger already in her hand.

As if in response, from the dark beyond the moonlight came a rustling and smacking of wet objects on stone. It shivered around them, like wind in trees, and Metsäron let out a quiet moan.

"Can you get past them?" Professor Odd asked, businesslike.

"On my own, easily," Elo declared.

"Then get back to the Oddity, we may need a bolt hole," she said, and stepped down off the dais.

"Hello there!" she called, loudly, as Elo slipped away into the dark. Alister wished he could join her, but he knew she stood a better chance of escaping on her own. Instead he backed himself against the Index, next to Kilni, and kept a sharp eye on the murky shadows.

"We were having such a nice *discussion* about you," Professor Odd continued. "Won't you come join us? I would *love* to hear your side of the story . . . "

From out of the shadows something large and dark appeared, taller than the Professor, hulking. It brought a strong smell of saltwater with it and glinted in the moonlight, as though wet. It walked slowly, deliberately, and creaked a little as it moved.

The first thing Alister thought of was a spaceman: the suit looked similar in that it was large and bulky, and had a big, bubble-domed helmet with a glass front. The suit itself seemed to be made of a thick fabric bound by metal, with big, pudgy arms and two stout legs which it used to waddle carefully up the steps. At the end of each arm (there were two) was a smooth, round ball, out of which sprouted delicate metal fingers. The legs had a metal attachment which put Alister in mind of a prosthetic leg, a bent piece of metal that acted both as a foot and a spring.

Though he couldn't help but admire the suit as a piece of engineering, Alister could clearly see that whatever was inside it could not move quickly or easily. As intimidating as its size and appearance was, he could hardly find it threatening.

He turned and looked accusingly at Kilni.

"The *orka* are aquatic creatures; they can't even walk on land without encumbering suits. How did they end up being your archenemies?"

Kilni glared back at him. She still had her knife out, but held it close to her side; hidden.

"They attacked our ships, kidnapped our children and dragged them underwater to drown. They exist in the shadows of the deep; they are *evil.*"

"*They* might say the same of *you,*" Alister pointed out.

Kilni bristled, but was distracted by a guttural, buzzing voice that emanated from the *orka's* suit.

"We have . . . been watching . . . you," it intoned. It was not as artificial as Dave's translator, but it had clearly been heavily processed. Alister guessed there must be a system of microphones and speakers mounted in the suit.

"Then you have me at a disadvantage," Professor Odd said cheerily. "*I'm* Professor Odd. What's your name?"

The *orka* hesitated, and Alister fancied he could hear a sort of sloshing coming from inside the suit. It must be filled with water. He wondered if the *orka* were like whales; their bodies weren't built to withstand the full force of gravity without water to help them float. The suit wasn't just so the creature could breathe. It was a pressure suit to keep them from sustaining internal injuries.

"My . . . name . . . " said the *orka*, "is not . . . important. What you . . . possess . . . is." Slowly it raised a tubular arm—*all that water is heavy,* Alister thought—and a single skeletal finger extended, pointing at Kilni.

"Deliver . . . the invader . . . to us . . . " it said. "And . . . we will let . . . you go."

Professor Odd still smiled, but it had gone brittle now. Her eyes rolled around in their sockets as she took in the muffled sound and half-seen shapes of dozens more *orka*, carefully arranging themselves on the edge of the moonlight. Her tentacle curled tightly at the back of her neck.

Metsäron slumped his shoulders, looking dejected.

"I'm sorry," the Professor said, speaking around that frigid smile. "You can't have Kilni. She is under my protection—such as it is."

The *orka* in the light rocked backward, then forward. It took another step toward the Professor.

"Give us . . . the invader . . . " it said. "Or . . . we will take . . . you . . . all."

Though all Alister could see of Professor Odd was her back, he could tell that this caused her to relax, for some unfathomable reason. The tense line of her shoulders eased, and her telltale tentacle uncurled to droop casually over her back.

Then she turned and marched over to Alister and Kilni, where she inserted herself between the two of them, taking a hand in each of hers.

"You'd better take us all, then," she said cheerfully.

Kilni protested, but Professor Odd silenced her with a look. Alister had to use all his will power not to panic and run as the *orka*, at least twenty of them, appeared around the base of the dais and began ascending the steps. They put Metsäron aside with surprising tenderness, but nevertheless forced him to the back of the crowd. He gazed at them helplessly, defeated.

The tramp of their metal feet was loud on the stone, and a faint buzzing filled Alister's ears. He fancied it was them talking to each other over some sort of radio.

Hard, claw-like hands grabbed his arms. There was a moment of frantic scrambling as they took hold of Kilni—who promptly tried to stab all comers—and then they were being marched down the steps toward another stone archway.

As they approached, Professor Odd's head jerked up, and she called out to no one in particular:

"It's now or never—take us home!" And she broke for the door, dragging Alister and Kilni with her.

This action confused the *orka*, who had been moving them in that direction anyway. They hesitated a moment, and that moment was all the Professor needed.

The dark of the archway was suddenly lit by multicolored lights, and Alister threw himself up the stairs and into the Oddity with a will, Professor Odd pushing Kilni up after him. She seemed dazed. He took her by the arm and pushed her into a seat at the table, then turned to find the Professor at the door, struggling arm to arm with an *orka.*

At first Alister thought she was trying to prevent it entering the Oddity, but then he realized the opposite was happening. With a great heave the Professor brought the suited creature down onto the steps, and called up in a hoarse voice:

"All in, Elo! *Disconnect!"*

There was a musical *hum!* and the confusion of *orka* beyond the door was abruptly cut off. All that remained was the confusion of a single *orka,* sprawled on the Oddity's steps.

It thrashed about wildly, its arms flailing, leaving great smears of water and grime on the hallway's cushioned walls. Its skeletal hands clawed, leaving deep gashes on the upholstery and scraping horribly.

Professor Odd leapt out of reach of the clawing hands and crouched at the top step, watching intently.

Eventually the creature realized no one was trying to harm it and pushed itself up onto its knees, looking around with understandable consternation.

"Hello," Professor Odd said cheerfully, and waved. Her cheek was smeared with grime and her wig had been knocked askew, making her look even more strange and desperate. Alister found he could not blame the *orka* for stumbling backward and pressing itself against the Oddity's closed door.

At length it spoke, with the same filtered quality as the other, but by the tone and timbre of its voice Alister guessed this was a different individual.

"Am I . . . a prisoner?" it asked, and now Alister could see the little speaker lodged against its throat. A little flap, like an eyelid, blinked open and shut as the sounds came out.

Kilni, who had recovered so far as to recognized her enemy, grabbed up a piece of piping from the jumble on the table, and made to run at their new addition.

"Nothing of the kind," the Professor said, smiling, and stuck out an arm to block Kilni.

She needn't have bothered; Elo had already seen to it by grabbing the elf about the legs as she passed, and she collapsed in a heap at the Professor's back.

"What are you *doing?*" she hissed, practically in Professor Odd's ear. "That is the *enemy!*"

"I don't believe anyone need be *anyone's* enemy," the Professor returned mildly, and she rolled an eye in Kilni's direction. "You said you would accept the truth, Miss Kilni," she said. "Well, here it is: the *orka* are not monsters, they are the original inhabitants of this planet. By rights they should be trying to drive *you* off, not the other way around."

"That changes *nothing!*" cried Kilni. "They are still *monsters!*"

"*Are* they?" Professor Odd said, turning her head to fix Kilni with a look that, even from his safe distance, made Alister's stomach curl. "Were they *ever?*"

Kilni had no answer to that. Her eyes grew big and impossibly deep blue, and with a cry of frustration she tore herself away from Elo, leaving the pipe on the floor, and stormed off to the opposite end of the Oddity, where she disappeared into the Rejuvenator Room.

Professor Odd sighed and turned back to their guest. "Alister," she said, without turning around, "*could* you try to talk some sense into her?"

Alister felt like he would much rather stay and watch the Professor convince the *orka* to help them—which was clearly what she intended to do—and made a noncommittal noise.

"Are you sure I'm the best one for that, Professor?" he asked. "I don't think she likes me very much."

"Yes, but between the three—er—four of us," said Elo, climbing out of the pilot seat. "I think she *dislikes* you the least." She gave him a wolfish grin.

Alister groaned and tried to run his hands through his hair, forgetting that all he had at the moment was a bristly pelt, and settled for rubbing the fuzz at the back of his head. He took one last envious look at the *orka,* and reluctantly turned and threaded his way between tables and chairs toward the back of the Oddity.

* * *

The *orka*, all this time, had been crouched on the steps, twisting the head of its suit around, taking in its surroundings. It visibly relaxed when Kilni left, and cautiously extended what passed for a hand—it was essentially a ball with skeletal metal digits protruding—and pulled itself further into the Oddity. Elo counted six metal fingers on the ball-hand, before they were retracted. The suit went still, as the creature inside it seemed to be focused on something inward. Then the reflective plating on the interior of the helmet was abruptly rolled back, and Elo found herself looking into the eyes—all seven of them—of a live version of the image they had seen in the library.

This *orka* was a light pearly blue, and its eyes reflected the multicolored lights of the Oddity like flashing mirrors. Its mouth was a tight mat of feelers and pedipalps, tucked close upon one another, which was the only indication of expression: its head was made of plates of hard skin, as immovable as solid armor.

It leaned forward, and Elo saw with interest that its eyes could move independently, and indeed they were darting around the Oddity, taking in the lights, the cockpit, the table, the alcoves and the windows. Their movement meant they caught and released the reflected light, giving the head a twinkling appearance.

Movement inside the fluid-filled dome, and Elo saw the mouthparts move. She even caught a faint sound through the water and glass, but a moment later it was relayed through the speaker at the neck of the suit, overpowering the original sound.

"If I . . . am not a prisoner . . . then why . . . can I not leave?"

"Well, *technically,* you can leave any time you like," said Professor Odd, going down on one knee. "But it would be a little awkward, and mostly . . . the *thing is* . . . we rather need your help."

The *orka* shifted back, straightening its unusual spine, and Elo saw two of its eyes flash toward her.

"What . . . *help* . . . might I provide?"

"Information," Professor Odd replied promptly. "There's *something* happening here. Something *big.* I can't quite see it, and that bothers me. I *think*... I think you might know. Or you might know things that'll help me figure it out."

The *orka* considered this, its mouthparts pressing in on themselves. *Like a human pursing their lips,* Elo thought.

"And if I ... answer your questions ... you will ... let me go?"

"If that's what you want," Professor Odd said. "Though I'd appreciate any other help you can give. I have a *feeling* we're going to need all the help we can get."

"This is ... acceptable," said the *orka*. "As long ... as you ... answer my questions ... first."

"Fair enough," Professor Odd said, sitting down cross-legged on the Oddity's floor.

"Then ... " the *orka's* eyes glanced at all the Oddity's dark windows at once, "*where* are we?"

Elo sighed as the Professor, after a moment's thought, launched into the usual explanation.

Kilni sat in a corner of the Rejuvenator Room, holding her knees to her chest and trying not to cry. The cool blue light was soothing and the racks of clothes provided a comforting surrounding. They reminded her of the hangings in her Grand Mother's old rooms, even though she could tell they were strange, foreign clothes.

Alister stood awkwardly on the threshold, shifting his weight uneasily from foot to foot, and feeling intensely uncomfortable.

What did you say to a person in Kilni's situation? *I'm sorry, but the history you've been fed all your life was fabricated to give your race precedence over others, and your violent racism (speciesism?) was founded on a lie. Take a deep breath and move on* ... seemed to be asking a bit much. Alister could sympathize, also, with the feeling of having your world tipped upside-down and then shredded to pieces. He thought back to that frightening period when all he could do was grasp at straws of his old life, even as they were torn from his hands. What could he say to that person?

"You get used to it, eventually," was what came out of his mouth, rather before he had thought his words through.

Kilni's head jerked up, and he saw that her eyes were flaming red around the edges; he looked away instinctively.

"That knowledge brings me no comfort," she snapped.

Alister had to concede this.

"I am damned either way," she said, waving a hand to illustrate. "According to the teachings of the *vanhemari* all *orka* are evil by nature and will bring only sickness and destruction and in standing by I am complicit in evil ... "

"That is a reasonable assumption," Alister said, coaxing. "They might have carried diseases that your people had no natural immunities to. Of course, the reverse could be true for *them* ... "

"But according to the Index ... " Kilni went on, as if she hadn't heard him, "I would be in the wrong *not* to learn and approach with an open mind, and it is *everyone else* who is in the wrong."

"Try not to think of it in such black-and-white terms," Alister suggested, moving slowly into the room.

"Then I should become like the low dragons, and see only in shades of gray?" Kilni said, the sneer audible in her voice.

"Shades, yes," said Alister, moving between the racks of clothes. "But not necessarily of gray only. In my experience the multiverse doesn't operate on strict lines of black and white. It's all different ... well ... colors."

He was standing right next to her now, but separated by one of Professor Odd's similarly multi-hued dressing gowns. The sight made him smile.

"What sights have you seen, in your short life ... " said Kilni, her normally musical voice gone hoarse, "that I, in five hundred years, have not?"

Alister was a little staggered at this. Gedan years or Earth years, five hundred of either was a very long time.

"Maybe that's the problem ... " he whispered aloud.

"What is?" came Kilni's response.

"Your people," Alister said. "You live forever?"

"Practically," said Kilni. "We can be killed, or die of a broken heart, or choose eternal sleep. But we do not age unless by choice, and we know no diseases."

"Sounds nice," Alister admitted. "But I think maybe that's your problem. See, if you live one way for ten years, it's hard to change. But if you live by one set of beliefs for *five hundred,* it might very well be impossible. What I'm wondering," Alister went on, wondering to himself the wisdom of speaking these thoughts out loud. "What *I'm* wondering is . . . how many more of you elves think or suspect the truth, but can't be bothered to *change.* Because things have *always* been this way?"

The Professor's dressing gown was swept violently aside and he found himself staring into Kilni's furious red face.

"And what if, then? Are you saying my people are liars? That they are *dishonest?*"

"Think about what *you're* feeling," Alister said, wincing but holding his ground. "Would it be easier to just forget what you saw, go back to your old life, or accept it and try to change things?"

He caught a moment's glimpse of a despairing expression, and then the dressing gown swung back, hiding Kilni from view.

"What shall I do?" Her words came muffled through the fabric.

"You're asking my advice?" Alister asked, surprised.

"I think you may be right," Kilni said. "Perhaps my long years, though they give me knowledge and wisdom, make me stiff in beliefs. Tell me what you, who can still see the world in all its colors, would do—were you in my place."

Gently Alister pulled back the dressing gown and gazed down at the elf. He schooled his face into what he hoped was an understanding but firm expression.

"I would be upset," he said frankly. "I would feel *cheated,* and maybe a little ill, for quite some time. It's all right to feel these things. But what I would *do. . . . *" He took a breath. "That is, what I think *you* should do, is follow the Professor."

"Follow the Kumallinién?"

"Follow the Kumallinién," Alister repeated. "Follow close. Stay right behind her. Try to see things from *her* perspective. *Watch* what she does, *listen* to what she says . . . and if she ever tells you to do something, do it."

Kilni didn't answer. She didn't even raise her head. After a few moments of silence Alister backed slowly away.

"Oh," he added when he had reached the doorway. "Ask questions."

Kilni's head came up at that: she gave him a blank, despondent look.

"Yes," said Alister. "Questions. Lots of them." And he left the room, hoping he had done more good than harm.

" . . . and so we can bring any doorway from any universe to fuse with the Oddity's door, thus allowing us to travel between them." Professor Odd finished.

The *orka* regarded her gravely. Elo, in turn, watched the creature closely, tensely alert for any signs of agitation. When it showed none, she cautiously leaned forward and asked a question of her own.

"So, what do we call *you?*"

Seven glassy, mirror-like eyes turned to her, like searchlights being redirected.

"You mean . . . my name?" it asked.

"Your name," said Elo. "If it's not *forbidden* or something. Maybe your gender . . . I mean, are you a boy *orka* or a girl *orka?* Or something-in-between *orka?*"

Professor Odd gave her a puzzled look, but the question got a reaction. The creature straightened, gaining several inches, and fairly glared down at Elo.

"I am . . . no *orka.* I am . . . a *native.* In my language we call ourselves the *votak.*" In its indignation its words came faster and with more confidence. "And I am an *adult,* of course I am . . . *male.* I am called *Tafo.*" The eyes flickered as nictitating membranes wiped over its eyes, like a rolling blink. "And . . . you?"

Professor Odd made a brisk introduction, concluding with: " . . . and *this* is Mister Alister," as Alister emerged from the Rejuvenator Room.

"I am . . . pleased by your names," said Tafo diffidently. "They are not . . . presumptuous."

Alister did not ask what the *orka*—native—*votak*—*whatever,* thought of as a "presumptuous" name, because out of the corner of his eye he saw movement at the doorway to the Rejuvenator Room, and suspected Kilni was eavesdropping.

"And I am pleased by yours," said Professor Odd, beaming. "Now, you come and make yourself comfortable—sit, stand, recline, whatever suits you best—and explain to me what has *really* been going on."

Tafo lumbered forward and stood awkwardly next to the table. The little skeletal fingers at the ends of his ball-hands twitched.

"You looked into the Index," said Tafo, seeming bemused. "You already know."

"*Yes*, but!" Professor Odd actually wrung her hands in excitement. "What is *going on* between the *votak* and the Luiniset? If the *votak* are aquatic, why do the Luiniset make them out to be natural enemies? What do the *votak* think of that?"

Tafo, evidently aware of one said Luiniset watching intently from across the room, stiffened inside his suit and considered his words carefully.

"*Votak* . . . " he said eventually, "are of three minds. Mostly. Some . . . *small number* . . . they hate the invaders. They say . . . *we* should have risen out of the ocean long ago had they not come. Had the dragons not come. Most . . . most I think do not care. We keep the deep, we do not belong out of water. We have no love for the invaders . . . but we do not hate them. Then . . . was a small number, but now growing . . . are some who worship the invaders. Learn their writing, their language. Like them. Want to study them."

"And which one are you?" Alister asked sharply.

Professor Odd shot him a glance that said she would have preferred he had not said anything, but Tafo seemed unperturbed.

"I . . . have not decided," he said, with studious diplomacy.

"Tafo," said Professor Odd. "Have you ever heard of the Vesil Tarkaliya?"

"I hear . . . rumors," said the Votak. "Invaders. They go into deep places, bring dragons. Talk."

"Yes, but what do they talk *about*?" the Professor asked, even as, behind her, Kilni's mouth went into a great 'O' shape of realization.

But Tafo blanked at this. It was, Alister supposed, a long shot: as Geda was mostly water, he assumed the *votak* were at least as widespread and diverse as humans on his home world; how could they expect one to know what their distant cousins were doing on the other side of the planet?

"Here is the thing," said Professor Odd, and she shot a glance over her shoulder at Kilni, to include her in the discussion. "There is a group of Luiniset who have begun *talking* with the *votak*. In secret. I *hope* they are trying to find a way to end a millennia of racial superstition and xenophobia, but I'm not *sure*. Would you be willing to *help* us *find out?*"

Tafo rocked gently back and forth, and his mouthparts worked furiously. Alister found himself thinking of a person wrinkling their nose and frowning. At last he said:

"Will you . . . take me home . . . after?"

"First thing!" Professor Odd promised, so loudly Alister almost didn't hear Elo's little snort of derision. She was ignored, however, as the Professor went on: "Elo, prepare to re-engage. We're taking Kilni back to Gilsufar!"

Part Two

GILSUFAR WAS BUILT on a headland that jutted out into a wide, crescent bay with two long peninsulas, like arms reaching around to either side. The continent itself was small, an island, really. It was a mountainous, forested place, called in the language of the local dragons: *land of two stones*. The elves assumed this was because of the way the bedrock changed color sharply from reddish to gray in a seam that ran down the center of the island to the bay of Gilsufar, and didn't ask more.

The city itself was built in layers over the bedrock, arches of pink and silver stone rising in a complex multitude typical of the elves. It was said that, just before dawn and just after sunset, Gilsufar would alight with the sun's rays, and on occasions looked as magnificent as the lost city of Amnós.

Gilsufar also extended down, down into the bedrock, notably in the form of the Ronduath, the great cavern which contained the thing with many teeth, and above which was built the palace of Suvién Vanasil, the heart of the city. But deeper and darker, and more secret than the Ronduath, other caverns lay.

It was in one called Tal Goléria that the shadowy figures met, bringing dim, fireless torches into the darkness, and standing in a line below the Wall of the Eye—so called because, jutting from the pale reddish rock of the ceiling, was an outcropping of jagged gray stone surrounding a craggy seam which, when viewed from just the right angle, might have been a giant eye, squeezed shut.

From below the eye the cave floor sloped down to where it disappeared into black water. In the pale greenish light of the glowstones the water glimmered, smooth and dark as obsidian.

Of the five shadowy figures, three were recognizably human-shaped—elves—but the other two were strange indeed: one was little bigger than a dog, but stood erect on its hind legs, its feathers glossy red. The second was wide and tall, and took up most of the wall. It had a fine crest of triangular plates running from its disproportionately tiny head up and down its spine, to where its tail ended in a wickedly spiked ball. It was brownish green except its spiny plates which were tipped with vivid orange.

"They will not come," said the little dragon. "We have been too aggressive; they were offended."

To a human's—or an elf's—ears its words would have sounded like a meaningless hiss. But one of the elves—a female with snowy-white hair and visible signs of age—translated what the dragon said for the benefit of the other two.

"We can but hope," murmured one of the younger elves, and made a complicated gesture over his breast for luck.

"They . . . will . . . come," intoned the large, small-headed dragon. It had a voice like a tree creaking in the wind, and its words were all moans and snaps. "We . . . know . . . this."

Again the white-haired elf translated, but this time her companions remained silent.

Above them there was a cracking sound, like a gunshot muted by several layers of rock, and a faint rain of dust fell from the ceiling. When it had finished and they dared look up again, the group could see that the seam of the closed eye had widened.

A tense silence filled the room, broken only by further distant cracking noises. All eyes, except for those of the large dragon, turned nervously toward the ceiling. So it was that most of them missed the ripple that appeared on the glasslike surface of the water, though they all turned to look when they heard it break upon the rock.

The large dragon moaned, staring keenly at the water with dark little eyes.

"They come," said the white-haired elf.

More ripples now, and the light glanced off a place in the water that appeared to be boiling, the effect of deep water being forced upward and out of the way as an object rose to the surface.

With a faint *gulping* sound something dark and angular appeared from the midst of the water, and suddenly the little cavern was filled with the hissing and splashing of water as it ran and dripped from the ledges and crevices of the object. Amidst the pouring water three domed heads emerged, shiny in the dark, and arms ending in balls with skeletal fingers gripped the object and began moving ponderously toward shore.

The three *orka* climbed carefully up onto the stone bank, water streaming from their pressurized suits and their strange cargo, splashing on the rock and running back into the pool. The five who waited pulled back respectfully to allow them to set their burden down in the middle of the room, where it rested, glistening in the light of their torches.

The three *orka* did not speak, but moved around the strange object, fiddling with controls hidden in nooks and crannies. Then with a faint *hiss* the thing began to change shape: blocks slid forward and out, or to the side, and it began to take on a form not unlike a lumpish, two-legged table. One *orka* stood on either side, holding it steady, while the third, who was somewhat taller than the others, stood between them and carefully inserted its skeleton fingers into some hidden crevices in the blocks.

The whole contraption hummed, and the seams between the blocks ran white with light, and a small hologram appeared on the flat surface of the table.

It looked like a sort of dome-shaped dwelling, complete with little models of furniture and elves on the inside, visible through a cutaway at one side. The three *orka* looked blankly at the waiting group, their faces unreadable behind their masks.

The leader of the elves, who wore a circlet of silver around his head, came forward and inspected the hologram thoughtfully. When he raised his face to the waiting *orka*, there was wonder in his blue eyes.

"You have wrought this?" he whispered, in the language Alister would have recognized as English.

"We have made . . . one," said the leader of the *orka*. "It will serve a clutch of your people. Choose who you would send . . . carefully."

The younger elf made a despairing sound.

"Only *twenty?*" he wailed, ignoring his leader's warningly raised hand. "You promised sanctuary for our people!"

All three visored heads turned to look at him, and he became acutely aware of his position all at once.

"We have done . . . " said the leader of the *orka*. "What we . . . *can*. We had to do all . . . in secret. . . . Our . . . Queen . . . she knows not. She would not . . . allow . . . *invaders* . . . into her country."

The large, spiky dragon spoke, in a string of creaking moans that sent vibrations even through the rock of the cave. The white-haired elf translated:

"It is a good start," she said. "If twenty survive, then that will be twenty more than survived the last rising."

There was a rumbling in the caverns above them, and a small shower of dust and stones clattered down the cave walls.

"This is a hard fate," she went on, now clearly speaking for herself. "Who shall bear the burden of choosing the twenty? How shall we, who know what is to come, prepare to face an end?"

The two *orka* holding up the table made unintelligible noises—presumably their own language—and glanced at their leader, who shook its head.

There was a string of whistling hisses as the little red dragon spoke. The white-haired elf inclined her head, and after due time she said:

"The dragons know of this. Already some have left Gilsufar, others have sought refuge on the far end of the island. When the tremors reach the surface more will leave."

"And what will happen then?" asked the younger elf, a note of panic in his voice. "What will my people do when we find the dragons have deserted us? We cannot all crowd into the eastern canyons, we cannot escape into the sea but for the intervention of the *or*—" but he was prevented from saying something truly unfortunate by a soft shuffling sound coming from near the floor of the cave, and a pale head with bright orange hair thrust its way between the legs of the table. It turned around, stared at them with wide, amber-colored eyes, and wrinkled its hairless brows in a look of surprise.

"Oh dear," said Professor Odd, shoving her shoulders the rest of the way through the table's legs. "Looks like we missed the entrance a bit. Well, could have been worse," and she wriggled out from under the table, much to the surprise and shock of all present, and stood up, brushing cave dirt off the knees of her pinstriped trousers.

The dragons and the elves and the *votak* stared at her. They saw a tall, more or less elf-shaped person in a drab green coat and dark brown trousers, with a ragged scarf draped around her neck. Out from under the scarf crept a pale, flesh-colored tentacle with suckers on the underside, mottled with green leopard spots. It waved around, appearing to take stock of the situation.

The *votak* looked at her, and masked as they were they almost appeared unmoved. The three elves gasped in varying degrees and pulled back, while the dragons lifted their heads and stared in amazement.

The group was then obliged to stare some more, as this extraordinary creature was followed from between the table legs by another *votak,* in a suit a little smaller and more dingy than the others, then another elf-like person with only a dark fuzz of a hair on his head, then an animal covered all over with soft, golden fur wearing an unlikely purple jumpsuit, and finally another elf, who stared back at them wide-eyed and said nothing.

There was a moment of shocked silence, and then everyone began talking at once. Kilni threw herself at the older, white-haired elf, crying "*Korkéna!* You are *here!*" Both the dragons exclaimed: "*Kumallinién! Kumallinién!*"—but in their own language, so no one understood. Tafo began talking very fast (for him) to the other *votak*. Something about "Contacting an elder . . . " but he was drowned out by the other voices. Alister was surprised that he spoke English at all, but then supposed that, like humans had many different languages, so probably did the *votak*. English might be their best bet for a shared tongue. And indeed the other three were answering Tafo, though what they said Alister didn't catch as the Professor was talking to herself right in his ear, and what she was saying grabbed his attention entirely.

"Fascinating device this, holographic is it? Let's see if it can show me a little more of the land around here—*oh.*"

It was the "*Oh!*" that got Alister. It was the tone of voice she used when there were reality schisms, or killer robots, or giant, sentient machines. So he turned toward her and saw that she had what looked like a hologram of a city displayed on top of the table. As he looked it shrank down, revealing a crescent-shaped bay, and a high, mountainous land behind it. It appeared to be thickly forested, dotted with smooth domes of elvish installations.

The hologram was a little hard to make sense of, because it was drawn in lines of white light, and the Professor had somehow made it go see-through, showing the inner architecture of the island as though it were the schematics of a building.

Lit from below by the pale white light, Professor Odd gazed across it at Alister, her face tight and intent. She did not look frightened, exactly, but enormously concentrated. It made the hairs go up all over Alister's arms and the back of his neck.

"Do you *see* it, Alister?" she said.

Alister looked, and had to admit all he saw was a city between two rocky peninsulas with mountains rising behind it.

Professor Odd sighed, and said something to Elo, who nodded.

The golden wolf jumped up onto the table (her legs went right through the hologram in a confusion of light), and setting her stance wide, she raised her head to the ceiling and *howled.*

The noise was unlike anything the elves, *votak,* or dragons had ever heard, and they all stopped talking immediately out of surprise.

"Now if you'll all *please* listen to me," said Professor Odd through the little window of silence. "I think I understand what's going on here, and we're going to have to act quickly if I'm right." For some reason, she kept glancing up at the ceiling as she spoke. Alister looked, and saw an odd sort of rupture in the stone, with a thick, dark crack running along it. The fissure was easily six feet long, jagged and uneven, but overall it ran in a rough arc, with a little spiderweb of cracks at either end.

Even as he watched, there was the sharp *crack* of snapping stone, and it widened before his eyes.

"Professor . . . " Alister said nervously, reaching for her coat-tails, but Professor Odd ignored him.

"You elves," she was saying. "You live *so long* in comparison to humans, you think you've lived here a long time. But you *haven't* really, not in *dragon-*time. Not in planet-time—you're not even *from this planet.* You came here from another world—the planet just next door—to get away from something. What you maybe didn't know was that the dragons—or should I say *dinosaurs?*—did the *exact same thing* millions of years before you!"

This caused a new commotion. The elves gasped and began shouting denials. The *votak* exclaimed, but in a way that suggested they agreed with the Professor. Alister heard Tafo say: "This is what I *tried* to tell you—" but he was cut off by Kilni of all people, who stepped to the front and said to her fellows: "You brought this flag, now watch it unfurl!"

Alister blinked at the strange saying, but the other elves fell silent. For their part, the dragons watched Professor Odd with a sort of wary reserve.

"In most universes," Professor Odd went on, "the ones with dinosaurs, anyway. In most of them, the animals we think of as dinosaurs went extinct about . . . " she paused to calculate in her head, "a hundred million years ago. Local years. The planet they lived on suffered a huge natural disaster: sometimes it's a meteor, sometimes it's a super volcano. Either way, the climate changes, and those that can't survive go extinct. But *here,* in *this* universe . . . something different happened."

She looked keenly at the dragon that resembled a *stegosaurus,* who gazed back serenely.

"In *this* solar system . . . there was another planet. *Another* planet with liquid water, and land, and the right kind of seismic activity," Professor Odd continued. "A place you could *escape to.*" She paused, frowning. "The compatible atmosphere is understandable, since the *votak* could not have evolved without a similar primordial process—cyanobacteria and all that—and perhaps you brought along your own *flora* along with the *fauna* and *megafauna*. But what I didn't understand until now is *how* you did it. Jumping planets, I mean. It's something very few *humans* can manage. The elves could build ships to take them . . . but *you . . .* you were *carried*. Carried by something bigger and older than all of us put together. Something that could fly through outer space." A small smile flitted across her face, and she turned back to the table, motioning Elo off it.

"It bothered me the first time I came here," she said conversationally. "Now I understand. Kilni, come here. This should also explain why the Luiniset and the *votak* have finally agreed to work together."

Again the hologram of the city sprung up, and again Alister looked: but saw nothing unusual.

"Life evolves into the most amazing things," Professor Odd said wistfully. "There are tiny creatures, you call them *tardigrades*, that can survive even in the vacuum of space. Is it so impossible to imagine, then, *giant* creatures that have evolved to live in the vacuum of space? Giant, slow-living creatures that feed directly on starlight, who coast from planet to planet the way an albatross flies from island to island?"

Alister blinked, an incredible image slowly forming in his mind.

"That's impossible," he whispered.

"This is a universe of elves and dragons," Elo said softly. "Nothing is impossible."

"Here, I will help you to see," Professor Odd said, reaching out and running a finger into the hologram. She pointed carefully at the central headland, where the towering buildings of Gilsufar were, and moved her finger down, carefully outlining a specific shape that, despite being somewhat craggy, was still recognizable. "This is the head," she said. Then ran her finger across, down one of the curving peninsulas. "Left wing," she said, and repeated the action along the other strip of land. "Right wing . . . " She moved her hand down the island, following a line of mountains. All of a sudden, like finding an image hidden in a mess of random lines, Alister saw it.

There was the unmistakable shape of a dragon trapped under the earth. The peninsulas of the crescent bay were its wings, and it lay so that its spine formed the central range of mountains, with its legs making the smaller curving ridges on either side. Its tail trailed off into the ocean in the form of a chain of small, rocky islands.

Now that he looked closer, Alister realized that the neck twisted, and that the dragon's head was resting on its side, with most of Gilsufar being built on its upturned cheek.

Unthinking, Alister looked up at the widening crack. If they were in the caverns under Gilsufar, then *that* could be . . .

"The thing with many teeth . . . " whispered Kilni at his elbow.

"But . . . " said Alister, whose brain was having difficulty catching up to what his eyes were telling it. "That thing . . . must be *miles* long."

"When you live most of your life in outer space," Professor Odd said reasonably, "size is relative." She looked up at their audience of elves and suited *votak*, and the dragons who regarded her with wary hopefulness. "You have to be big enough to sustain your own internal fusion engine," she continued, absently though, as if her mind were somewhere else. "Easily big enough to carry living plants and animals . . . big enough to cause serious damage if they crash-landed . . . "

"Or," said Elo, "when they *wake up*."

"Let me make sure I've got this right," Alister said, rubbing the back of his head. "These dinosaurs—er, *dragons,* were carried to this planet from *another* planet by giant *space dragons* that can fly through outer space . . . and then the elves came here and *built a city on top of one?*"

"We did not intend to," said an elf—the older one with white hair, who had still not let go of Kilni's hand. "This dragon was deep asleep and buried. We only discovered what truly lay below the caverns of Ronduath when new mapping techniques were developed. At that time we realized we would need an evacuation plan, should the dragon ever wake."

"And because Geda doesn't have very much land, you looked to the *sea,*" said Professor Odd. "Not a bad idea, except it took longer than you thought to bring the *votak* over to your side."

"The fault was ours," admitted the white-haired elf. "It has been considered treacherous to consort with the *votak* . . . "

"Because the *votak* are the true natives of Geda," Elo said, sniffing disapprovingly. "And you were afraid of what would happen if that became widely known."

"Never!" cried one of the younger elves. "It is what we were *taught*. What we *believed*."

"In your old world," Professor Odd suggested kindly, "perhaps there was a race that was your mortal enemy, and when you came here you just applied the old prejudice to the new world."

The stegosaurus spoke then, in a string of grunts and growls, and the white-haired elf translated:

"How it began is unimportant now. The dragon under Gilsufar is waking up. It will shake us off like the dust and twigs we are, unless we act."

"Unless you *run*," said Professor Odd. "When it takes off, I doubt anything living on the surface within ten miles would survive the blast."

A dismayed silence filled the little cavern. The elves looked at each other uncertainly, and Alister read in their faces what they thought: how would they evacuate a city, much less the whole island, into the sea?

"How much time do we have?" Elo asked, all business.

The little red dragon chirped.

"Less and less," Kilni translated.

"Let's look at what we have, then," the Professor said, rubbing her hands together. "You have been making arrangements, yes?"

"Some," said the leader of the new *votak*. "We have built them an undersea shelter, large enough for twenty. We are ready and willing to escort their delegation there, where they will be safe from anything that befalls the surface."

"That's hardly going to save a city," Professor Odd said, deflated. "What we really need is a way to carry a great deal of animals a great distance away . . . very, very fast. I mean, the space dragon isn't the only thing here: there will still be *an island* left for you to resettle afterwards."

This caused a thoughtful silence to befall the elves, while the *votak* seemed suddenly agitated. Tafo was speaking fast and forcefully to the other three, and seemed to be winning whatever argument they were having.

"Speak plainly, friends," said the Professor, folding her arms and tapping the end of her tentacle against her collar.

Tafo broke away from the others. Under the shield of his helmet there appeared to be a multitude of little feelers falling out of his mouth, twining around in the water. Alister guessed it was the *votak* expression for excitement.

"There is . . . one other thing . . . we can try . . . "

Professor Odd nodded, encouraging.

"No guarantee . . . " added *votak* leader, warningly.

"Yes, *what is it?*" Kini snapped.

"We could . . . we could ask for help . . . from the *elders.*"

"The elders?" Kilni repeated, nonplussed.

"You would perhaps call them . . . the *females,*" Tafo said. "They are the oldest, largest, and strongest of us all. Some of them remember Amnós. You know by name one of the legends . . . that of the great Basa-Moranth."

There was a sharp intake of breath from the elves, and even the dragons looked alarmed.

But before they could say anything there was a horrible cracking sound, and light poured into the room. It was bright white and terrible after so long in the dim glow of the elves' torches. When Alister could at last look about him again he saw it came from the ceiling, where the seam in the rock had split wider still, and now an intense light was filtering down through the rift.

"When space dragons hibernate, they shut down most of their vital systems." Professor Odd said conversationally. "But they get their energy from nuclear fusion. Just like stars . . . though on a much smaller scale. Still . . . fusion . . . " she trailed off, eyes narrowing at the huddle of *votak.*

"Go get your elders," she said, making shooing motions with her hands toward the group of three. "Tafo, you stay with us, we may need you."

One of the elves cleared his throat uncomfortably. "It would be inadvisable for a *votak* to go openly in Gilsufar," he said.

"Elo, see that no one hurts Tafo," said Professor Odd. "They'll have to get used to them quickly, or they won't survive."

"Aye," agreed Elo, and trotted over to stand next to Tafo.

"You too, Kilni," said the Professor. "They might actually *listen* to you."

Kilni, whose face had run the gamut of emotions since crawling into the little cavern, suddenly went stock still and blank.

Oo-er, moment of truth now, thought Alister. But to her credit she only hesitated a moment before crossing over the cave floor and joining Elo. Tafo looked at them uncertainly.

"Now go, *go!*" Professor Odd commanded, practically herding the other *votak* back into the water. They went, with several backward glances, before disappearing into the depths.

"And *you,*" said the Professor, rounding on the remaining elves. "You've got a city to evacuate and not a lot of time to do it in. *Spit spot,* as they say in Alister's universe. Get your people organized!"

"What good will it do?" asked the male elf, the one who hadn't wanted Tafo to stay. "I doubt these *votak* elders will be willing or able to help, and even if so, there are too many elves who would sooner die than accept the aid of an *orka.*"

"And if the elders *do* come, and they *can* help—" cried Kilni with sudden vehemence, "—and we have not made even the slightest attempt to prepare? Then what?"

The *stegosaurus* grumbled and turned ponderously around in the small space. The elves had to move aside to allow its spiked tail to swing around.

"The dragons will go," said the white-haired elf.

The little red dragon added something in a warbling chirp.

"To survive, one must be allowed to accept help," the elf continued. "We learned this long ago."

Things got a little hard to keep track of after that, although at first it was easy enough: the elves led them out of the cavern by a large, rough-hewn tunnel, up and up through twisting spirals. Tafo had trouble in the steeper parts, and took to walking with one claw-hand hooked in Elo's jumpsuit, and Kilni pushing from behind. When she wasn't doing this she spoke in her own language with the white-haired elf, who Alister surmised was a relative of hers.

The other two elves—a younger, dark-haired man named Kemenkavel and a blond man called Melonilma—walked on either side of him, and one in front and one behind when the path got too narrow. Alister tried not to take it personally.

For her part, Professor Odd walked with the dragons, deep in conversation with the *stegosaurus* via Kilni and her relative. This puzzled Alister, for he distinctly remembered *stegosaurus* as notorious for having a small brain and being quite stupid. But then, he reasoned, this was not *stegosaurus*, but the product of millions of years of evolution from that point. Who's to say it mightn't have developed a bigger brain along the way.

After an interminable amount of climbing, during which the cave walls shook periodically and the air in the tunnel would suddenly move in harsh gusts of wind, they emerged in a circular chamber with a vaulted ceiling. This chamber, unlike the previous tunnels, was covered in blue and green tiles and lit with fixtures of the same glowing greenish stone as the elves' torches. The center of the floor was flooded with water, and its ripples reflected the light in dancing squares all over the domed ceiling.

It was quite beautiful, but Alister had no time to admire it. The white-haired elf—Alister had still not learned her name, but Kilni kept calling her *Korkéna*—spoke a few ringing words, and a large elevator car was lowered to the surface of the water, and stepping stones rose from beneath the surface, leading to it.

Alister had developed misgivings about elevators, but his feet were beginning to hurt so he piled in gratefully with the rest.

It rose fast, and through the little window he was pressed against Alister saw flashes of other tiled rooms, growing brighter and brighter as they moved upward. The conversation petered out, until, when at last the elevator arrived, it opened in deathly silence.

They stepped out into a grand hall. Alister had a glimpse of massive, towering stone arches and a great airy space filled with light and streaked with cool shadows, before they were surrounded by angry elves.

Instinctively, he grabbed for the Professor's coattails. He felt Elo grab him, and looking around saw that Tafo had had the good sense to keep a claw wedged in the belt of Elo's jumpsuit. He had pulled a tinted visor over his clear one, so his face was hidden, and appeared to be trying to make himself look as small and inoffensive as possible.

Kilni, he noticed with relief, seemed to have firmly taken their side. She was shrieking shrilly in her native tongue at anyone who came near, while her *Korkéna* spoke more softly and reasonably.

The dragons let them bicker for a short while, but eventually the *stegosaurus* shouldered his way into the group (elves went flying in all directions to keep from being impaled on his horns or trampled) and boomed some very large hoots into the crowd.

The white-haired elf translated.

The elves shrank back from her words. They began to speak again, and even though Alister could not understand the language, he could follow their tones.

Some of them didn't believe it. Some of them believed, and were gripped with despair. Others were angry that they hadn't known. Most seemed to want to form a circle and discuss the matter further, but they were interrupted when a giant, orange-tinted shadow fell across one side of the hall.

Alister looked, and saw two huge, blade-like wings, and a long, pencil-thin head. A *pterosaur*, or one of its descendants, had come to perch beyond the high columns. A small figure slid down from its back and came pelting across the stone, shouting something incomprehensible even to the other elves. They made her sit down and speak slowly.

Kilni gasped, and translated:

"She says there has been an eruption in the bay. An eruption of *stone*, black and shiny, unlike any other."

"That will probably be one of the space dragon's forelegs," Professor Odd remarked. "Think about it," she said, when they all looked at her. "You're asleep with your head pillowed on one hand, like so . . . " she demonstrated, laying one cheek against her hand, with the other resting in front of her face. "You wake up to find this little *thing* has been built on your head. It buzzes and probably itches. What do you do?"

When her audience said nothing, Professor Odd significantly raised her free hand and brushed violently at her head.

"You must evacuate—*NOW*," said Tafo, and Alister realized that of all of them, Tafo was probably the bravest. Here he was across the world from his home, trapped in a pressurized water suit, in hostile territory that was about to be wiped—*literally*—off the face of the earth, and yet seemed to be reacting the most reasonably to Professor Odd's statements.

The elves were arguing again. Some of them seemed to think they could evacuate to the beaches—and Kilni's *Korkéna* was having a hard time convincing them this would not work.

Out of the corner of his eye, Alister saw the little red feathered dragon exchange a few words with the *stegosaurus*, and slip quietly away.

Less than a minute later the hall was shaken by a terrific blast, like a hundred dragons roaring in their ears. The sound went on and on, and Alister had to clap his hands to his head. The elves fell silent—it was impossible to speak during that sound—and when it had finished there was a mad rush to the end of the hall where the sun came streaming in.

Alister felt a tug on his arm, and found that Professor Odd was leading him to the side, to a small balcony that looked out over a sprawling forest of white towers and arches. This fell away to a deeply blue sea—in which, sure enough, there was a spike of shiny black rock in the midst of a churning cauldron of white water.

But Professor Odd was not looking at the rising rock. She looked to the side, where in the distance a long peninsula stretched out over the ocean.

Moving along that peninsula, in a riot of colored scales and iridescent feathers, was a teeming mass of dinosaurs.

"Every elf in the city will have heard that," said Elo, sounding pleased.

"If they will not trust the dragons, they will die," Tafo pronounced, and did not sound terribly put out by it.

Alister turned, wide-eyed, to Kilni. "You *have* to get your people out of here," he gasped. "Tell them to follow the dragons, tell them to get to those peninsulas, tell them—"

His words were swallowed up by a roll of thunder. It went on and on, echoing around the great hall. Down in the city, elves whose day had been interrupted by the cry of the dragons were now pouring out onto the street, looking around in bewilderment.

As the sound went on, Alister changed his mind: it was not quite thunder; it pitched and waved about too much, as though there were words hidden in the noise. It reminded him of a voice he had heard not so long ago, on another world, from another giant, impossible animal.

Tafo's head came up with a snap, and he began moving—really *moving*—across the hall and out, down a wide flight of steps. Kilni and Elo were hard pressed to keep up with him, and Alister and the Professor fell behind. He saw Tafo lean toward Kilni, asking a question, and in return Kilni took his nearest arm and began leading him through the streets.

At any other time Alister would have liked to stop and stare, tourist-like. It was a beautiful city: built of bluish-gray stone with lots of colored windows and steeply slanting roofs. Long-haired, graceful heads kept being thrust out of windows to stare at them, and Alister stared back, astonished.

He had not quite realized what a city of elves *meant*, exactly. Now he saw it meant that everyone appeared to be more or less the same age. There were no children, no teenagers, no one old or sick. What a paradise they must live in, when no one was troubled by the effects of age or disease.

Or, he thought, perhaps more reasonably, *maybe they just had different things to make themselves miserable about.*

Kilni led them up stairs and down streets, moving sideways in relation to the freshly risen black rock in the bay.

As they reached the edge of the city, climbing up a steep set of stairs which caused Tafo to slow so that Elo had to get down on all fours and push him, another blast of sound rang out over Gilsufar. It sounded like a vast horn, blaring a bleating note, and this time Alister had no trouble guessing what it was: the elvish equivalent of a klaxon—an alarm bell.

Behind them the streets were filling up with curious and concerned elves, but Alister had no time to watch: Tafo, Kilni and Elo had reached the broad walkway that led to the penin-sula, and were fairly pelting along it, Professor Odd hot on their heels. Alister caught one last glimpse of a city full of elves, con-fused and increasingly frightened, with a few flashes of color as the remaining dragons tried to herd them toward the arms of the bay.

Alister stumbled, fell, pushed himself up, hardly minding his bruised and scraped hands, and continued running. It was somehow harder now, and he realized it was because the very earth was shaking under his feet. A slight tremor ran through the ground, like an animal twitching in its sleep.

Or waking up, he thought desperately, and put on a burst of speed to catch up with the group.

The peninsula must have easily been at least three miles long, and they hadn't run a quarter of that before Tafo tired. Ordinarily Alister wouldn't have had a hope of keeping up, but in the Gedan atmosphere he found he could run much longer and faster than he thought.

But Tafo was built for swimming, not running, and as soon as they reached a rocky promontory where the path curved close to the water's edge he collapsed to the ground. Kilni dithered at his side, uncertain, but Elo snapped: "Get him in the *water!*" and together they carefully lowered the bulk into the shallows.

This was how Alister eventually caught them: as they stood around the edge of the water, while Tafo frantically undid the snaps and valves of his suit.

He didn't take it all the way off: just enough for the dark, dirty water to wash out, replaced with relatively fresh water from the pool. His whole body was heaving, moving the water across his body, like panting.

While they stood there another wave of thunder rolled across them. Now they were out beyond the buildings Alister was able to tell where it came from.

It wasn't coming from the city, or from the land at all. It was coming from far, far out to sea.

Alister looked up sharply, shading his eyes with one hand and straining them to see into that blue, blue distance.

There was something dark on the horizon, growing slowly larger, and soon joined by other large, dark shapes. They were low and rounded, like the backs of whales, but must have been bigger than any whale. Alister saw an explosion of white near one of them.

Half a minute later they were hit by another thunderclap, louder this time.

"Thirty miles out," muttered Professor Odd. She turned to the prone form of Tafo. "Your people worked fast."

"I did not think . . . they would succeed at all," Tafo admitted weakly.

Professor Odd shrugged. "Will you walk with us, or swim?" she asked.

"I will . . . walk," Tafo said, pulling the panels of his suit back into place. "They may not recognize you, else."

It took all four of them together to drag Tafo back up onto the wide path, and everyone got wet. The day was warm, however, and Alister didn't mind.

They walked slowly after that, ambling toward the head of the peninsula, where it terminated in a jumble of rocks. Behind them was a commotion as the population of Gilsufar began to trickle out of the city and onto the peninsula—but they were delayed even more by pushing handcarts full of belongings, carrying baskets or struggling under enormous packs, and never really caught up.

Ahead of them black shapes kept appearing on the horizon, stretching out across it in a line of little dark humps. The closer ones disappeared into the blueness of the sea, but Alister could just make out the leader, now closing in on the bay. Every time he saw a little puff of whitewater from it, he counted the seconds before the thunder hit them.

"Is it very silly of me to ask what those things are?" he said after a thunderclap that had rocked him on his feet.

"Not particularly," Professor Odd said pleasantly, but didn't answer the question.

"Do you know what . . . most confused me about the in-vaders?" Tafo remarked, apparently at random.

"Luiniset, please," Kilni said.

"Luiniset, then."

"What was it?" she asked obligingly.

"That you are born different," said Tafo. "You have what you call *male* and *female* Luiniset, but all of the same age. It's confus-ing to us, because we *votak*, we all hatch the same. We are . . . children. Sexless . . . no parts. Then, as we grow up, we become adults. All adults, we have what you call . . . hum . . . *male* parts."

Alister frowned. "But you mentioned females," he said. "Where do they come from?"

Professor Odd turned around and walked backward in front of them, grinning. "Well, Mister Alister, when two adult *votak* love each other *very* much—" she began, but Tafo cut her off.

"When we . . . reach a certain age," he said. "Our bodies cease to function . . . productively. So two adults who have formed an accord will . . . " he paused, as if this next bit gave him trouble.

"You know how caterpillars will eat and eat and eat and then turn into a chrysalis?" Professor Odd suggested. "And then, a little while later, come out as a butterfly or moth?"

"We have crosswings," Kilni said. "They spend the first half of their life in water, the second in the air, in between they have a changing stage."

"Yes, just like that," Professor Odd said cheerfully. "Well, with *votak* it's like *two* caterpillars getting into the same chrysalis, and coming out as an *eagle*."

"Wait," said Alister, as the picture being painted came into focus. "You mean . . . "

"The two *votak* will . . . *join*," said Tafo. "Their bodies become . . . one. Their minds . . . meld. They grow and grow to enormous size, and develop the ability to bear eggs. We call them elders, but they are what you seem to think of as *females*."

"And how long do *they* live?" Elo asked.

"We don't know," Tafo said. "They can be killed in battle, or go to sleep forever. But it is impossible to know whether an elder is really dead, or only sleeping."

They walked on. The heavy Gedan sun beat down on them— Alister was sure his face would be red as an apple by the time this was all over. The path was wide as a road and covered in a thin layer of bright white sand over equally bright rocks, and Alister had to squint so his eyes were almost shut. Every few minutes they would hear the thunder of the approaching fleet of *votak* elders, and now he also was noticing a change in the waves that broke upon the rock: where before they had been regular white breakers, now they ebbed and surged, sometimes so high they broke over and spilled across the road. Everyone was splashed and a little damp by the time they reached the headland.

Now the rising rock in the bay was visibly shaking, and there was smoke rising from the city. The peninsula road was packed with refugees, and the other arm—just visible across the bay— was teeming with motion as well.

Out to sea, the nearest black humps were close enough that Alister could see they were bigger than he thought: some looked to be the size of a city block, with rough crags like horns ringed around the edge. Each one brought with it a small wave, which ran along the surface before it in a white line.

Then, just as the first refugees from Gilsufar were arriving, the lead elder—who more resembled an island in her own right—dropped completely out of sight.

Professor Odd leapt to the top of the crag of rocks that overlooked the sea, and peered out at the water. For some minutes they all stood, waiting, and then the wave the *votak* had brought hit the shore, crashing over the headland and soaking everyone. By the time Alister spat the saltwater out of his mouth and wiped it from his eyes he saw with incredulity that Professor Odd still clung to her rocky perch, and had even turned around to wave at him.

There was a deep, piercing moan. Alister felt it in the soles of his feet. It reverberated in his ears and made his teeth ache. While he was still reeling from the noise there was a roar of displaced water, and from behind the Professor, like a submarine rising from the deep, came the most enormous creature Alister had ever seen.

It—*she*—was a deep glossy black, her face alone was the size of a house, and her eyes—there were *fourteen* of them—were like windows, lit from behind by a dim blue light. From what Alister could see of her mantle—which was still mostly underwater—it stretched almost halfway into the bay, and then as far out again to the open ocean on the other side. The bottom half of her face, now emerging in a torrent of water and foam, was comprised of a complex mess of feelers the size of trees and tentacles like fire hoses.

There was screaming behind him. A flurry of motion as the evacuees retreated down the peninsula. Tafo fell sideways in shock and clutched at his arm, the skeleton fingers of his suit digging painfully into Alister's flesh. But he was able to hear the *votak* when he said, in a voice that was hoarse and strained even for him:

"That is no ordinary elder! That is *the* elder. That is *Basa-Moranth!*"

"She who birthed the *orka?*" hissed Kilni.

"She who carried the city of Sark on her back for thirty years!" gasped Tafo.

"She who looks like she's about to squish my Professor!" growled Elo, and leapt forward.

But the *votak* elder seemed fascinated by Professor Odd, not hostile. Alister could see all the eyes focused on her, like search-lights, and very slowly a single tentacle the size of a tree trunk detached itself from the writhing mess. For one horrible instant Alister thought it *would* wipe Professor Odd clean off the rock.

Instead it bent, sharply, and bent again, forming itself into a simple, angular—and utterly familiar shape.

Alister stood and gaped at the sight of the giant sea monster calmly holding out one tentacle in the shape of a triangle.

Wait a minute! Alister thought, and looked again. And stared. And felt his mouth fall open in shock.

There, plastered in the center of the creature's forehead, be-tween the four central eyes, every arm twined and curled to hold on as tightly as possible, in that vast expanse of blue and black was a little splotch of bright green. Alister thought he could just spy a speck of orangish yellow in the middle of it.

"*Dave!*" screamed Professor Odd, putting her hands on her hips. "What *have* you been doing?!"

Like the walls on a movie set being rolled away, Basa-Moranth's mouth opened. Alister felt the rush of air as the crea-ture *inhaled*, and then . . .

He had just the presence of mind to clap his hands over his ears before the roar hit him. Even so the force of the air alone made him rock backward, and the sound shook him down to the bone. He didn't know how Professor Odd could stand it, but there she was, still balanced on her rock. Indeed, she was shouting back.

"No! No! No, it's no good!" she hollered over the dying roar. "Better just *give him to me* and let him explain things!" and she reached forward and laid her hand on the nearest branch-like feeler. Dave took that as all the invitation he needed, and slithered down from the *votak's* face, across the appendage, over Professor Odd's arm, ripped off her wig with one tentacle and clamped himself onto her head.

Professor Odd twitched a little, like it tickled. She got an inward, concentrating look on her face, and Alister knew Dave was talking to her directly: not through an awkward translator, but with his own psychoactive slime.

It was like listening to one end of a telephone conversation.

"Oh, oh so *that's* what you were doing. Oh, oh I *see*. Yes, yes that's *fantastic*. Yes, well, the elves aren't too keen on the *votak* either, but they'll just have to lump it. Unless they want to take their chances with a space dragon eruption. Yes, yes it's really a space dragon. Yes, it's an *unconventional* creature, I'm sorry. Okay. And you'll thank her for me—oh, she can *understand?* That's wonderful—" here Professor Odd paused to wave cheerfully at the house-sized face of Basa-Moranth, "—all right, I'll hand you back over."

Dave neatly picked himself up and writhed back across the living bridge and settled himself between Basa-Moranth's lower eyes.

Professor Odd wiped a glob of slime off her head and stuck her wig back on.

"Pass this message along, Kilni," she said, hopping down from the rock. "The *votak* elders have come to serve as evacuation ships. They will line up along the peninsula with their backs out of the water, and your people are to climb onto them. There is to be no fighting, no violence of any kind. After the, er, *eruption*, they will take you back to whatever is left of Gilsufar, or to the nearest habitable land. Any hint of aggression, and they *dive*, is that understood?"

Kilni, still a little awestruck, nodded.

"Then get going, woman!" cried Professor Odd, flapping her hands at the elf.

Kilni went, but Alister had no time to see how she organized half the population of Gilsufar. He had eyes only for what was rising out of the sea all around them.

From what he could tell, the *votak* elders were shaped rather like flattened turtles, with wide backs rising to a gentle dome in the center. Around the edges they were studded with rough, horn-like protrusions, and their skin was covered in barnacles.

They rose from the sea, streaming water, and came as close to the shore as they could manage. Alister guessed they went on a long way under the surface, like icebergs, because there was still a wide gulf of water between the nearest back and the shore.

Some of the *votak* solved this problem by raising huge arms, as wide as the peninsula road, to serve as bridges. Others just waited patiently while the braver elves swam across and pulled themselves up the sides, using the barnacles as handholds.

They lined up along the peninsula—both peninsulas, Alister saw when he thought to glance across the bay. More elders had emerged there, and he could just make out the frantic flashes of color as the dinosaurs crawled aboard. Clearly they had found ways to communicate without the Professor's help.

The ground beneath his feet trembled. At first Alister thought it was just the *votak* speaking again, but now he saw the actual buildings of Gilsufar *heave,* rise, split and fall aside. A great burst of steam shot up through the central dome, and Alister saw it explode: pieces of rock and masonry flying everywhere.

A second later he heard the boom. It seemed small and weak, after Basa-Moranth's greeting.

But if the elves had been hesitant and cagey at first, this sent all their reservations packing. There was a mad rush to get off the land, and Alister felt himself being pushed forward by the surging crowd.

They were stopped by Basa-Moranth, who raised a single arm and pointed it at Tafo. She didn't speak as far as Alister could tell, but Tafo seemed to understand. He crawled awkwardly over the rocks, and let the arm wrap gently around him. Then Basa-Moranth lifted him up, up, to place him gently on her knobby forehead. Then she turned and appeared to move away, but Alister could see she was only turning so her vast side was presented to the land. By leaning forward he could see the shape of her, like a giant rocky ray fish, sliding past under the surface.

Then she rose, the water sliding away, an equally knobby and barnacled arm rising like a bridge between her back and the land. Alister could believe she had once carried a city on her back, for now that it was out of the water he couldn't see clearly to the other side, and Tafo was a tiny dark speck on the peak of her head.

The crowd behind them surged, shouting angrily, and Alister, Elo, and Professor Odd, being the nearest, were forced to run helter-skelter up over the arm and scramble up onto her back or risk getting crushed.

Basa-Moranth's skin was hard and wet and treacherously slippery—there seemed to be algae growing on it—and Alister found he had to go on all fours, and wouldn't have stood a chance of making the climb without the barnacles. It was like climbing up a strange, smooth, slightly soft hill. But Alister went, as fast as he could for fear of being trampled, until he found a spot near one of the horns that marked the edge of her back. He threw his arms around it and clung there.

Some of the other elders were already leaving, while new, empty backs rose to take their place. It looked to Alister that the limit would not be how many elves could they carry, but how many could they take on before the city exploded.

There was a deep roaring noise. Alister looked and saw that the pillar of rock that had emerged from the bay was clearly moving. It was rising, rising, rising, and as it rose Alister saw the shape of it at last: a giant claw at the end of an equally giant arm, and it rose out of the ocean—sending a wave of water rippling across the bay—and reached up, back, its rocky skin cracking.

Still having a hard time believing his eyes, Alister watched the giant arm—easily as long as one of Gilsufar's main streets—spread its claws, and plunge in amongst the houses and buildings, bridges and towers.

He could have been horrified at the destruction, but he was too astonished by what happened next.

The city tore away, crumbling to dust as the very earth it was built on heaved and cracked open, and with a violent wrench a head twisted and jerked up into the air.

From this distance Alister could see the entirety of the space dragon's head. It looked rather like a dinosaur, he decided, with a long snout and a wide mouth. It seemed to be made of the same smooth, gray stone as the rest of the island, and when it blinked, its eyes glowed brightly, even in the sun.

The city was in ruins now, lying in dust and rubble around the space dragon's chin. Now also the hills and mountains behind the city were quivering, and Alister felt a little sick as he realized what was about to happen.

By now the peninsula was almost empty. Most of the elders had moved away and were streaming into the distance. Basa-Moranth, because she was so huge, waited the longest, until the last of the stragglers had been helped up over her side. Then, with a gentle heave, she pushed herself off the peninsula, and out into the open ocean. The crowd on her back collectively turned to watch the land as they began, at last, to move away.

It was not so much land anymore but a writhing heap of earth. The dragon which had lain asleep for so long—longer even than Basa-Moranth—was shaking off millennia of earth and forest. The mountains cracked along the ridge, and the dragon thrashed to free its wings, hurling chunks of mountain out into the sea, where their fall caused waves that beat upon the shore, tearing more land away.

From this chaos something giant emerged—a vaguely reptilian shape, with four stubby legs and a long neck. Its wings, still trapped beneath the peninsulas, quivered, and the white road that Alister had trod minutes ago was scattered like dust.

The space dragon's wings were not like bird or bat wings, but closer to those of the pterosaur: angular and blade-like. Caked in mud and sediment, it was hard to imagine them carrying anything through the air.

All this Alister nearly missed because he was trying to find Kilni. He hadn't seen her come aboard with the last of the evacuees, and though he told himself she could well have gotten onto one of the other elders he still felt a swell of panic rise in his throat.

It's stupid, he thought. Lots of things are going to die today. There were probably elves who did not get out of the city in time. Animals who had nowhere to go. Forests that *couldn't* go. You can't evacuate a whole city in a matter of hours, much less an *island*.

Basa-Moranth's back was not as crowded as he had first thought, she was so huge. But many of the elves were clustered at one side to watch the destruction of their homeland, so it felt that way. Once Alister got clear of the crowd he found he could actually walk fairly freely across the slippery, living surface.

He caught a glimpse of the Professor's orange wig toward Basa-Moranth's head, and made for that. When he got there he found not only the Professor, but Elo, Tafo, *and Kilni.*

Kilni was sopping wet, and Tafo looked smug even under his suit. Alister decided not to ask.

He wasn't given the opportunity anyway. Professor Odd, it seemed, had been speaking with Dave. Basa-Moranth had instructions.

"Tell everyone to *lie down,*" she was saying. "*Lie down.* And hold on to something."

"Why? What's going on?" Alister asked. "I thought we escaped."

"We haven't yet," said Elo grimly.

"That dragon didn't just get up to use the loo," Professor Odd said. "It's *leaving,* Alister. Where do you think *space dragons* go when they *leave?*"

"It's . . . going to take off?" Alister said blankly.

"Launch, more like," Elo said. "They don't fly like birds, they launch—like rockets. What do you think a rocket that size would do to the earth underneath it?"

Alister thought his mouth was dry, but he managed to swallow anyway. Glancing back, he saw they were only half a mile from where the space dragon was shaking bits of island off its back. Even as he watched, the swell from an earlier wave caused Basa-Moranth to rise and fall with the moving water.

"We need to outrun the blast wave," Professor Odd was saying. "Actually, we're *going* to outrun the blast wave."

As she spoke, Alister noticed that the wind seemed to be picking up.

Wait. No, it wasn't. Basa-Moranth was moving faster. Faster. *Faster.*

"Hold on everyone!" Alister hollered, throwing himself down. The wind was serious now, pulling at the skin of his face. Alister tucked his head against his arm and looked back, over the dark swell of Basa-Moranth, now covered with bedraggled elves. They seemed to have gotten the idea; the *votak* was ripping through the water at such a pace you had to hold on otherwise you'd be blown off.

Something changed then. There was the sensation of lifting, and Alister got the feeling that, instead of swimming through the water, Basa-Moranth was now running on its surface, using her wide mantle like a rudimentary wing. In their wake he saw a frothing foam of white water.

Makes sense, Alister thought numbly. *Air is thinner than water; you can move faster through it.*

He could hear nothing but the buffeting of wind in his ears, but looking back he could see clearly enough.

They were maybe a mile from the island. The dragon, smaller from the distance but still huge, had sat up and was stretching its wings. The sediment flaked off them, and they now appeared to be made of many glinting platinum blades, arrayed like the petals of a flower. It seemed not to notice or care about the fleet of comparatively small *votak* elders skimming away across the sea. It turned its head from side to side, like it was working out a kink in its neck. Then it folded its wings close along its sides and spread its legs out, crouching over what remained of the island of Gilsufar.

Alister saw the flash of light long before he heard the rumble. They were maybe five miles away now, and his hands were growing numb from holding on in the wind.

The space dragon surged forward as it jumped, and it looked as if a small sun exploded on the horizon. It sent a wave of air and water shooting out into the sea, and the space dragon shooting up into the sky.

It rode a stream of brilliant yellow fire, and as it rose, streaming through the air, still more pieces of earth and rock were stripped away. Something silvery and shining emerged. The space dragon's true skin was like plate metal, and it shone in the sun as it hurtled up into the sky. Up, up, in a gently sloping arc, too distant now for Alister to see it in any detail. It was a shining dot at the head of a tail of white fire streaking across the sky, growing fainter and fainter, until it winked out all together.

A few minutes later the wave caused by its launch caught up with them at last, and Basa-Moranth's back tilted steeply as she rode it, treaded water at its crest, and finally slid down the other side, letting it move on out into the ocean.

The *votak* slowed, sinking back into the water. The wind ebbed, and Alister pushed himself up on shaking arms to look around.

Professor Odd was already on her feet, straightening her wig and brushing off her damp coat. She smiled brightly at him.

"*Well,*" she said. "That went well!"

At her feet, Elo laughed weakly.

In the end the elves decided not to return to Gilsufar, but to follow the dinosaurs to what they called "the Living Islands."

"They're just volcanos," Professor Odd explained. "Only one still active. Nothing compared to a space dragon."

They said good-bye to Kilni on the edge of Basa-Moranth. Five other, smaller elders had come to take her load, and they had knotted their huge arms together to create slippery bridges between themselves. Alister was glad to see that, among the elves who crawled carefully over the bridge, one was the white-haired elf Kilni had called *Korkéna*.

Kilni herself was one of the last to go. After she bid brisk but respectful farewell to Tafo, Elo, and the Professor, Alister lay on his belly and helped her down Basa-Moranth's side.

"I've been thinking," he said quickly. "You mentioned this *Basa-Moranth* earlier, didn't you?"

"According to our *legends,*" Kilni said, and had at least the grace to look embarrassed. "She was a monster of the abyss, out of whose belly came the first *orka*. She opened her mouth wide and they came pouring out."

Behind and above them, Tafo made a sort of snorting noise.

"What if that wasn't *entirely* wrong?" he suggested. "What if . . . well, what if someone *did* open their mouth, and something else *did* come pouring out? Just not Basa-Moranth, and not the or—er, *votak*."

Kilni put her head on one side and blinked thoughtfully at him.

"How do you mean?" she said.

"I mean—" Alister took a swallow of the dense, clear air. "I mean, how did the dinosaurs get to Geda? Did they ride on that space dragon's back? Through the void of outer space? I know the Professor was talking about tardigrades and things but *dinosaurs* aren't like that."

Kilni had her feet on the writhing tentacle-bridge, where she balanced, expectantly.

"No," Alister called down to her. "I think they rode *inside* the space dragon. And when it got here, it opened its mouth and . . . " he trailed off, making a little walking motion with his fingers. "They all came marching out."

Kilni looked around at the giant sea monsters waiting patiently to take her people to their new home, and shrugged.

"Perhaps," she called back. "I should not concern myself overmuch with the content of legends; they do not appear to be at all reliable." She waved, and began making her way carefully across the bridge.

"You might want to concern yourself with thinking about your neighboring worlds," Professor Odd called over Alister's shoulders. "You never know when the next batch of settlers will show up!"

Kilni was too distant now for Alister to make her expression, but he thought she nodded.

Tafo did not come back with them.

"I have been offered a position with the Mekar," he explained, as if they would all know what the *Mekar* were. "If . . . it is all the same to you . . . I will leave you here, and return to Amnós by my own means."

"Which is a very nice way of saying you don't want to risk getting dragged into any more adventures," Elo said brightly. "I *completely* understand."

She and Alister shook his strange claw-hand, but Professor Odd grasped him by the arm and pressed her forehead to the dome of his helmet. She tapped at it lightly with her tentacle.

"Next time," she said. "I will come and visit you, and then it will be *me* in the awkward suit."

It was hard to tell with the glass visor in the way, and with how different *votak* faces were from human faces, but Alister thought Tafo smiled at that.

He did not climb down Basa-Moranth's side, but leapt gratefully into the water, disappearing in a splash of white foam.

The journey back to Gilsufar took a lot longer than the flight from it, because Basa-Moranth clearly didn't feel like pulling her flying trick again. They passed the time by talking to Dave, who came crawling back and draped himself lazily over the Professor's shoulders. It turned out he had stumbled onto Basa-Moranth quite by accident, and had been told the whole story of Geda directly from her. It had been Basa-Moranth who felt the space dragon begin to wake up, and after some encouragement from Dave agreed to help evacuate the elves. He had been quite surprised to arrive there with the rescue party only to find Professor Odd at the head of the line.

"Yes, *well,*" said Professor Odd with a shrug. "We were rather surprised to see *you.*"

"Explains why the elders showed up so fast," Elo remarked. "Tafo only thought of asking *them* for help at the last minute."

The elders had not been all that eager to help, Dave admitted. They had, in fact, taken quite a bit of *persuading.*

No one asked how Dave had gone about doing that.

It was dark by the time they reached the shore, but Geda's two moons were both rising in the sky and they could see well enough to make out the smoking heap of rubble that was all that remained.

The peninsulas were gone, and where the city had risen, spire over spire, there was now only a water-filled crater with a few bent and broken piles of rock. Here and there a column or a piece of roof was recognizable, rising out of the moonlit water. One of the larger domes had landed more or less upright, and it was to this makeshift island that Basa-Moranth eventually took them, weaving and heaving her way through the wreckage.

It was a hard scramble from Basa-Moranth's limb up onto the dome, and Alister's tired muscles protested the whole way.

He reached out a hand to cling to the steep slope, and found the stone still warm to the touch and scorched black.

Professor Odd, with Dave still around her neck, was the last to leave, and stood for a time before Basa-Moranth's house-sized face. They waved good-bye, one green and yellow tentacle, one white hand, as Basa-Moranth ponderously sank back into the sea. Elo and Alister waved too, as soon as they realized she was leaving them.

The water lapped at the dome, rising slightly at the bulk of the creature disappearing into it. When these waves had subsided, Dave also slipped down into the sea, diving swiftly out of sight.

"Where is he going *now?*" Alister asked as Professor Odd climbed past them up the dome.

"Why, back to the *Oddity,* of course," she replied over her shoulder. "Or did you forget we'd left the portal under five hundred feet of rock and water?"

Alister had actually assumed Professor Odd had a way around that, but he supposed having Dave go on ahead and pick them up was as good an idea as any.

The top of the dome had a little balcony with a pointed roof supported by columns, mostly intact. Wordlessly the Professor pointed, and went on climbing. Alister sighed, and heaved himself after.

Elo, as comfortable on four legs as she was on two, kept trotting ahead and then looking back, thoughtfully. The third time they caught up with her, she said:

"Looks rather like Amnós, don't you think?"

Alister looked around at the ruined wreckage and had to admit there was a certain similarity. Except Gilsufar looked like it had been burned into the bargain, and there was no building that remained more than half out of the water.

"Professor," said Elo, "*was* Amnós another space dragon?"

Professor Odd seemed surprised. "Nothing of the sort. Space dragons only spend enough time on a planet to lay their eggs. This one was highly unusual. No, Amnós was a victim of geography: they built it over a sinking fault. One day they had an earthquake, and the ground sank lower than sea-level . . . and . . . well . . . *gravity* and all that."

The going got easier as they neared the top of the dome: the sides grew gentler and gentler, and Alister walked the last few feet upright.

They sat on the edge of the balcony, looking out at the moon-lit ruins and drinking the last of the water from Elo's bottle. Alister's face still felt hot, and he suspected he would have a rather bad sunburn the next day. He was so tired his bones ached, and he couldn't be bothered even to worry about Dave, swimming through the treacherous wreckage, searching for a portal that might or might not still exist. The night air was cool and sooth-ing against his burning face, while the warmth that remained in the stone kept him from becoming chilled. The water lapped peacefully at the ruins of Gilsufar, and a gentle wind blew away the smell of burned earth, replacing it with the pleasant scent of clean air and seawater.

He had almost fallen asleep where he sat when he heard a humming sound behind him, and bright, multicolored light spilled out onto the side of the dome, dimming even the light from Geda's two moons. Blinking, Alister twisted around and saw that between two columns and the roof, the Oddity's door had now opened. There was a trail of slime and water running up the steps, and Alister had to steady himself against the wall to make sure he didn't slip in it as he made his way wearily up them.

Standing aside to let the Professor go next, Elo took one last look out at the forest of stone and water, raising her eyes up to the heavens and their strange stars. Out there were other suns and planets . . . and now, she realized, at least one giant, dragon-shaped being with blade-like wings and a head the size of a city. She shook herself at the thought, and went inside.

"Don't forget," she said as she came up the stairs. "We still need to go pick up Dave's suit!"

Epilogue

IN A GRAY DAWN the beach lay deserted. The night's tide had swept clean the footprints and scars from the day before, and all that remained was a single, roughly barrel-shaped object that sat by one of the tidal pools. It had a dome-like top cracked halfway open, and the inside seemed to be filled with water. There was a faint dew upon its outside, and the man who bent over it leaned close, but was careful not to touch.

He was a tall man dressed in a neat black coat with neat black trousers. He had a pale face and black hair, slightly in need of a trim, swept severely back from a high, sloping brow. He had a long, inquisitive sort of nose, and a small, thin-lipped mouth— the corners of which twitched, as though a smile had attempted to form, only to be cut back before it could really get anywhere. His eyes were bright and improbably green, and there was something of the snake in the way he moved. He slithered a hand over Dave's suit—careful not to actually touch it—and wrote down some notes in a neat little black book. Then he went carefully away.

He walked so carefully that, when Professor Odd came striding down the beach with Dave on her shoulder an hour later, they found no trace of him.

Dave did hesitate before climbing back inside, but didn't say anything. He couldn't figure out a way to explain that he had smelled an echo—an echo he had felt before, no less. But the first time he had been rather preoccupied with extracting Alister's mind from the clutches of a giant machine, so he allowed himself to believe he could be mistaken.

Professor Odd was in such a good mood, anyway, going on about her precious *space dragons* and how she had finally gotten to see one. It seemed a pity to bother her.

There would be bother later. Dave knew it in the tips of his tentacles. But for now, he thought as he piloted his cumbersome suit back across the beach toward the waiting Oddity, for *now* they could take some time and relax. Dave felt they had earned that much, at least.

ESCAPE VELOCITY

Apsis Fiction 2.2: Perihelion 2015 will appear in December 2014. In it you can look forward to:

"The Stone Man"
"The Withered Hand"
"God, or Aliens"
"The Monster's Daughter" (Parts 1 and 2)

and more!

Find the entire library of *Apsis Fiction* issues at

heliopauseweb.com/fiction/apsis-fiction

Apsis Fiction is a Heliopause Production; written, illustrated, edited and designed by Goldeen Ogawa.

More from Heliopause

The Adventures of Bouragner Felpz, Volume I: A Study of Magic

Professor Odd Novellas:
#1: The False Student
#2: The Slowly Dying Planet
#3: The Promethean Predicament
#4: The Elder Machine

Coming soon:

#5: The Dragons of Geda

Driving Arcana: Rotation One

heliopauseweb.com

About the Author

Goldeen Ogawa is a writer, illustrator and cartoonist. She is the creator of *Year of the God-Fox*, an online manga-style comic, and has written numerous short stories and novellas. In her spare time she likes to ride her bicycle and sing. Sometimes simultaneously.

She lives in California.

About the Text and Design

The body of this book was typeset in Elysium using LaTeX. Cover art and design by the author.